INFERNAL SIN

PRIMAL SIN #3

ARIANA NASH

Infernal Sin, Primal Sin #3

Ariana Nash - *Dark Fantasy Author*

Subscribe to Ariana's mailing list & get the exclusive story 'Sealed with a Kiss' free.

Join the Ariana Nash Facebook group for all the news, as it happens.

Copyright © May 2021 Ariana Nash

Paperback Cover Design by Covers by Combs

eBook cover design by Covers by Aura

Edited by Rascon Revisions / Proofreader Jennifer Griffin

www.ariananashbooks.com

CHAPTER 1

 evern

A DEMON KISSED his angel in a starlit field and all the lies crumbled to dust. It was a careful kiss, the kind that told a story. Beginning soft and tentative, full of reverence and hope. There was love in it too. In the way Mikhail's light fingers skimmed Severn's jaw, in the way his soft lips gently parted Severn's and his tongue teased. They'd kissed before, but not like this, with Severn in his true skin. No more lies between them. And no more hate.

Whatever he and Mikhail faced, whatever battles they fought, they'd survive them all. Together. No force in the world was strong enough to destroy this love. The kiss almost said all that, until its end. Because Mikhail's face—cupped in Severn's demon hands—suddenly turned away. Then he tore free of Severn's hands with a savage hiss.

He doesn't love me... Severn's heart stuttered, his worst fears realized. Mikhail had seen his true form and turned away in disgust. But a sudden understanding soon chased that thought back. It wasn't disgust on Mikhail's face, but pain.

Mikhail stumbled in his haste. He twisted and fell to a knee.

Severn reached for him, so thoroughly afraid. Was Mikhail's pain Severn's doing?

"Mikhail?"

Mikhail breathed hard, teeth gritted in agony.

Severn withdrew his hand, not wanting to further hurt him. He was all right, wasn't he? Just shock. That was all. "Mikhail?" he whispered, not knowing what else to say. Could he hastily reconstruct his illusion, make himself angel again? He'd do it, he'd do anything to have Mikhail look at him in love, not in... whatever this was.

Something glinted in the glossy black feathers of Mikhail's left wing—something foreign and sharp. Severn blinked. His stumbling thoughts tripped over the hurt from Mikhail's rejection, but his thoughts were clear enough to recognize the barbed whip head.

Djall's whip.

An inferno of rage surged through Severn's veins. Mikhail wasn't turning away in disgust, but in *agony*. *Djall was here, and she dared hurt Severn's angel!*

A demon rushed from the darkness—angular wings held back. Her dagger flashed in her left hand as she held the whip in her right, keeping the line taut with Mikhail hooked at its end.

Severn lunged, forearm raised to block the dagger's

2

downward strike. Her wrist struck his, and they crashed together. Her eyes blazed with the desire for vengeance. Damn her for this. He'd kill her.

She gritted her sharp teeth, pivoted on the balls of her feet, and tried to spin away. Power and heat and rage poured over Severn. His true body was his own again—his *demon* body. Full of strength and heat and fury. Nobody had defeated Konstantin in battle, only Mikhail. Djall would not defeat him now. He captured her wrist, hauled her smaller body against his, and flung her facedown in the grass. She let out a muffled grunt and tried to scrabble forward. Severn planted a boot on her back, pinning her still, and yanked her arm awkwardly behind her. Her right wing flapped, the left trapped beneath her. She still had hold of the whip, her grip on its handle hidden between her chest and the ground.

"Severn?" Mikhail spluttered. He knelt, braced against the ground, shoulders and wings heaving with every breath. He should have been able to shrug off the whip's barb. He should have easily knocked her aside. Why wasn't he rising? What else had she done to him?

Severn leaned into Djall's back. *"Let him go."*

"Never!" she spat.

He caught her flapping wing, tucked it under his arm, and leaned into the bone, bending its arch against its natural angle.

Djall's breathing sawed through her sharp teeth. "He dies here!"

"Let. Him. Go."

Mikhail was still down. His great, feathered wings sagged. Blood from the barb dripped into the grass. *Get up,*

Mikhail, he silently urged. "Let him up, Djall, or Aerius help me, I will tear your fucking wings off!"

"Kill him!" she screamed. "Kill him, brother. It's the only way!"

"I'll fucking *kill you*." He knelt on her back; following the tail of the whip with his hand under her arm, he tried to ease the tension on the whip's line, but she rolled into it, into him, keeping the whip tight and tugging again on Mikhail.

Mikhail's cry sailed far into the night.

"Stop!" Severn pulled at her arm, desperate to free Mikhail's wing from its hook. Striking her across the jaw briefly rolled her eyes and split her lip, but she smiled as scarlet blood ran between her jagged teeth.

This wasn't working. He had to get the whip handle free from where she had it pinned under her. He kicked her hard in the ribs, intending to expose the whip. Her dagger flashed, slicing too close to his face. He snatched her wrist and slammed it into the dirt, pinning her to the ground under him, then dug his fingers into hers, trying to pry them open.

She suddenly fell still. "It's too late." Djall's wide, fear-filled gaze locked on something over Severn's shoulder, *behind* him.

"Tell him we planned it together." Her panicked gaze found his face. "Your lies. All of it. We planned to get him here, for you to *kill him*." The words gushed out of her, driven by desperation. "Please. Lie for me, Stantin... just one more time. Kill the angel so Red Manor lives. The Manor is all." All the rage had cooled, leaving only fear in her eyes. Fear for him? No, fear for the Manor, their family, and everything they stood for as demons. There had been a time he'd have agreed with her and would have gladly killed one angel to protect them, but not anymore. It couldn't be us versus them. The divisions had to stop.

Severn glanced behind him. Countless demon wings blotted out the starlight, and at their front loomed the unmistakably jagged silhouette of High Lord Luxen.

In his own skin, Severn could fight Lux, one-on-one, but not with so many backing him up, and not while protecting Mikhail.

The flap of so many demon wings was deafening now, rumbling like thunder that had no end.

"Brother, please." Djall writhed. "Mikhail dies here. We survive, Red Manor wins, and you take Luxen's place as High Lord! The guardian dies now. He must, or we're all finished, and what will it have been for? All the battles, all the lives lost. *He's just an angel!*"

He stared down at his sister, barely hearing her words over his thumping heart. Mikhail wasn't just an angel, he was Severn's angel.

Mikhail was still down, still struggling to breathe. His shoulders heaved. Whatever pain he was in, it couldn't all be from Djall's whip. "Mikhail? What's wrong? Talk to me."

He didn't reply, maybe couldn't even hear the question. Severn grabbed Djall by the neck and squeezed. "Did you poison him?! What did you do?!"

Panic raced through him, splintering his thoughts. The Manor was all. It lived in his veins, in the blood of his ancient ancestors, but so did love. He'd die to protect Mikhail, and he'd take Djall with him. "I swear, sister, I'm going to gut you—"

"*Tien,*" Mikhail gasped.

5

Tien? Was that even a word? Severn rocked back on his heels, still pinning Djall's chest, his bulk more than enough to hold her down now her fight had turned to fear. "Mikhail—Lux is coming, can you fly—"

"Tien injected me—*Poison*," Mikhail hissed. "I thought it gone, but... just... catch my breath..."

Shit, shit, shit, if Mikhail couldn't fight or fly, they didn't stand a chance. The demons would hang them both from a tree, flay them alive, and that would be just the beginning. They'd take Mikhail's wings for the thousands he'd killed, and nothing Severn could say would stop them.

"Give me the fucking whip, sister." Severn tore at the whip in her hand. She scrabbled, desperately clinging on. The heavy *thwump-thwump* of demon wings grew louder still. The air stirred, grass hissing. "Damn you!" Finally, the whip unraveled from her fingers and the tension in the line slacked, but the barb was still lodged in Mikhail's wing. Snatching Djall's dragger from her fingers, he dashed to Mikhail's side.

"We don't have long. They're coming." Severn skimmed a hand down Mikhail's wing and found the barb lodged deep inside a joint. "This is going to hurt." He plunged the dagger in.

Mikhail groaned through clenched teeth.

I'm sorry. So sorry.

Exposed muscle glistened beneath the bloody feathers. Severn sliced around the barb and dislodged the horrid thing, tossing it aside.

"Lord Konstantin," Luxen's suave voice announced. "What a wonderful surprise, and in your true demon skin too."

Mikhail's wings shuddered closed, but he stayed down.

Pain had etched deep lines into his pale face and washed out the blue in his eyes, turning them gray. A silent plea widened his eyes. Whatever Tien had done to him had been working its way through him since they'd left Haven, and he wasn't shaking it off. He couldn't fly, couldn't fight.

Severn had no choice but to negotiate their survival.

He cupped Mikhail's cheek, briefly startled by the contrast of dark skin against light and of how small Mikhail now seemed against his demon hand. "Trust me," he whispered.

Mikhail swallowed and nodded. Severn must have looked like Mikhail's every nightmare. The worst kind of demon, a concubi lord. His enemy, back to haunt him. There was true pain in his eyes, but from the agony of losing Severn as an angel, or from whatever the drug was doing to him? If they just had some time together, if the rest of the world would just leave them alone, they'd get through this, he knew it, but Lux and Djall clearly had other ideas.

Severn drew in a deep breath, filling his lungs and his body with strength, and slowly rose to his feet. He spread broad wings, stretching them high and wide, as a deliberate threat and a shield, and turned to face Luxen.

The High Lord was wrapped in leather and buckles, his armor dark against his bronze skin, designed to blend into the night. A two-handed axe-head poked out from behind his left shoulder and daggers gleamed at his narrow hips. His wings had been closed, but now Severn had spread his, Luxen's parted, slowly opening, their great arches rising.

The demons behind him—easily thirty in all—had all come armed for battle. They looked at Severn as though they'd gladly bring him down. The Lost Lord Konstantin was dead to them. Severn was a traitor.

"My name is Konstantin, Lord of Red Manor." He paused, letting his words and their meaning fill the quiet. "And this angel is mine."

The resonating words faded until the quiet claimed the night once more. Demons glared back, united in their hatred for Mikhail. Some tried to lean out and get a look at the fallen guardian behind Severn's wings. They would cut Severn down to get to him. All that stood between them and Mikhail's horrible death was whatever Luxen said in these next moments.

Luxen's lips tilted sideways. He stepped forward, wings opening wider with each step, and stopped a stride from Severn. An abundance of ether made his wings shimmer, and while physically slimmer, he'd be quicker than Severn. If they threw down, the resulting battle would be brutal and bloody, and only one of them would live.

Severn raised his top lip, baring his teeth in a snarl.

Lux's dark eyes scanned Severn's face, and the quiet dragged on. Minutes turned into what felt like hours. Lux closed the gap between them with a single step, bringing him eye-to-eye, chest-to-chest, wings raised, each mirroring the other. He hadn't gone for his weapon. This was all posturing.

"I have no wish to fight you," Severn said carefully.

"*Skree.*" The word could only be said through a snarl.

Lux hadn't gotten to his position as High Lord by making foolish decisions. He knew Severn was capable of killing him. He likely wouldn't want to fight either. Severn had to believe that because if they locked horns, he couldn't protect Mikhail.

"Our battle is with angels," Severn said. "But not *my* angel."

Lux stepped back, breaking the standoff. "He is wounded?"

He must have seen him fall from Djall's whip as he flew in. There was no denying it. If he were fine, he wouldn't have been hiding behind Severn's wings. "Poisoned."

Lux snorted. "The angels finally saw the truth of their butchering bastard, *a truth we have always known.*" He raised his voice, and the demons behind him cheered in agreement.

Gods, they'd kill Mikhail. None of the demons here were ready to hear their war was a lie, that demons and angels could love. "Lux—"

"High Lord Luxen," he corrected sharply.

"High Lord Luxen, Mikhail is under my protection and the protection of Red Manor—"

Lux laughed. "Red Manor is long dead." He twitched his wings wider. "As are you, *Konstantin.*" Luxen's wandering gaze caught on Severn's wings. His eyes narrowed as he absorbed their expanse, and then his steady gaze found Severn's. "I think it best for us all that this ends now." He reached behind him and freed the axe.

Djall was right. There was only one way out of this, and that was to lie all over again. To tell Lux this had been his plan, to bring Mikhail down for demonkind. The lie might keep them both alive until he could figure out an escape. But Severn was so damn tired of fucking lies.

Djall had quietly climbed to her feet to Severn's right, keeping well back, probably so she could flee as soon as blades began to swing. He resisted glancing at her. She was just as likely to stab him in the back as she was to fight for him.

Severn slowed his breathing. He had his sister's tiny dagger, wings he hadn't yet adjusted to, and a substantial body broadened with muscles he hadn't used in a decade. He'd bested Djall, but he had the weight advantage over her. He'd have bested the old Lux in seconds. But the High Lord had clearly changed too, grown confident in Severn's absence, his reign strengthened by the demons behind him.

Lux flexed his fingers on the axe's handle, testing its weight. His smile had grown. He'd decided, and the outcome was not the one Severn had hoped for.

"Don't do this," Severn said.

Lux backed up another step, not to retreat but to get a look at where Mikhail lay panting. "That angel is a monster. A ruthless butcher of our kind, and you protect him behind your wings? I am ashamed for you, Konstantin. You have fallen too far. Red Manor dies with you."

Djall drew a small breath. "Lux—"

Severn spread his stance, readying to defend. "Touch Mikhail and I will fucking destroy you all."

"Lord of the Red Manor turned traitor." Lux's grin was all teeth.

"No. Never that. I am Red Manor, as I am demon, and we've all been lied to. All of us—"

The axe whirled in Lux's hands. "We are all aware of your lies!"

Severn dodged the first swing, but the second came just as fast, barely missing his shoulder. He lunged off his back foot and plowed into Lux's chest, tackling him backward, into the waiting line of demons. *Mikhail, run!*

Mikhail had to get away. If they caught him, they'd kill him. Run, fly, do whatever the fuck he had to do, but he had to escape. They hadn't survived everything destiny had thrown at them to die now. The truth had to survive. Severn landed a punch in Luxen's gut and the High Lord crumpled around the impact, but even as Severn lifted his head, he feared it was too late. Demons rushed forward, around him and *toward* Mikhail. Djall among them, her whip lashing at her side.

Mikhail still knelt, vulnerable and bleeding from his wing. He struggled to get his feet under him. Rose, but fell again.

He looked up, met Severn's gaze, eyes blazing with defiance.

The demons plunged in, and he was gone, vanished among bodies and wings. "No!" Lux swung his axe again. Severn skipped back, and the second Lux tried to recover the heavy axe, Severn landed a devastating right-handed punch into his face. Blood sprayed, and he reeled backward with a roar.

Severn whirled, desperate to find Mikhail among the chaotic flap of wings. Fingers snagged Severn's right wing. He roared and jerked free and tried again to rush into the fray for Mikhail.

Arms locked around his waist and tried to haul him off his feet. "He's mine now," Luxen hissed against Severn's ear.

Brilliant white light flooded the field, turning night to day in a blink. It was so bright it burned. Severn recoiled, turning his face from the sudden glare. Luxen's grip vanished, the demon similarly blinded and stumbling.

Severn reached for the blurred shades that could only

be demons. One would be Luxen, and in the chaos, maybe he could bury his sister's dagger into his chest.

A shadow consumed the light, absorbing it, forming the shape of six great arches. His eyes adjusted, squeezing out useless tears, and there, at the dark heart of the light, was Mikhail, his head thrown back, raw power blazing through him.

A small sob of relief fell from Severn's lips. He was all right... He'd get away.

The light stuttered. Mikhail's great wings suddenly retracted around him, the light blinked out, the night rushed back in, and Mikhail fell.

Severn forgot Lux, forgot the fight, forgot Djall and her whip. He tore through the awestruck demons and skidded to his knees beside Mikhail, who lay on his side in the scorched grass. Gods, he was out cold, eyes closed, his six wings collapsed about him, their feathers ragged. "Mikhail?"

The demons crowded around, coming closer. But they hadn't rushed in, so there was hope, wasn't there? Severn twisted, trying to block Mikhail with his own wings, keeping their line back. They stared at him, half stunned from the sight of Mikhail's *other* form, but coming back to reality. "Don't touch him. Just... just listen. He didn't hurt you. He could have. Please... he's changed."

Closer, they loomed, all horns and wings and bristling weapons.

"Stop, wait." Severn desperately held out the small dagger, like that alone could hold back a demon army. "He's different."

Lux's firm muscular arm hooked around Severn's throat from behind and locked there, sealing off his air. Severn thrashed his wings, but Lux hauled him back against his chest. His vise-grip tightened, slowly wringing the consciousness from Severn's pounding head.

"Oh, he's changed all right," Lux growled into Severn's ear, "and whatever he's become is all mine."

Those final words chased Severn down into an endless dark.

CHAPTER 2

$\mathcal{M}$ikhail

YOU WILL ONCE AGAIN BE the guardian you were destined to be...

He opened his eyes, expecting Tien and her needle to be looming in front of him, but the simple windowless room was dark and empty. What was this place? A single light shone its harsh glow from above. He hung from his wrists against a wall, his feet far off the floor, his wings trapped behind him. Was he still in Haven?

A fiery agony blasted down his neck, scorching his spine. When it did eventually subside, the afterburn left him panting. His breaths came too fast, his cold skin slick with sweat. Something had happened. Something bad. He couldn't remember... Sickness sweated from his skin.

Haven. He'd been in Haven. He was sure. There had

been angels, and Severn had been there... They'd danced, made love, and...

The Haven angels were going to kill *Severn*!

He tried to pull against the restraints. The metal clasps groaned but didn't give. Trying again, the metal bit into his wrists, and his efforts only left him limp and bleeding.

Severn, he had to find him.

He was in danger.

This was Mikhail's fault. If he hadn't been so blind to his own feelings, if he hadn't tried to flee from the truth, Tien would never have managed to get that wretched needle into his arm. Whatever the drug was that ravaged him now left him confused and adrift. Disconnected and weak.

Gritting his teeth, he clenched both hands into fists and heaved his body from the wall. Metal groaned. Blood trickled down his trembling arms. With a cry, he collapsed, still strung up like a trophy.

Panting, he dropped his chin.

He was stronger than the shackles holding him, stronger than this room, stronger than any cell. But the drug... Tien had made him weak, made him susceptible to whatever they did to emotional angels.

The more he tried to cling on to his thoughts, the more they fractured and fell apart. He'd been in Haven. Severn had been with him. Of those two things he was certain. Everything else was... missing. How had he gotten from Haven to wherever he was now?

Something had happened, something terrible. And now he was here, fixed to a wall in an empty room with just a single buzzing light.

Angels didn't do this to him. Angels would not sling him up, like an animal to be slaughtered.

A memory twitched, a blade in his back. *"Your love dies with you."* Remiel. More memories and madness spilled in, so many that their onslaught summoned cold tears and crushed his heart. The guardians... Tien and Remiel. They'd turned against him. His whole world had turned against him.

He heaved again at the restraints. More blood spilled. The air was thick with the smell of it. He pulled until his biceps burned, muscles threatening to snap, but the chains held.

He heaved and thrashed and strained until sweat and blood soaked into his feathers, until his vision blurred the single light, smudging it into a throbbing ache.

Rest. He had to rest and regain his strength. He had to escape, to find Severn and make him safe. Severn with his sly, blue eyes and lopsided smile. The way he looked at Mikhail sometimes, as though he couldn't understand him but loved him all the same. They'd found something together. Something special. Two angels...

His memory flashed.

He blinked at the buzzing light.

Why couldn't he remember how he'd gotten here? He must have fought. He wouldn't have surrendered.

He drifted, lost to his own thoughts. Hours passed, maybe days, it all blurred together in a broken stream of waking and restless sleep.

The sound of the door opening roused him.

Mikhail peered through his lashes at a demon filling the doorway. He wore a strange mix of buckled leather.

The jacket hung open, revealing a lean but defined muscular chest beneath.

Demons in Haven?

No... this was... something else—somewhere else. He was not in Haven at all. And that changed things.

Two steps inside the room and the demon's wings bloomed behind him. Two enormous canvases of featherless leather towered over him. Mostly black, with some gold accents along their boned arches. When spread, they'd reach from wall to wall. Two horns curved backward over the demon's head and flicked up at their tips. A concubi, he'd know their kind anywhere, and this one had the look of a lord.

Mikhail bared his teeth. His heart thudded, breaths coming too fast. Tien's drug had left him vulnerable and exposed to his enemy. Somehow, between her work and now, demons had captured him. If he couldn't escape his restraints, this room, he'd die here.

"My name is Luxen." Luxen's voice was deep, rich, smooth. He grabbed the single chair and sat, leaning forward, accommodating his relaxed wings. He could illusion them away so they didn't snag, but displaying them revealed his prowess as demon. Though, such a thing was wasted on Mikhail. He'd taken wings just like those and hung them on his wall.

"Where is Severn?" Mikhail asked. His voice compared to this demon's was a mangled wreck of rasping hitches.

"We'll get to that," the demon said calmly. "How do you feel?" He almost sounded as if he cared.

"Release me." Mikhail's head throbbed, as though the act of speaking was breaking his skull apart. He leaned back, hating how weak he appeared to this creature.

Closing his eyes eased the pain some. The drug would have to wear off eventually, and then the chains wouldn't hold him. He'd break these walls and any demons who'd dare try to stop him to find Severn. He didn't care for anything else. Just Severn. Did they have him strung up here too?

"You do not seem like yourself," Luxen said, his melodic voice weaving its way into Mikhail's mind, somehow soothing out the ache. That seemed wrong, but he couldn't deny the relief was welcome.

This is not the way of angels.

This has always been our way.

The memory had his body flushing cold all over again. "How did I get here?" Mikhail asked, opening his eyes to fix his blurred gaze on the demon once more.

Luxen tilted his head. "You don't remember?"

Mikhail shouldn't be speaking, shouldn't be telling him anything. This demon. His enemy. But there was something about him that made Mikhail want to talk, to answer his questions. "Tien... a guardian, she tried to..." He trailed off. There was a trick here, a lie... The demon was concubi, and concubi manipulated with their every breath.

His memory flashed, bright and blinding. *Be the guardian you were destined to be.*

A growl bubbled up his throat and left his lips. His own mind was sabotaging him. He'd been with Severn. He'd gone to Haven to save them both. Tien had been there. She'd agreed to help. So why then did his mind trip every time he tried to recall what happened after?

A sting jabbed at his arm. He looked at his bicep now, held tight above his head. Another memory. Something injected. But the skin had healed over any mark that might have been there. "What have you done to me, demon?" He flung the accusation at the smug-looking lord.

"I've merely restrained you for my own safety. So you tell me, what happened, Mikhail?" Luxen asked, his voice so soft now, like a friend's might be. If Mikhail had ever had one to know what that felt like. "What happened in Haven?"

Cool water ran down Mikhail's face. He blinked, dislodging more tears. "I don't..." Memories assaulted him. His own kind had betrayed him, betrayed themselves, and he might have killed the one thing in this world he loved. Severn. His laughter so carefree, his demands always pointed and edged, like he had the authority to issue Mikhail orders. His heart ached from loss. Had he been too late? Had the guardians taken him. "Where is Severn?"

"You seem confused."

This was wrong. He couldn't be here. Couldn't be restrained. Something was very, very wrong with *him*.

He yanked at the restraints, heard them groan, and pulled again, funneling every quivering muscle into breaking free until his body burned. He couldn't be kept here. There was something he had to do, it ate at him, rattling his mind, silently screaming inside his thoughts. He didn't know what it was, but this demon couldn't help him. This room couldn't help him. He had to escape... He had to find Severn.

A shout rose. Luxen was moving. More demons spilled into the room, filling the small space with their huge bodies.

Mikhail bared his teeth at them. Power washed through him, scorching his veins, bringing him alive at the same time as it hollowed him out, making him cold. A tiny new prick of pain barely registered in his arm.

Then Luxen was in front of him. Warm, strong fingers sealed around Mikhail's throat. "Easy..." the demon purred softly. "Easy... there... there, relax, you're safe." As quickly as he'd realized the demon was not a friend, he began to fall again, and the strength, the light, it all slipped away, draining his consciousness out of him until there was nothing left but blessed silence.

 evern

HE WOKE in a hard bed that was nothing like Haven's fluffy duvets and pillows, in a room with stained wallpaper and filthy windows, but more worryingly, he woke without his warm angel beside him. For a few seconds, he lay still. Was the nightmare real? Being angel, living that life, loving and lying to Mikhail for so long... until the lie had become real.

But it hadn't been a nightmare. Not really. He'd turned angel, and then turned back again. He lifted his hand. Soft light played over dark fingers and pooled in his palm. Demon. He was demon again. Konstantin. He had his body back. The body he'd abandoned for ten years. He slipped the hand down himself, not looking—feeling. A broad chest, ripped with muscle. Wide hips. And there, through the stretched Haven slacks... a cock he couldn't wait for Mikhail to—

Mikhail.

Severn shot from the bed, almost fell over his slow-moving feet, and swayed, readjusting for the sudden weight. Samiel lunged from the chair across the room and was suddenly in front of him, blocking the door.

The smaller demon glared back, his face full of defiance, his wings spread in warning. He held out a hand, as though that would be enough to stop Severn from shoving him aside. "Think, Stantin, before you go charging into Luxen's den."

Severn loosed a growl. Luxen, the bastard, had Mikhail. "I am thinking of all the ways I'm going to rip his wings off. Get out of my way, Samiel, or I'll do the same to you."

Samiel's face, always so full of smiles, turned hard. "No angel is worth dying for."

"Mikhail is worth *everything.*"

Remembering he had wings, he revealed them now, flicking them out in a threat, and stalked toward Samiel, towering over the demon who had once been his friend, his lover. Gods, it felt good to be in his skin again, and even better now he carried the body to back up his threats. "I will cut down every single demon who stands in my way to get to Mikhail, starting with you, if I must. Don't make an enemy of me, Samiel. You won't survive that fight."

His small hand pressed against Severn's chest. "I'm stopping you because I care," he said in a small voice. "If you charge into Luxen's den, he'll kill you."

"He can fucking try." He shoved Samiel aside and tore open the door, vanishing his wings before striding out into a hallway. A door marked FIRE EXIT drew his eye. That would take him to the roof. From there, he could get his bearings. Lux's den was on the top floor of one of only a handful of London's remaining high-rises. He'd have Mikhail inside it. Lux wouldn't kill him, not yet. He was too curious since fucking Severn to end Mikhail quickly.

Gods, Severn had to save Mikhail before Lux got his claws in him. Before the prick proved to Mikhail that all demons really were the monsters he'd been raised to believe. He had to get to him for other reasons too. Mikhail had only just seen him as Konstantin. The love they had, it was real, but fragile. And having your lover turn from a fluffy golden-haired angel into a featherless, horned demon was a test even established lovers might fail.

What if Mikhail didn't want Severn?

He couldn't think straight. His heart was a hot, heavy thing thumping inside his chest, making his fiery veins burn. Maybe Mikhail didn't want to see him, but Mikhail needed him now. Severn couldn't lose him again, not for anything. He'd tear the whole fucking world down to find him.

"Konstantin," Samiel said, striding to catch up. "The Manors will turn on you. Lux has seeded doubts, made them think you're a traitor. Don't prove him right by doing something stupid."

Fucking Lux. "I don't care what they think. I'm getting him back." He took the short flight of stairs up to the roof two steps at a time and pushed through the fire exit door onto the roof. A strong wind swirled about the roof and shoved at him, urging him to *fly*. He hadn't flown in over a decade, not properly. He'd fallen from Aerie. There was little skill in falling. Flying took years to master. Could a demon forget how to fly? Jumping off a high-rise was one way of finding the knack again.

"Stantin, please!" Samiel yelled, chasing after him.

Severn approached the edge. Early morning mist swirled off the silvery line of the Thames snaking through the heart of gray London. Old, half-broken high-rises stabbed the clouds. Luxen's was the shining glass one, half encased in scaffolding. It shouldn't be too hard to fly there. What was it... maybe a mile?

He rolled his shoulders.

Walking would take too long.

Luxen would already have his claws in Mikhail.

Oh gods, he had to find him, to know he was okay. Severn tipped his head up. "These bastard wings had better hold, Amii." He flung them open, caught a gust, and jumped.

"Wait!"

Rushing air tore the sound of Samiel's voice away. Severn scrabbled at nothing—definitely falling, not flying. *Shit.* He flexed the wings, thrusting their sail-like membranes outward, caught an updraft, and lurched higher. Right, he'd forgotten how the swirling drafts around the high-rises were always a fucking death trap. But he had it now.

"Still got it." He grinned. The updraft vanished. He dropped, guts suddenly in his throat, and then snagged another swirling column of warmth and shot higher. "Mostly still got it."

The wind corkscrewed, unpredictable and choppy. His wings ached and burned and twitched, making it clear he was abusing them, but he held on, clumsily flapping like a wounded bird to gain height whenever the wind dropped out from under him. It probably looked awful from below, like a pup's first fly, but it was damn well the best he could do with wings he'd only recently grown.

Mikhail would raise an eyebrow and laugh.

If Luxen had touched a single hair on his head...

He'd be all right. Severn had to believe it. Mikhail was strong, stronger than anyone Severn had known. Oh, but by the gods, he was naïve and stupid too, and Severn's heart ached to think of a master concubi like Luxen slipping into his mind. He'd resist. He was Mikhail. No demon would ever get the better of him.

But hadn't Severn done exactly that for ten years? And if Severn could manipulate Mikhail, Luxen damn well could too.

Severn forced his wings to beat harder, sending agony down the previously unused quivering muscles. A mile's flight around high-rises on temperamental air currents may have been too ambitious, but he was committed.

Finally Lux's huge high-rise loomed close. Buffeted by the wind, it took several attempts to grab the scaffold poles and haul himself onto rickety, rotten boards, but he eventually managed to find a sturdy enough one to land on and retracted his wings so the wind didn't grab them and yank him into the air again. The steel frame groaned under his weight. There wasn't much holding the steel poles up now but moss and rust.

Carefully crossing the soft, flaking boards, he approached the massive windows. Half the glass was intact, but some windows had either never been installed or had been blown out. The scaffold made a perfect perch for demons entering and leaving Lux's building.

"Stop!"

Severn growled a curse, grabbed a scaffold pole, and flung a snarl at Samiel. "Go back."

"I can't..." He alighted perfectly, feet first, wings back, so graceful, unlike the mess Severn had made of it. "If you go in there, he'll kill you, Stantin."

"More like I'll kill him."

"Maybe you will, and then what?"

Samiel loved him. It was all over the rawness in his face. He always had loved him, since they were both pups, too young to know what to do with love. And now he looked at Severn—with the new wings and body to back it all up—and saw Konstantin, who had once wholeheartedly loved him in return. But Konstantin was still dead. He hadn't suddenly forgotten his love for Mikhail just because his skin had changed. Is that what Samiel hoped for?

"I love Mikhail," Severn said, raising his voice over the howling wind. Samiel flinched. "I look like the demon you know, but I'm not him, Samiel. I'll never be him again. You have to let me go."

Samiel crossed the groaning boards, grasping the scaffold poles. "I won't." The wind pulled at his clothes and hair and made him raise his voice. "You're so stuck in the illusion, you still think you're Severn, but you're not. Konstantin doesn't love angels. You're Konstantin." His golden eyes glowed. "Have you seen yourself?" He gestured at the windows where their twin reflections hovered in the glass.

Severn glanced across, expecting to dismiss what he saw, but the demon staring back with his own eyes was spellbinding. Skin as dark as night, etched with simmering veins of fire. A body built for battle, muscular and proud.

Great, arched horns, passed down in the genes of long-dead Red Manor ancestors.

"You're magnificent," Samiel said. "I thought I'd lost you, but you're right here. You can have Red Manor, you can have it all, more than before. You'll lead us as Konstantin, like you always should have. But not if you go in there for an angel. Let Mikhail go."

Severn felt his insides twist, like the wry smile on his lips. "You're not listening, Samiel. I don't love you anymore."

"No!" he snapped. "You're not listening! If you go in there, you'll fuck it all up. Don't throw *us* away! We're worth more than that, more than *him*."

He couldn't deal with Samiel's jealousy now. "Leave." He turned toward the open window. "We'll talk later—"

Samiel's fingers wrapped around Severn's arm and yanked. Severn spun and delivered a fist to Samiel's jaw, knocking him back. Samiel's foot punched through a rotted board. His whole body yawned backward. Wood splintered, cracked, taking his leg. Samiel grabbed for a pole and the rusted length twanged off in his hand. The entire scaffold shuddered a warning. Clamps sprang loose, popping free of their joints. The platform was about to collapse.

Severn bolted for the window. A scaffold pole struck him on the back of the neck, knocking him out of his stride. He missed his footing. Metal and wood rained, and the board beneath him suddenly vanished. He dropped, stomach whooshing up, and somehow snagged the window's lower lip with one hand, but gravity grabbed a hold and poles clanged, knocking him free, and then he was free-falling, plummeting among shattered wood and bent poles.

His wings reflexively sprang free. A pole struck his left arch and tore into the membrane, spinning Severn in the air. He scrabbled for purchase, for any kind of updraft or air current. More poles fell out of the sky, skimming too close. He pulled his wings in, making less of a target, and *dove down*, out of the tumbling wreckage, beating his wings once he was free to climb higher again and watch the mess of scaffolding rain toward the ground.

Samiel struck him like a wrecking ball. He hadn't even seen him approach. The impact slammed the air from Severn's lungs. Glass suddenly shattered, sinking thousands of tiny teeth into his arms and face, and then he slammed into something only marginally less solid than a wall, punched through it in a shower of dust, and came to a skidding halt on his back among bits of raining plaster. Spluttering, he rolled onto his side, shaking some balance back into his vision. Plaster fell from his hair and clothes. *Fucking Samiel!*

Samiel's hand twisted into Severn's hair, and suddenly his snarling face was all Severn could see.

Severn thrust his head up, striking his horn between Samiel's horns hard enough to stun him. He brought his knee up, lodged a boot against Samiel's chest, and kicked, sending him flying across the room. It should have been enough, but Samiel never had known when to quit. He landed on his hands and feet. His wings sprung out, and digging in, he charged at Severn with a roar.

As Severn-the-angel, Samiel may have stood a chance. Now, Severn flipped onto his feet, pivoted as Samiel plowed toward him, grabbed his right wing, and using

Samiel's own momentum, spun him around and slammed him facedown into the floor.

Samiel stayed down, eyes closed but fluttering. Plaster dust settled on the string of blood dribbling from between his lips.

Stupid fucking fool. He'd get himself killed.

Severn's heart stuttered. He freed Samiel's wing, letting it flop to the floor. He'd never wanted to hurt him. But Samiel had left him no choice. He looked up and through the settling dust and spotted the faces of a few demons at the doors and internal windows, watching on.

Lux's entourage. They'd probably seen it all.

Severn freed a snarl, left Samiel out cold, and shoved through the high doorways into the inner hallways, keeping his wings out as warning that he wasn't in the mood to fuck around. At least nobody tried to stop him. After what they'd just seen, they'd likely reconsidered.

"Mikhail?!" he called. Demons scattered like rats. He broke into a jog up a small set of stairs until finally reaching Lux's penthouse.

"Hey, you can't go in there!" someone called.

"Watch me." The door gave way under a swift kick. The large, sumptuous bed dominated the room. The same bed where Lux had salivated over Severn and they'd gotten really personal for a few days. He'd half expected to find Mikhail spread there. But it was empty, the sheets tucked in and pillows fluffed.

No Lux.

No Mikhail.

The air was stale. Nobody had used the room in a while.

Severn tore the sheets from the bed. Lux's scent filled

the air, trying to sooth Severn into thinking the High Lord was *desirable*. Fucking concubi. If he tried that shit on Mikhail, Severn was going to dehorn him and shove those horns up Luxen's ass.

Where else would Luxen take an angel if not his own den?

Shit, he could be anywhere in north London.

All of the demon territory had hundreds of buildings, any one of which Lux could hide Mikhail in.

Rage set him ablaze. He flung open his wings and let loose a roar. It wasn't supposed to be this way! They'd just damn well found each other. He needed Mikhail to see that nothing had changed, not on the inside, but how could he when Lux had him hidden away and was probably feeding him all the lies?

He grabbed a bedpost and tore it free, crippling the bed at one corner. Using the post as a bat, he swung it into a bedside cabinet, splintering it to pieces. The noise and destruction at least felt good, as did using his considerable strength, even if it was just to trash Lux's belongings. A vase went next, exploding into a thousand shards. The more he destroyed, the more he hungered to destroy, like the anger was a living, breathing thing inside him, driving him forward, making him powerful, making him unstoppable. He'd tear them all down, every last fucking one.

When there was nothing left in the room that hadn't been broken into bits, he stood among the wreckage, no closer to Mikhail. And that hurt the most. If Lux wanted a fight, he'd give him one, like he should have done years ago.

Demons fearfully peeked through the door.

Severn spared them a glance over his shoulder.

He swung the battered bedpost at the window, shattering the glass, and ran at the open skies, spreading his wings the moment he leaped from the building.

The wind caught him, and he soared. London blurred below as vengeance fanned the fire in his heart. The love between a demon and an angel had been destroyed before. That would not happen again, not for as long as Severn's heart beat for Mikhail. He'd find him, he'd save him, and in doing so, maybe he'd save them all.

CHAPTER 4

ikhail

"I ASKED myself what I should do with you? The simple answer was to kill you, obviously. But that seemed like such a waste."

This demon, Luxen, liked the sound of his voice, and Mikhail—still strung up on the wall—had no choice but to listen. But he didn't have to like it. So he stayed silent and watched the demon pace back and forth, enjoying his own drama. He'd hidden his wings and changed his clothes into something less warrior-like and more tailored to fit his frame. When Mikhail had rounded the concubi up to kill, most were larger beasts. Konstantin was definitely heavier than most and more substantial than this Luxen.

Konstantin.

Severn.

He'd remembered most of it during the night. The

memories had tumbled forth like waking dreams. Konstantin and Severn were the same, but different too. And Mikhail wasn't entirely sure what that meant. In fact, he was still trying to piece together what any of this meant and how exactly he'd come to be this demon's prisoner. Or indeed, why he was still alive. If the positions had been reversed and the old Mikhail had held Luxen prisoner, Luxen would have been dead already. Now? Mikhail wasn't sure what he might have done. Severn had changed things. Changed *him*. For the better.

Luxen strode up close and peered into Mikhail's eyes. "I could take your wings as you have done to so many of my kind. Cut them from your back and make you cry for them." He leaned closer. So close Mikhail could see every one of his black eyelashes—so soft, like an artist's paintbrushes. "But I am not you."

The taste of him tingled on Mikhail's lips. So very demon. And so very like Severn. He turned his head away to wrangle his thoughts back under control.

Severn was surely alive. They'd left Haven together. He remembered that now too. It was all coming back, but in pieces that didn't quite fit together. Like the kiss in the field, with Severn so thoroughly demon. His dark skin stunning in starlight, his amber eyes full of luster, a touch so warm and soft—so simply Severn's that he knew the demon was the same person Mikhail had come to love. But there was fear too. Severn had shaken off his angelskin. Did that mean his feelings had changed with it? There had been no time to really understand any of it before the demons had descended on him, and then after that, he recalled nothing. Just waking up here, his head full of nonsense.

"Hm." Luxen made a deep, throaty sound of appreciation. "I cannot deny I find myself somewhat... torn."

His warm fingers pressed to Mikhail's jaw, forcing him to straighten his head and meet Luxen's gaze.

"But one thing is for certain, angel. Your reign of terror has ended here, with me. You're mine, to do with as I please."

Mikhail was no expert in emotion, and certainly not in lust, but the heat in Luxen's gaze wasn't all murderous glee. Severn had sometimes looked at him the same, in the beginning, when the allyanse had first been sealed. As though Mikhail were a feast. He'd spoken of ether and wondered what kind of emotion Luxen sensed in him now. The allyanse may not have been real, in a way the angels believed it to be, but there was no denying the very real desire in Luxen's dark eyes every time he fell silent and *observed*. Desire for angel.

Mikhail jerked his head free. "Where is Severn?"

Luxen's emotive face revealed a strange kind of amusement. He waved a hand. "How did this attraction between you come about?"

"Is he alive?" Mikhail asked, ignoring his question.

Luxen held his gaze. "Are there others like you? Other angels who desire demons?"

"I'm not answering your questions, demon, until you answer mine."

A knock sounded at the door, drawing Luxen's gaze. He stared at the closed door, considering whether to answer.

"High Lord?" a muffled voice said from outside.

Luxen's gaze slid back to Mikhail, holding a dangerous edge. He was sly. And now he knew Luxen was socially powerful too, their *High Lord*. Mikhail hadn't been sure. He'd heard of Luxen, but they'd never met, only catching glimpses in battle. He didn't look like he could control a rabble of demons, let alone their entire force. So his strength lay in subterfuge, like Severn's had. Just how alike were they?

Luxen opened the door, keeping whoever stood outside from Mikhail's view. "Yes?"

"He trashed your den," the newcomer said out of sight.

"How juvenile." Luxen left, the door swung closed, and voices soon faded.

Mikhail flexed his fingers, trying to keep them from falling numb. Moistening his lips, he blinked at the room with its single chair and naked light bulb. He had to get out of here. Whatever Luxen had planned, the High Lord would eventually kill him. But whatever concoction Tien had given him still ravaged his body, and his mind was not as it should be. This room, Luxen, he couldn't be entirely sure any of it was real. The drug's purpose had become clearer alongside Mikhail's own thoughts. The substance had made him suggestible, muddied his memories, leaving him open to whatever truth the guardians would have told him. He'd escaped before they could fulfill their plan, but the drug hadn't left him. Not fully.

He'd have to be careful around Luxen. If the High Lord realized just how weak he was, he might not be able to defend against him.

Mikhail sighed. Tired of looking at the same walls, he closed his eyes and tried to recall the last and first real kiss he'd shared with Severn in the field—Severn as demon. The memory seemed so far away that he had to fight to recall the tingling warmth of Severn's lips against his own.

The truth of them as they stood together against the world. Demon and angel. And the wonderful glow he'd felt inside, of what he could only name as love, when it had been just them.

No drug, no guardian, could ever make him forget that.

CHAPTER 5

evern

HE TWITCHED AWAKE, saw a pup sitting at the end of the bed, and jerked upright, onto his ass. "Fuck, Ernas."

"Sorry, didn't mean to startle you."

Groaning, Severn dragged a hand down his face. After destroying Luxen's den, he'd wandered through the streets, daring anyone who looked his way to attack—itching for a fight. To his disappointment, nobody had challenged him. Then the pup he'd met months ago, Ernas, had fearlessly swaggered into his path and told him to follow. With nowhere else to go, Severn had followed him to the corner of a derelict warehouse. The tin roof leaked like a sieve and there was a faint smell of urine in the air.

Ernas had then offered him a ham sandwich, said little, stoked an oil-drum fire to keep them warm, and given Severn his makeshift bed for the night. The wind had howled and moaned through the place, flapping the plastic sheets and making trash dance. It wasn't the best place to sleep, but it was better than the street. He was definitely a few rungs down from his nice, plush Aerie bed.

"How you doin'?" Ernas asked now, tossing a hot breakfast wrap at him.

Severn snatched the paper packet out of the air a fraction of a second before it would have hit him in the face.

"Breakfast in bed. Five-star accommodation, eh?" Ernas winked, then flopped back against the wall. "Sorry it ain't the Hilton."

Severn sat up and winced around all the aches. His sore wings would be making their presence known for days. The "bed" he sat on was a few pallets stacked high, some old newspapers, and a stiff old duvet Ernas had probably dragged from the local recycling center. He couldn't complain. Severn probably looked as though he'd been dragged from the recycling center too. Blood stained his Haven-issued clothes. He still had plaster dust in his hair and on his face, probably had the same dust all over his wings too. "It's good," he said. "I was in a pretty shitty mood last night. So thank you for this." He patted the bed and waggled the wrap. "I needed it."

"It's all good." Ernas beamed. "Red Manor gotta stick together, right?"

Yesterday had been a disaster. From attacking Samiel to failing to find Mikhail. He was no farther forward, just more pissed off. "Right," he muttered, biting into the bacon-and-egg wrap. He was starving, and the wrap hit the spot, making him moan.

"Can't fight a war on an empty belly."

"Who told you that?" Severn asked around a mouthful.

"My sire. He died when I was little. Maybe he didn't eat enough." Ernas chatted about his family and his one surviving sister. She'd left for the countryside, somewhere up north. He hadn't seen her in a few years. He'd been rattling around the docklands, learning to fight since then, searching for a manor to take him.

While listening, Severn finished the wrap, threw off the sheet, and sighed at the wreckage of his wrinkled and torn gray angel slacks and sweater. The fabric had stretched over thick demon muscle, but there wasn't much give left in them. He probably looked like a Rottweiler shoved into a sweater. Nothing felt like it fit, or maybe it was his skin that no longer fit. His thoughts didn't fit his head either. He was a fucking mess.

He'd given up hope of ever having his true body back again, but here he was, fully restored as Konstantin. At least on the outside. On the inside, things were more complicated.

He ran a hand through his hair and brushed dust from his horns. "I have to find him."

"Find who?" Ernas asked. He'd moved to the oil drum and was stoking the fire inside again, building it up with anything flammable he could find. Old shoes, bits of wood, newspaper, plastic bottles. It all went in.

Mikhail. But Ernas would look at him like he was mad too if he told him the truth. "Luxen... I have to find Luxen." He tossed the wrap's paper wrapper into the fire and watched the flames hungrily devour it.

"Oh yeah, I heard all about you beating ten shades outta Samiel and trashing Lux's den. Wha'd he do?"

Everyone would be talking about *that* display. At least

they knew Konstantin was back. Though, he could probably have made a better entrance. "Stole something."

"Must be something special."

"There's no other like him." Severn cleared his throat. "Thanks for inviting me here. It means more than you know."

"I figure we all need help sometimes, even the legends."

He chuckled. "I'm not that."

"You were to some of us. Still are to me." He smiled sheepishly, then tossed bits of splintered scaffold board into the fire. "What you said before, about me joining Red Manor. Did yah mean it?"

Severn clearly needed all the help he could get. He had no plan and no idea where Mikhail was. "Honestly, you've got more to offer me than I have you, right now. But sure, if you want to, you're in."

"Yes!" He fist pumped the air, then said more sedately, "I'd like that. The other manors won't take me. Said I'm too small." He tapped his stubby right horn. "These don't help."

"They'll come in, give 'em time. Mine were late too. An' don't listen to the others," Severn said. "How many are left in Red Manor?"

"I think it's just you and me, and Djall, I guess."

And an angel. Ernas didn't need to know Severn had claimed Mikhail for Red Manor. Not that it had helped much. Luxen had still stolen him. The bastard.

If Severn was going to have any weight among demons, he needed more than Ernas behind him. He needed power and control. He was Konstantin again. A lord of Red Manor. Others *would* follow him, eventually. He just had to prove to them he was trying to end the war to stop demon deaths. He needed allies. "Do you know a demon, goes by the name of the madam?"

"Sure do. She's set up a little, er... after-dark club around near Abe's store. Some of the concubi go to her. Not me," he hastily added.

He wasn't surprised the madam had fallen back on her talents. "Can you ask her to meet me here?"

"Is this, like, *official* Red Manor business?" Ernas's eyes widened. "Is she gonna join us?"

Severn smiled. "Let's not get ahead of ourselves. She's always been independent. But she has connections. Can you find her?"

"Fuck yeah." He tossed something plastic into the fire that quickly caught and churned out black smoke, then brushed his hands. "I reckon there's others too, that'll follow you. I mean... like, Samiel, maybe? I know you kinda kicked his head in, but he's had it comin' for a while, so..."

Severn probably shouldn't have smashed Samiel's face into the floor of Luxen's building. But they'd fought before, and he always came around. "I'll talk with him. If you see him, tell him to meet me here too."

Ernas bounded off, his wings falling open and flapping haphazardly behind him.

Severn stared at the drum's contained flames. The fight with Samiel had been avoidable. He should have handled it with more finesse, but he hadn't been thinking clearly. He'd wanted to get his hands on Luxen, and Sam had been in the way.

He needed his friend, now more than ever. Samiel was usually reasonable. If he'd stop being an emotional demon for ten minutes and actually listen, he might come around, at least enough to want to stop the war.

The madam would help too. She was loyal to Konstantin, but she wasn't a fighter, and Mikhail had shredded her wings. Shit, was there anyone Mikhail hadn't fucked over? They all wanted him dead. He'd have to tread carefully, maybe lead with stopping the war and not so much with saving Mikhail from Luxen. The madam had connections and Ernas had excellent local knowledge, but Severn needed fighters. He needed someone the demons already looked up to. Someone with clout, who might know where Luxen was keeping Mikhail.

He needed his sister.

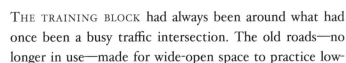

THE TRAINING BLOCK had always been around what had once been a busy traffic intersection. The old roads—no longer in use—made for wide-open space to practice low-level flying, and the underpasses provided both shelter from the rain and any spying angels.

The trainee numbers were slim today. In Konstantin's days, the roads were packed with demons practicing their moves. Today, only a handful of demons attacked dummies and one another. All of them stopped and stared as he passed by. They were all armed too. Their crawling gazes made his back itch. Clearly he had a long way to go to make up for the past and Luxen's slur campaign against him.

Luxen hadn't sent his guards after him yet. Either he didn't think Severn a threat, or he was too busy with Mikhail...

Shoving that last thought aside, he climbed the vine-covered trellis up one side of a crumbling multistory parking lot and hauled himself over the short wall, onto the large flat roof. He could have flown in, but then Djall would immediately see him and ready her whip. He was hoping a nonthreatening approach on foot might keep her from lashing out.

When they'd both been pups, he'd free-ran with Djall through the battle-scarred remains of London's streets, over rooftops, through gutted houses, and down London's hidden tunnels. All of his siblings had done the same. Always ending on *this* parking lot. Now they were the last two of their bloodline. Survival of the fittest, or the luckiest.

Djall was up ahead. She hadn't seen him, so he hung back. The last thing he wanted was her dagger to land in his chest. They'd always fought. A lot. Then more recently, he'd tried to kill her on the banks of the Thames to keep his demon secret from Mikhail. He'd failed then, and he was glad for that. Djall had done some fucked-up things, like plan the bomb on Aerie with Lux, but she did want the same thing as him. To end the bloodshed.

She cracked her whip and spun, dagger flashing toward the sparring dummy, and it wasn't any wonder he'd failed. She moved like light reflecting off a mirror. Fast and lethal. If light were barbed, had sharp teeth, and killed anything it touched.

"Sister."

With a yelp, she dropped, twisted and flicked a dagger in low. The damn thing nearly took his ear off. He danced aside at the last second, and the blade clattered against the wall behind him.

Lifting his hands in surrender, he backed up. She'd have multiple daggers hidden all over her, ready to launch with no warning. "I just want to talk. See, no weapons. Just talk."

"That just makes you easier to kill." She straightened and marched toward him, stiletto boots clicking on concrete.

He had a horrible feeling he was about to get his ass kicked again. "Djall..." Another step back and his legs nudged the low parking lot wall. "I didn't come here to fight. Again."

"You lied to me!"

Oh shit. He'd lied *a lot*. Which lie was she upset about? The whole Mikhail thing, or the finding his true body thing? "No, no... well, maybe... Probably. Okay, yeah. I lied. A lot. To everyone. But I really was trying to do the right thing for Red Manor, for all of us."

"By turning yourself angel?" She stopped within stabbing distance and narrowed her eyes. "You're so full of shit. You're a disgrace to demons, a traitor, and I should stab you in the heart right now." She punched him in the chest instead, rocking him back. She could have hit him harder, or shoved him off the roof altogether, so this was possibly progress. "I hate you and what you've done. Our kin look at me like I might fuck an angel next. It's embarrassing. You're a skree. Look at you. What even *are* those clothes —are those *angel* clothes? *Dafaq*, Stantin?! You really just walked through the area in angel-fucking-clothes?!"

He looked down at himself. Still wearing his angel clothes a dumb move, but he really hadn't been thinking clearly since Lux took Mikhail. The only words that came to his defense were the truth. "I love him."

She threw her hands up, retrieved her dagger beside his feet, then slipped it into its hip sheath, leaving the whip at ease in her other hand. "If our sire were here, he'd slap some sense into you. Thank Aerius he's not. You're mad. Driven that way by your own stupid plan to wear angel-skin."

"Maybe." He felt crazy sometimes. Right now, he was feeling pretty beat up and mostly tired.

"What am I supposed to say?" She folded her whip into a loop and hooked it to her belt. "I tried to protect you, but you keep doing stupid shit, so I'm done. Luxen will kill you for this. I can't blame him."

He'd come to ask for her help, or so he'd told himself. But mostly, there was one thing he really needed to know. "Where is he, Djall?"

She propped a hand on her hip and sighed. "Your fucking angel? I don't know. And if I did, I wouldn't tell you."

He scanned her face. Thin lips, pressed tight. Golden eyes, looking at him as though she could drill him to the floor with her gaze. She wasn't lying. "Do you have any ideas?"

She sighed again. "Are you going to fight me over this, like you did Samiel?"

He dropped his ass on the low wall, deliberately putting himself in a less threatening position. "Samiel attacked me. He wouldn't listen and then lost his shit with me."

She snorted. "It's a shame he didn't beat you senseless."

Just because they were talking didn't mean she wouldn't do exactly as she'd said and stab him in the heart.

But she had sheathed all her blades, so maybe she would hear him out. "I went to Haven."

"Hooray for you," she scoffed.

"It's not some utopia where angels go to fuck. It's a brainwashing facility. The guardians wipe young angels of all emotions to keep them controlled. They strip every single angel of emotion, but mostly their love. We've always called them machines, with no heart and soul, because they are machines. They've been conditioned that way by their own people."

She blinked. "That's some twisted bullshit. How do you know all this?"

"I've seen it. I know it because I've felt it. Inside. Ten years, Djall. I know them. They're victims, most of them."

"Victims? You sound crazier the more you talk." She turned, opened her wings, and hopped off the roof, landing on the street below.

Severn quickly followed, landing behind her. Again, the training demons all looked at him like he'd sprouted a third horn. Some backed off when he locked gazes, some snarled like they'd love nothing more than to be the one to take Konstantin down.

He jogged to Djall's side, earning her raised eyebrow. "Go away," she grunted. "You're making me look bad."

"Demons were made to love angels."

Her expression darkened. "There's stupid, and then there's you. You're real close to a punch in the face."

"Seraphim fucked up. He made demons full of emotion and love because his angels were shit at all those things. He was trying to make it right. And then he fell in love with his own creation. He fell in love with Aerius."

"Did it take ten years for you to think up this shit?"

"Seraphim loved Aerius."

She spat a laugh. "I don't know what's funnier, the fact you think Aerius could fuck an angel's ass, or the fact you think any of those fairytales are based on real people."

She was laughing at him, but she was listening and not attacking, and that was progress. "Djall, the guardians killed Seraphim. They killed their own god because he loved a demon."

"That sounds more likely."

"They tried to kill Aerius. Seraphim saved him and died as a result. Guardians have been hushing it all up since, making angels war against us for an age-old mistake. Guardians buried the truth because they're afraid of love. They told me."

"Who told you?"

"The prick Remiel. Before he threw me off Aerie."

"That bastard angel leading Aerie right now? *He* threw you off Aerie?"

"Mikhail caught me."

She stopped marching and stared, her face screwed up in some kind of mash-up of disgust and horror. "Mikhail what now?"

A few demons lingered nearby, pretending to focus on their sword thrusts instead of listening, but their argument had gotten real loud and Severn wasn't sure he cared. Let them listen in. It'd give them something to think about.

"He pulled me out of the air. He saved my life—the life of a demon—in front of all his angels."

Her mouth fell open. "Even knowing you're Konstantin," she uttered. "After all that bullshit, taking your wings, learning you're not a real angel, and he *saves* you? That doesn't make any sense."

There wasn't any right way to view Mikhail's actions. He was everything she hated about angels. "He's fucked up, I get it. He gets it. But he saved me. Then Remiel stabbed him for it and pushed him over the edge too. His own people wanted him dead because he's the proof they're so afraid of. Mikhail isn't the monster we all thought him to be. He's changing. He *cares*. They're all capable of it. And once those angels know the truth, they won't fight. I promise you this."

Her horror softened some, until she just looked confused. But the softness soon vanished beneath the hard mask of a warrior-sister he knew too damn well. "He cared a great deal when he took the heads of all the Red Manor concubi and displayed them like trophies as a warning to the rest of us. It makes me sick to think I share the same blood as someone who believes he loves that monster."

"Djall—"

"No!" she snapped. "Get out of my face, Stantin, or I'll stab you in yours." She marched off.

That could have gone better, but also much worse. She had listened. Even if she didn't believe him, she'd *heard* the truth. Hopefully now, she'd think on it.

Severn regarded the demons staring at him, like he was some foreign thing. Baring his teeth, he snarled, spread his wings, and took to the air. Maybe they'd never believe him, maybe they would kill him, or maybe everything he'd said would trigger a tiny spur of compassion in them. Either way, he'd tried, and right now, that was the only weapon he had.

CHAPTER 6

*M*ikhail

SMOOTH, light fingers stroked over Mikhail's wrist, skimming the sensitive skin near where the restraint rubbed. Luxen smelled of musky spices, cinnamon, and citrus. And when his sly, dark-eyed gaze briefly skipped to Mikhail's face, a skitter of *something* quickened Mikhail's heart—some emotion he couldn't identify. The restraint holding his wrist gave suddenly. Mikhail's tingling arm flopped forward, and to his shame, Luxen caught him. His hands branded where they touched at his chest and waist. When the second restraint let go, Mikhail pushed from the demon's hold and fell back against the wall. A shudder rippled through his weakened body, foggy thoughts blurring. He fluttered a twitching hand to his forehead, trying to physically move the pieces of his mind back into place.

Luxen—now a few steps back—offered a bowl of soup. "Eat."

"Why am I still alive?" Mikhail eyed the bowl. Hunger chewed on his insides. Surrendering to Luxen in any way seemed like a failure, but he had to eat. Sliding his back and wings down the wall, he dropped into a cross-legged position.

Luxen had moved farther away, as though sensing Mikhail needed space, or perhaps needing it himself, and leaned a shoulder against the opposite wall. "We took some of your blood while you were out. Had a closer look at it. Found a potent substance that likely explains your mental and physical dissonance. You *were* poisoned. Why?"

Mikhail reached forward, gripped the edge of the bowl, and scooped it into his lap. He grabbed the chunk of bread that accompanied the soup and took a bite. Once he'd begun eating, there was no stopping it. The soup may have been the most delicious meal he'd ever eaten. He washed it down with a cup of water and slumped against the wall, waiting for his heart to slow and the aches to pass.

Luxen had observed in silence.

The door was a few strides away. It didn't appear to have a lock. But if he dashed for it, he likely wouldn't get far in his current condition.

Luxen shoved from the wall, crossed the floor in two long strides, and crouched. He had his wings hidden, but he still carried a formidable presence. Concubi always did. They could fill a room with their allure, make their rapt audience fall over themselves in awe, exuding ether for their leech-like existence to drink down.

"Is Severn alive?" Mikhail asked. He'd asked it so often the words no longer had meaning.

Luxen smiled. "If I tell you, what will you do for me?"

"Nothing," he rasped, hating that he was still so damned weak. If he could just summon the gods' power, no demon would stand in his way, but any effort to reach for the power just fizzled to nothing.

Luxen huffed a rich, humorless laugh. "Negotiating means I give you something and in exchange you give me something."

"I don't negotiate with demons."

He sighed as though genuinely disappointed. "And Konstantin said you'd changed. But you are the Mikhail you've always been, aren't you? Is Konstantin blind or did you lie your way into his demon heart?"

The idea that Mikhail would have lied and pretended to love Severn was abhorrent. He stared the demon in his dark eyes. "I don't lie either."

"Then how did you trap him?"

"I didn't."

"You just"—Luxen touched his lips with his fingers and fluttered them into the air—"fell in love with another angel? Does that happen often?"

"The allyanse..." *was a lie.* "Is Severn alive?"

Luxen straightened, making Mikhail look up the tall length of him. He shuffled back, disliking their positions and how this demon towered over him. Once he was back to full strength, Luxen would kneel to him and this whole charade would be over.

"Konstantin is very much alive," Luxen said finally, with no fanfare. "In fact, he's exactly where he should be, as a lord among his manor, among his demons. I don't think he's mentioned you at all. It seems his infatuation with angel has... worn off."

The relief almost made him weep. Severn was alive! And then the other words sank in, but Mikhail found those hard to believe, especially coming from the lips of a demon. "You think me naïve enough to fall for more concubi lies?" He chuckled darkly, liking the sound.

Luxen shrugged. "Lies or not, you're here, and he is not. If your love were so fierce a thing, why has not come for you?"

Mikhail couldn't trust this demon. He'd say anything, lie and trick to have his way. "What do you want from me if not to kill me? Why are you keeping me here?"

Luxen tilted his head. He reached up. His fingers stroked Mikhail's cheek. Instincts demanded Mikhail turn away from the touch, but to do so would be to give the demon a win. Mikhail glared back, the soup in his belly roiling.

"You had six wings in that field," Luxen said softly. "Your light was like nothing I've ever seen, brighter than the sun. You are not like other angels. Why is that?"

The demon's gaze drilled into Mikhail's. His lashes were dark, his eyes the color of warm caramel, and Mikhail could feel himself falling into a place where his body no longer hurt and his head cleared. It would be a relief to surrender to this one. To give him everything he wanted. He *desired* it...

Mikhail grabbed the demon's throat, swung him around, and slammed him against the wall. Or at least, that had been the plan, but Mikhail's arms felt like lead and as soon as he'd committed to the attack, he knew it to be a mistake. Luxen got a leg under him and vaulted away, only to spin lightly on his feet.

The wall was suddenly at Mikhail's back, Luxen's fingers at his throat. All the air lodged in Mikhail's lungs, trapped there by the demon hand at his throat.

"Consider this... angel," Luxen snarled, filling Mikhail's vision, "I am not the monster here. You are." He grabbed Mikhail's wrist, hauled his body high off the floor, and clamped his wrist back into place.

Mikhail tugged at the vice-like grip on his neck, desperate for air. Luxen freed him suddenly, but in the next second, he slammed Mikhail's opposite wrist high and clamped that back into place too.

Luxen backed up, admiring his prize. But he didn't look pleased with his catch. With a snort, he ran a hand over his right horn and tugged his shirt cuffs back into line. "It's a sorry state of affairs when the only angel worth a damn thing was a demon in disguise."

"You can't hold me here for long, demon. The poison will wear off. When that happens, these restraints won't hold."

"And will you kill us all, Mikhail? Scorch us all from this earth with that righteous light of yours like the monster you are?"

Mikhail heaved against the horrid wrist clamps until his arms trembled all over again. "I'll burn you all to the ground!"

"You haven't changed at all." Luxen left with those words resounding in Mikhail's ears. He *had* changed. Luxen was wrong, but only the opinion of one demon mattered. A demon who was back among his own kind, a demon lord, once respected and revered. He would be again. What place would Mikhail have with Severn then? Severn loved him, that was for certain, but he also loved his people, and if Severn had to choose, Mikhail feared he knew which way Severn would eventually fall.

He did not belong here, among demons. But he didn't belong in Aerie either.

He folded his wings' dark fronds around himself, as much as their pinned angle would allow. He *had* changed. But he'd changed for Severn, and without him, there was no place in the world for a broken angel.

CHAPTER 7

Severn

WATER DRIPPED from the warehouse's vast roof, and a cold wind rippled the plastic sheets protecting Ernas's den from the elements.

"Lux hasn't been seen in days," the madam said, arching an eyebrow as Severn stripped off the filthy angel clothes and buckled himself inside the clothes she'd brought for him. Nothing fancy—he didn't want to draw more attention than he already had. Just black trousers, a plain purple shirt, chunky black boots, and a three-fourths-length coat that he buckled tightly across his chest. He could maybe pass for any demon like this. The madam wore tightly fitting purple velvet pants and a black lace waistcoat, revealing enough that the rain glistened on her purple skin.

"The rumors say he's working on a weapon to finally

bring down the angels," she added. "But if that's true, he'd better hurry. The cambion report Remiel is building a flight of battle angels that makes our measly three-thousand-strong rank of demons look pathetic. Thousands are gathering in Whitechapel, and more angels have come from afar to shore up Aerie. It seems you shook a hornet's nest."

Fucking Remiel. The angels would follow that golden-tipped asshole to their deaths for a cause entirely built on lies. And Remiel *knew* the truth. The guardians were the root of the problem, but they were also tough bastards to get rid of. As Mikhail had proven for ten years.

"Remiel means to attack," Severn said, shrugging the coat into place.

If he could rally their forces, they may have a chance at defending against the angels, but only because Severn knew how they fought. Luxen wasn't capable—and the prick was holed up with Mikhail somewhere. A fact that made Severn want to rip every last building down to rubble to find his angel.

Ernas had been combing the streets for information, but either nobody knew a damn thing, or nobody was talking to the angel-loving traitors of Red Manor. Demons loved to talk, so the latter was more likely.

He paced to the broken warehouse window. Rain hissed against the street outside. Mikhail wasn't dead. He knew that much. Luxen would have his head paraded on a stake if he'd killed him. The High Lord's plan was more insidious. Lux was concubi, and concubi thrived on ether. And there was no better source of ether than an angel like Mikhail.

Mikhail wouldn't have stood for it had he been at full

strength. So, Tien's poison was keeping him weak. The guardian had likely planned to use the drug to fill Mikhail's head full of lies, to recondition him and send him back to Aerie like the good guardian angel he was supposed to be. Tien was gone, Mikhail had seen to that, but her drug wasn't. If Luxen sensed weakness, he'd go in for the kill.

That fucking snake was manipulating Mikhail. Severn was sure of it. Otherwise, Mikhail would have brought all of London to its knees by now.

Severn braced an arm against the wall and bowed his head. Knowing Mikhail was out there—knowing he needed help and not being able to get to him—hurt worse than any physical wound.

The flap of plastic announced another arrival. "We need to build a counterforce." Rainwater dripped from Samiel's coat and pooled on the floor around his boots.

At least Samiel was still with him, even after their spat. The madam was here, and Ernas would be back from his patrol soon, hopefully with some lead as to where Mikhail was being held. So he wasn't entirely alone in all this. He was making progress. Even if it was slow.

"If the angels attack now, we'll lose," Samiel continued. "Luxen is AWOL. I can't even find Jeseph. Djall is the only one who seems to have any sense of urgency. She's forming a rank, but it won't be enough, and she can't do it alone."

His own kind thought him a traitor when his only crime was loving an angel. Part of him wondered why the fuck he was even here. Why should he help the demons when they'd written him off? Most wanted him dead, and all would kill Mikhail the first chance they got.

He flicked his coat collar up and sauntered between the madam and Samiel, pushing back the sheet to enter the main warehouse. The wind instantly blew grit into his face and rippled his coat.

"Konstantin, wait," Samiel called, chasing after him. "I... I'm sorry, about what happened. I was a dick."

"Yeah, you were." Severn mustered a smile. "But you're here."

"Yeah." Samiel thrust his hands into his pockets. "For what it's worth, Remiel's forces aren't going away. We need you. You're going to stick around, right?"

"I'm not going anywhere." He had to find Mikhail first. Everything else could wait.

Samiel puffed out a heavy sigh. "Okay... I mean, you can use my den, if you want? This place is a bit"—he frowned at the yawning space full of trash and old storage crates—"draughty."

"Thanks." Severn turned away and headed for the doors.

"Where are you going?"

"Out." The rain wasn't going to stop him from spreading his wings and taking to the skies over London in the hope he might catch a glimpse of Mikhail, or something—standing around and waiting for news was killing him slowly. Revealing his wings, he shook out their stiffness, broke into a run, and launched into the rain-heavy air. Spiraling higher in the air revealed Samiel standing in the rain, head tilted up, watching with a frown.

CHAPTER 8

M ikhail

Voices outside the door roused him from a restless sleep. One of those voices was Luxen's melodic drawl, but the second was more difficult to define.

By Haven, how long had it been? Days? No more than a week, surely. Luxen had brought food, talked some, asked him the same questions, but he hadn't hurt Mikhail, hadn't tortured him like angels would have tortured a demon.

The voices faded and Mikhail drifted again, lost halfway between sleep and wakefulness.

"Holy shit."

Mikhail blinked, thoughts swimming back together. A demon pup stood, wide-eyed, in the middle of the room. Water dripped from his horns, hair, and clothes. He panted hard, like he'd been running. The door hung open.

"Fuck," the pup gasped.

Mikhail eyed him carefully. His deep blue skin and short horns were familiar. They'd met before, but he couldn't recall where.

The pup straightened and stepped closer. "Wow." His gaze darted about Mikhail, skimming his face, body, and then the wings.

"Who are you?" Mikhail narrowed his eyes.

"You don't remember?" He snorted. "Typical. You attacked the med ward? I was there. Tried to stop you. You punched me into the floor."

Oh yes, he recalled this fiery little demon now. He had come at Mikhail like an insane creature seeking its own death. And now he was here. Was this revenge then?

The pup took another step and tipped his head back, taking all of Mikhail in. "You deserve this."

Mikhail swallowed. "Yes, I probably do."

The answer surprised the pup. He opened his mouth to say something, then glanced at the door. "Shit, someone's coming. I'll bring him to you. Just... hang tight." He snorted at the pun and dashed from the room.

Moments later, Luxen's voice sounded out, demanding to know why the door was open. The High Lord strode in and glared. "Who was here?"

"A draught," Mikhail grumbled. "Nothing more."

"Your attempt at lying is truly spectacular," Luxen growled. "It doesn't matter. I've doubled the guards. Whoever saw you won't be returning."

Mikhail's heart fluttered. The pup had said he'd bring *him*. Did he mean Severn? He just had to hold out a little longer.

Luxen withdrew a syringe from his trouser pocket and

held it up. "You remember I said we'd discovered a substance in your blood? Well, here it is. A powerful hallucinogen in humans, but in angels, not only does it appear to negate their innate healing abilities, but it also has the effect of dumbing them down, making them suggestible." He approached. "If I were to inject you with it, given you've already had a high dose, I might suggest a few things, and you'd likely believe them."

He was lying. It was just water, or saline solution, or some other drug that would have no effect. "We don't need to be like this," Mikhail said. "Seraphim did not intend for his children to fight. Release me and let us discuss the future between our two races."

"Suddenly talkative are we? What happened to not negotiating with demons?" He approached, the exposed needle glinting.

"You're concubi. I cannot trust you." Mikhail swallowed, moistening his suddenly dry throat. His gaze skipped between the demon and the needle. Luxen couldn't know the substance Tien had used. He had to be bluffing.

"Well, that's true. But you trust Konstantin, arguably the most powerful incubus concubi alive. And someone who lied to you for a decade."

"I love him. I do not love you."

Luxen's smile turned cruel. "That can soon be rectified." He lunged and grabbed Mikhail's left upper arm. The sting was instant, and a beat later, a chill spilled into his veins, traveling through his shoulder, toward his heart. He bucked, wings thrashing as much as their wedged position allowed.

Luxen staggered back and tossed the empty syringe to the floor.

He could feel it—whatever it was—creeping through him. "I'll kill you for this, demon!"

"No." He shrugged his jacket back into place, smoothing it down. "I don't think you will. But you will help me win this war. Once the angels see one of their own kind—one as powerful as you—kneel to me, they'll all fall in line. You're going to win this war for me, and you're going to fucking love me for it."

"It doesn't..." The drug pulled him down, blurring the edges, making everything numb, making the words slur. "... have to be this way." He'd have fought alongside them had he just asked. But Amii had been right. They weren't ready. Mikhail could only hope Severn learned of this and that he cared enough to stop Luxen before it was too late.

SUNLIGHT STREAMED in through a wall of windows, soaked up by stripped wooden floorboards and the crisp white bedsheets cocooning him in warmth. For a moment, he was back in Aerie, high above the clouds. His thoughts drifted, without a tether, wrapped in a contentedness that seemed almost too complete to be real. A cloud drifted in front of the sunlight, swallowing the room in shadows, and the demon sitting in a chair across the room became clear.

This wasn't Aerie.

Mikhail pushed upright in the bed. His wrists burned where they touched the sheets. He rubbed at them but found no sores or marks on his skin. He'd been... restrained? Or had that been a dream?

"How do you feel?" the demon asked.

Mikhail pressed a hand to his head. He felt... disorientated, out of place. "Strange."

The demon was well-dressed, attired in a suit, like humans sometimes wore when they wanted to impress others of their species. Was this demon trying to impress him? He seemed *familiar*. They knew each other. *Luxen.* And this bed was clearly his.

Mikhail threw off the sheets. Loose gray pants clung to his hips and skimmed his legs, brushing the tops of his bare feet. He had no memory of dressing, no memory of how he'd come to be in a demon's bed. He padded to the window. London sparkled all the way to the horizon with the broken disks of Aerie looming high above. Aerie was his home. He felt that as strong as he knew his name. "I need to get back."

"No, you don't. They don't want you there. They stabbed you in the back and threw you over the side, remember?"

Mikhail pressed his forehead to the cool glass and closed his eyes. He did remember. Remiel, a guardian, had tried to kill him. He'd fallen.

"I saved you." Luxen's soft words stole a small gasp from Mikhail's lips. He touched his head, trying to feel his way through the muddled memories. "You were wounded," Luxen went on. "You've been recovering here, with me."

Mikhail slid his gaze to the demon now standing beside him. A powerful specimen, clearly concubi, especially considering the soothing presence he radiated. But something wasn't quite right with all of this. The room, the demon, it all felt tilted, slightly off-balance, or perhaps it was Mikhail who was unbalanced.

Luxen's fingers found Mikhail's. He lifted them, his gaze on Mikhail's face, and brought Mikhail's fingers to his warm lips. A not unpleasant shudder ran through Mikhail at the demon's kiss. He had beautiful eyes. Beautiful lips too. The twin keratin horns with their glossy surface were... intriguing. His heart thumped, suddenly making him aware of the heat rushing through his own body.

The door flew open and a young demon stumbled in, shoved by a third, much larger demon.

"What part of *do not disturb me* didn't you understand, Samiel?" Luxen barked, his tone scything through Mikhail's soft thoughts, splitting them apart. Mikhail pulled his hand free of the demon's touch and eyed the concubi. His mood had switched from pleasant to lethal in a blink, further unbalancing the room and Mikhail's place in it.

"Ernas was the one who found Mikhail," the demon, Samiel, said. "I found him making a run for it. He's Konstantin's new recruit. Ain't that right, Ernas?"

Luxen grabbed Samiel by the throat and shoved him roughly out the door, slamming it behind them both, leaving Mikhail blinking at the disheveled pup. Well, this was unexpected. Smaller than the other two, the pup's horns weren't yet developed. He wasn't a threat.

Ernas shrugged his clothes back into place and quickly scanned the room, his gaze lingering on the bed. "Were you and 'im about to...? Oh, by Aerius, Konstantin is gonna lose his shit." He crossed the floor to the window and tried to yank open a pane. The units didn't budge. "Shit... I need to get out of here."

Luxen's raised voice permeated the closed door, chastising Samiel for interrupting a *delicate process*.

Ernas was in front of him suddenly, squinting up at Mikhail's face. "What's he done to you, eh? Are you even awake in there?" The pup waved his hand in front of Mikhail.

Mikhail grabbed him by the wrist and hauled him close. The pup yelped. Mikhail smothered his mouth with his free hand. Luxen would deal with this one. The little demon bucked, but his strength was meager.

"Be still," Mikhail warned. "He'll speak with you soon."

Luxen opened the door and ran a hand over his horn, slowing his pace as he saw Mikhail with Ernas in his grip. Samiel stared, wide-eyed, into the room, his shining yellow eyes locking on Mikhail. Tawny, golden skin, two C-shaped, curved horns. He had his wings hidden, but Mikhail knew his face. He'd seen him before. His memory was muddled, pieces of it broken off, but the instance he sought was old. The day of a terrible battle. The day Mikhail had cut down the great Lord Konstantin and taken his wings. Samiel had been there. Samiel had led Mikhail to his lord. Samiel had stood back as Mikhail had taken Konstantin's wings. Mikhail had suspected a trap, all those years ago, but none had come. Samiel was *untrustworthy*.

The torrent of memories poured forth, blinding Mikhail. The day he'd brought down his enemy. The demon, Samiel, had smiled when the deed was done, when the wings lay severed and Konstantin lay bleeding in the mud.

He wasn't smiling now.

"Fuck..." Samiel breathed.

Mikhail threw the pup aside and stumbled against the window, making it rattle. *Wait. This room, the demons. Liars.*

This was all wrong. Samiel... Samiel. He had a name now, a name for the demon-traitor who had helped him bring down Konstantin. Samiel. But the name brought with it more implications. Samiel... Konstantin's previous lover, the demon who had saved Severn from the rubble of Tower Bridge. Did Severn not know Samiel's betrayal that day? Did he still trust this one?

Severn had surrendered a memory to turn himself angel. A powerful memory from years ago.

Severn didn't know Samiel had betrayed him that day.

Samiel wasn't Severn's lover, he was his *enemy*.

These demons were both the enemy. And they'd done something to Mikhail, made him weak, fed him lies! The sudden weight of the truth hitting him doubled him over. He clutched at his head, trying to keep it all in.

"Hold him!" Luxen yelled.

Hands clamped ahold, fingers digging into his arms. Rage fizzled through his veins. These two demons were conspiring against Severn and had been for years! A cold sting pricked Mikhail's arm and the cascade of memories slowed, blurred, and wisped away, swept away like dust in sunlight.

It was all right. He was safe here. With Luxen. Luxen's deep, dark eyes and his soft, caring touch told Mikhail so.

"Shit," Samiel gasped, stumbling toward the door but hanging back. "Ernas ran." He planted his hands on his hips and stared at Mikhail. "Mikhail fucking knows me, Luxen. You said he wouldn't remember."

"Go after Ernas," Luxen said, sneering. "Make sure he never talks, and don't concern yourself with Mikhail. He'll remember only what I tell him." Luxen scooped Mikhail onto his feet and helped him to the bed. "Rest, my angel."

Yes, rest. That was the only way, and perhaps tomorrow, the strange fog in his head would lift.

CHAPTER 9

 evern

DEMONS DANCED IN THE SKY, not unlike angels, but Severn dared not tell them that, especially as Djall was the one directing them. They dove and swooped to the crack of Djall's whip, like an orchestra and their maestro. Only these instruments were all sharp-edged and brutal angel killers.

Severn took to the air, keeping an eye on their thirty or so number. It wasn't unheard of for such training sessions to get out of control and someone meet with an *accident*. He beat his wings, still learning their twitchy uniqueness, and approached Djall. She hovered outside the cloud of warriors, barking orders here and there. The higher Severn climbed, the more the wind battered him, trying to shove him off course. It would be doing the same to them—that was the point. Angels hated flying in anything but brilliant sunshine, lest they dirty up their feathers. Demons had no such hang-ups. A demon storm—where a large number of demons whipped up a gale, altering the weather—was one of the few weapons they had that worked to hold angels at bay.

Djall's whip suddenly lashed his way—a dark zip slicing through the damp air, heading straight for Severn's head. He plunged, raised an arm, looped the whip around his forearm, and jerked Djall *down*, turning her whip into her weakness. She growled, flapped uselessly, and shot him a warning look.

Before they were old enough to fight in the war, they'd often spring traps for each other and scrabble in the dirt until their sire tore them apart with a growl.

"We need to talk." He freed her whip. She snatched it back, looping it around her arm. Her wings gracefully stroked the air, keeping her aloft. Her demons had stopped their training, probably to see if she'd beat ten shades out of her brother.

She raised her arm and brought it down in a signal for them to disperse. Her demon rank scattered into the wind, dismissed.

"If it's about your angel, we really don't," she called over the buffeting wind.

They'd get to that. "It's about Remiel."

Jerking her chin in a small, tight nod. "Catch me, and then we talk, *brother*." And with that, she tucked her wings in and *dove*.

"Shit." He'd feared this would happen. Wings were important, not just for flying but for displays of control and prowess. Of which Severn had none. With no choice but to follow her lead, he pulled his wings in and chased after his sister's rapidly plunging figure. The patchwork of houses and streets grew, coming up fast to meet him. She'd leave it until the last second to pull up. They'd played this game a thousand times. Whoever pulled up first lost. Pull up too late, and your insides decorated the street. He'd always excelled, but that was before, with his old wings. The ones he'd learned to fly with. He was still working out the kinks in his new wings.

The wind tore at his face and brushed up his clamped wings, urging them to open and lift him far from the fall, but if he pulled up, she'd think him weak. There wasn't time for him to convince her otherwise. He had to do this.

His lungs burned. The air pulled through his teeth as thick as honey, and his vision fogged, eyes drying. Djall still plummeted impossibly fast toward the ground.

The rush of blood in his ears deafened him to the wind, and his racing heart pumping hot blood through his body defended against the cold.

Shit. The high-rises blurred past.

Djall let out a howl. Her wings bloomed, skillfully catching the air like twin parachutes opening.

Severn shot by her like an arrow, narrowly missing plowing right into her.

"Stantin!"

He sent a silent prayer to whoever listened that his fucking wings did as they were supposed to and flung them open. Gravity tried to yank his guts into his boots. His wing bones groaned, agony sparking through his shoulders and down his spine, like the air itself could rip his skeleton from his flesh.

He gasped, lurched, almost took out a lamppost, and somehow, by some miracle, missed the jagged edges of the buildings and sailed down to street level, scattering surprised demons out of the way.

Landing in a run, he skidded to a stop and whirled. *"Holy fuck."*

Djall hovered above like a black smudge against the sky. He couldn't see her face, but she had damn well better be impressed. Spreading aching wings, he lifted off the ground and climbed to her side.

"You're insane," Djall said, her hand on her hip, but her smile spoke volumes. "All right, you earned it. Let's talk."

"Not here…" He gestured for her to follow and took her away from the east end of London, farther north, away from the killing fields and demon territories, where humans still ran their little stores and went about their lives relatively secure in the knowledge that Seraphim's Law protected them. He sometimes envied their freedom. Demons and angels fought so they didn't have to, and they were clever enough never to pick a side.

Severn alighted alongside a bustling road and instantly illusioned his wings and horns away. His arrival drew a few glances, but most ignored him. It was more unusual to see an angel this far north than a demon.

Djall landed behind him, banishing her horns and wings to better blend in. He crossed the road and ducked into a small coffee shop to the jolly ring of a quaint bell.

"Why did you bring me all the way out here?" she asked once they were seated and the coffee ordered.

"You used to love it up here."

She glanced around them. The dozen tables were full of people. They laughed, stared at their phones, ate cake, and drank coffee. Always busy, locked in their little bubbles of humanity. Angels referred to humans as sheep, and the angels were, naturally, their shepherds. Demons in that analogy were wolves. All bullshit. If anything, angels were the wolves.

"You said it reminded you of what things could be like," Severn said.

"Yeah, if the angels left us all in peace." She'd agreed to talk, but she didn't look happy about it.

A smiling barista called out their order. Severn collected their coffees and settled back in the chair, leaning a shoulder against the wall so he could watch the oblivious people and Djall's scowl.

"Angels have forgotten why Seraphim made them," he said.

"Don't start with all that Seraphim bullshit again. You won the dive, doesn't mean I have to sit here and listen to your drivel." She sipped her espresso and sighed. "Damn, humans make the best coffee."

"Right." Severn grinned and tasted his own skinny hazelnut frothy latte.

Djall smiled, then chuckled.

"What?"

"You're such an angel. Skinny hazelnut latte? Seriously? You used to eat the beans raw!"

He snorted. "Tastes change."

Djall rolled her eyes. "Gods, stop with the heavy-handed comparisons. No, I don't know where your angel is, before you ask. But it's been long enough that Lux has either killed him or..."

"Or?" Severn asked carefully.

She shrugged a shoulder. "Mikhail isn't easily caught, so Lux has done *something* to keep him controlled."

As concubi, they both knew what that something was

likely to be. "Yeah, well, I'm not here to talk about Mikhail. Remiel is building a force like no other."

"Yes, I am aware."

"Luxen is distracted. Jeseph is incompetent, and seeing as nobody can find him, he's probably fled like the coward we all know him to be. We're a fucking joke. Remiel is going to annihilate us. Let me help."

She raised her cup, gave him a droll look over the brim of her coffee, and noisily sipped it. "You've been on the other side of the killing fields, killing demons *for* Mikhail. Why would I ever trust you again?"

"I fucked up... I get it. I left, and I should have been here to hold it all together. But listen..." He leaned in. "I know Remiel. I know angels. They all follow where their guardians lead. If we oust Remiel as the fraud he is, their faith will fall. Without faith, they're lost."

"And how do you intend to *oust* Remiel? You ain't an angel no more."

"Haven."

"Their little vacation resort?" She snorted. "Thought you already wrecked it?"

"Mikhail shook it to the core. We escaped, but there are angels there who weren't so lucky. On the surface, it looks harmless enough, but that's only for those who swallow the guardian bullshit. Anyone who doesn't gets poisoned and shoved somewhere else for emotional correction, probably below ground, out of sight. If I can get back inside Haven and find the damaged angels, the ones they're trying to fix, and free them, then it won't just be me and Mikhail telling the truth, it'll be a whole flight of angels—"

She laughed so suddenly half the people in the café

turned to look. "Have you looked in a mirror lately? You ain't a pretty blond no more. They're not ever letting you back into their precious little birdcage."

"All right, but they'll let other angels inside."

"Hm, fancy wearing your angel-skin again, do you? Why am I not surprised?"

"No, actually." He was done pretending to be someone he wasn't. Only the truth could save them. "But I know an angel who I think will help us."

She set her coffee cup down hard and leaned closer to hiss, "It's remarkable how nice they are to you, almost like you're *friends* with angels? Why would I ever trust anything you say again when you're telling me right to my face that you're friends with our enemies?"

"*Because* I am telling you. And I'm not friends with all of them, just one."

"Who?"

"Solomon. When I left, he was halfway to realizing the truth. He's not stupid, he'll be figuring it out. If I can get him into Haven, he'll discover the truth, just like I did. Nobody believes me on either side, demons or angels, because you all think I'm tainted by the other, but the angels will believe Solo. He's well-liked, honest, strong. They'll listen to him."

"You want to undermine the angels from the inside? Again?"

"Not undermine them, save them... It's the only way. We can't beat Remiel. That's a fight no demon walks away from. If we take away their belief that all guardians are sacred and make them see exactly what the guardians have been doing to them all their lives, they'll crumble from within. The truth will bring them down."

She frowned into her cup. "It has merit. If what you say is true, and the guardians are all bullshit liars, then their whole faith system could collapse."

He met her gaze. "It's true. If Mikhail were here, he'd say the same."

She pulled a face. "Can't you find a demon to love? It's not like you couldn't have your pick. Samiel—"

"Djall, who I fuck is not up for debate."

She caught his tone and backed off with a shrug. "The guardians are really lying to their own kind?"

"Yes. Through some misguided belief they're protecting them from love."

"Not just from love though, is it? According to you, the guardians are protecting angels from *loving demons*?" she whispered the last part.

He'd come this far, he couldn't back away from the truth now, especially when his sister was actually asking the right questions. "Exactly."

"Then what you're telling me is you want to find this Solomon and convince him to reveal their own ugly truth, which will bring down Remiel."

"I can't stop either side from fighting, not without evidence. My word alone ain't gonna cut it. I can't see another way to survive what's coming, can you?"

"That's a lot riding on one angel. Is Solo trustworthy?"

"Absolutely. I just have to get to him. The madam has access to nephilim, and nephilim love to talk. They'll know where he is."

"And he won't kill you the second he sees you... as Konstantin?"

Severn screwed up his nose. The last time he'd seen Solo, Severn had been about to be shoved off the edge of

Aerie. Solo had watched, but he'd also stood beside Mikhail, not Remiel, and that allegiance was an important one. "He'll try..." He'd clashed with Solo in Mikhail's gallery of wings, but the red-winged angel was fiercely loyal to Mikhail. That worked in their favor. "He's smart and he's already had his faith tested. He'll figure it out."

"I don't know, Stantin."

"Do you believe any of us have a choice? Remiel will wipe us from London in weeks, if we even have that long."

"All right. I'll support you in this, for Red Manor. But if you fuck up again, I'll kill you myself."

He smiled but quickly let it slip. "Now, tell me where Mikhail is."

"I don't know." Djall sighed. "There are rumors Luxen is torturing him somewhere, but the bastard is slippery. Wherever he has him, it's well hidden."

London was a large place, half-inhabited, half-barren from war, and Severn had flown over less than a fifth of it. There was a chance he'd flown over Luxen's hidden den and not known it. The bastard knew how to hide. "If you hear anything—anything at all—will you tell me, Djall?"

She rolled her eyes. "Stop with the sad face already. Shit... If you promise me you're on our side."

"I always was."

"*Convince me*. Like you'll have to convince *everyone*."

He held her gaze. "I am demon, Djall. I've been trying to end this war since I was old enough to lift a blade. Everything I did, it was for Red Manor, for demons. I'm not lying. You can trust in that."

Shaking her head, she glanced away, absently scanning the people who seemed to be none the wiser of the eternal battle going on for their freedom in the heart of London.

"You're all I have left." She faced him again and sighed. "Don't make me regret this."

She left shortly after. Having his sister on their side was progress, but his position was a precarious one. If he didn't produce proof of his claims, she'd turn on him. Along with the rest of her ranks and probably all of demonkind.

He left the café, tucked his hands into his coat pockets, and walked the bustling human streets. The rain had eased, but the people still carried their wet umbrellas aloft. Their black membranes reminded Severn of Mikhail's wings, and how those glossy feathers had sheltered him from the rain on a London rooftop. He drifted through the people, largely ignored, and jogged down the steps to the tube. Electric trains still thrust through parts of old London like pistons through an old combustion engine. Before Mikhail had taken his wings and his life had pivoted, he'd often deliberately ridden the tube on its loops under London, grounding himself in a different world where war didn't rage and people worried about things like making their rent payments, what to eat for the week, or whether someone liked them enough to ask them to be their mate.

It was all so... real. And it reminded him what they all fought for. Angels had lost their perspective long ago.

He caught the Baker Street line, which would take him closer to central London, and soaked up the visceral feel of the train rattling through dark tunnels, the flickering lights, and the people seated or standing, doing their best to ignore the strangers beside them—and Severn. He'd told Mikhail to get closer to the people he was supposed to be protecting. Half the problem with angels was how they saw themselves as *higher* than everything and everyone. They lived their lives high up in Aerie, presuming they were right about it all. Angels were so far up their own asses that making them see again was almost an impossible task.

Switching trains at Mile End, he rode the District line to Dagenham East. With each new stop, the number of humans dwindled, replaced by a handful of demons. Arriving at Dagenham, he flicked the collars of his coat up, strode free of the tunnels, shivered off the illusions, flexed his wings, and took to the sky.

Back inside the derelict warehouse, there was no sign of Ernas or the madam. Or anyone. Even the drum fire had burned out. Severn emerged onto the street, into the early evening light. The street was quiet, deserted. Coming from the bustle of the human world to this... It always soured his mood.

Leaning against the warehouse wall, he briefly closed his eyes. He had to get to Solo without alerting Remiel. He couldn't pretend to be an angel. Solo had made his thoughts clear on that tactic the last time Severn's lies had been exposed. And Mikhail wouldn't approve, and that mattered. Any conversation with any angel could not begin with more lies.

The flap of wings alerted him to an inbound demon. Samiel glided in to land in a run at the end of the street. He tucked his wings in and sauntered over. Wind-ruffled hair and glittering eyes spoke of a harried flight. It looked as though he'd picked up a bruise on his cheek too. Always brawling.

His quick smile faded when he saw Severn's face. "You all right?"

"Yeah, I just..." How much to tell him? Severn had no wish to fight him again. He might not love him like he had before, but he still cared for Samiel. "Just trying to figure things out."

His grin sprang back onto his face. "You look like you could do with a drink—or ten."

Severn's lips twitched. "Ernas hasn't returned. I have to find the madam—"

"Ernas? I just saw him." Samiel gestured with a thumb over his shoulder. "He said he's doing another loop or something. I wouldn't worry, the pup's always into something. He'll be back when he's ready." Samiel's smile gained a softness. "I've got a bottle of whiskey that needs finishing. I'd prefer not to drink it alone."

"Make that vodka, an' I could be persuaded."

"We could go check?" He looked hopeful. And maybe Severn could make an effort not to be a dick. There wasn't anything waiting for him in the warehouse, and the thought of sitting alone, doing *nothing*, while Mikhail was out there just might drive him insane. "All right."

They flew to the top of Samiel's building and entered through the rooftop fire escape. The small apartment hadn't changed since Samiel had brought him here after Tower Bridge. One large room with a kitchenette to one side, separated from the bed area by an island unit, and a bathroom through the door on the opposite side. Small. Functional.

"Ah ha!" Samiel grabbed a vodka bottle from a kitchen cupboard and tore off the lid. "Your favorite brand?"

It was. He'd remembered. He always remembered the little things.

Severn propped himself against the island. Samiel

poured the vodka into two glasses. He raised his, prompting Severn to do the same, and they clinked the glasses together. "To the end of this war," he said.

Severn could drink to that. The vodka went down smooth and easily, warming him through, wings and all.

"So, what's your next move?" Samiel asked.

"To bring Remiel down from the inside out."

Samiel grinned and leaned in. "Tell me more."

CHAPTER 10

 evern

WHILE SEVERN TOLD Samiel his plan to find Solo, they'd drained one vodka bottle, found another, and were halfway through that. He hadn't realized how much he needed this —just to stop and breathe and think, and maybe drink so much his wings had gone numb.

Samiel was sitting on the end of the bed, chatting freely and easily, the vodka having loosened his tongue. It hadn't been that long since Severn had fucked Samiel for ether, and the bed where much of that had happened lay neat and undisturbed behind him.

Severn had melted into a chair opposite the bed, letting his wings drape over its edges and trail on the floor. He'd sunk so deeply into the cushions, he wasn't sure he could move. Maybe it was selfish, coming here, pretending everything was fine, talking and drinking like nothing had changed between them. But despite the progress he'd made with Djall, the visit to human-side had left him hollowed out.

"Do angels drink vodka?" Samiel slurred, admiring his glass. "Do they get drunk?"

"No." Severn snorted. "They don't have vices. Or they *think* they don't. Honestly, they just need someone to tell them it's okay to have fun once in a while." Severn lofted his drink to his lips, recalling the time he'd returned to Mikhail sloshed off his head on gin. They'd made love in the shower after. Angel on angel, and Mikhail had come alive in his hands, like he always did.

"Maybe they'd quit fighting if they got laid once in a while?" Samiel chuckled.

"Probably," Severn mumbled, then downed the last dregs of vodka and weighed the advantages of prying himself from the chair for a refill.

Samiel must have seen the dilemma on Severn's face. He stood, plucked the glass from Severn's fingers, and refilled it in the kitchen behind him. Severn let his head flop back. Samiel's wings shimmered in the corner of his eye, their leathery surface pearlescent under the soft lights.

Samiel turned, caught Severn looking, and raised an eyebrow. "Eyeing my ass or my wings?"

Severn took the drink. Samiel's fingers brushed his. Probably by chance. Samiel stayed beside the chair, sipping his own drink. His golden eyes flicked to the bed and back to Severn's face, the direction of his thoughts becoming clear.

That wasn't happening, despite Severn being starved of ether. He'd promised Mikhail he'd never touch another and intended to keep his word, even if it pained him. "You told Luxen we fucked," he grumbled.

Samiel shrugged and sauntered back to the bed. He dropped, letting his wings hang low, and propped an ankle over his knee. "He asked. An' you fucked him too, so doesn't matter, does it."

Samiel telling Luxen how angel tasted led to Luxen drooling over Severn, giving the High Lord a taste for angel. A taste he was probably exploring with Mikhail right now. "You don't have to do everything he says," Severn grumbled, more pissed at reality trying to ruin his drunkenness than Samiel.

"I'm not like you. I don't have a name, or a rep as some badass demon. Luxen is our High Lord. I have to do what he asks. That's kinda the point of having a leader—not that you'd know."

Severn rolled the cool glass against his forehead. He'd never been very good at following orders. The demon hierarchy had always seemed to lack the impetuousness to actually try and stop the war they were all trapped in. It was part of the reason he'd infiltrated angels on his own. "You told Lux what it was like with me..."—he waved the glass aimlessly—"the whole angel-ass thing, and now..."

"Now what?"

"Now he has Mikhail. And I can't do a fucking thing about it."

Samiel snorted dismissively. "I thought it was *lurve* between you?"

"What the fuck does that mean?"

"You and him, you said it was *special*," Samiel slurred. "Eternal love or some shit. The *allyanse*. A fucking joke. You just like fucking angels."

"Well, yeah. I am concubi, so... kinda comes with the wings, but... I do love him."

"So if it's love, then Mikhail is yours and yours alone..." Samiel trailed off. "Unless maybe Mikhail doesn't feel the same?"

Severn didn't doubt Mikhail. At least, not his feelings. Mikhail was terrible at hiding his emotions now that he'd allowed himself to have them. His love for Severn was real. But then there was that kiss with Solo, which meant nothing, but still... and now Severn was a big-ass demon, not a fluffy angel. Mikhail had only just begun to understand he was an emotional creature. He might... experiment. "Mikhail is—he's still figuring out how emotions work."

"You think there's a risk he and Luxen might—"

Gods, yes. He did think it possible. And shit, he was jealous. He'd spent long enough with Luxen to know the High Lord had perfect control over his allure. And Mikhail was vulnerable. "Mikhail wouldn't... But Luxen might twist it all up in his head."

"Like you did?" Samiel blinked innocently.

Severn opened his mouth to deny it but couldn't. He absolutely *had* manipulated Mikhail. In the larger perspective, Severn had been his enemy longer than they'd been lovers. He knew he loved Mikhail, but Severn knew love intimately. Mikhail was still figuring it all out. And there was a lot to discover. All Luxen had to do was tell a few lies, flutter his wings, and... oops, Mikhail's cock was in Luxen's mouth.

Samiel dipped his chin and peered through narrowed eyes. "Do you think there's a chance he's chosen to stay with Lux?"

"No." He replied it too quickly, and Samiel heard the

too-hard denial. Dammit. With a growl, he left the glass on the floor, levered himself from the chair, and drifted toward the small windows overlooking London's twilight skyline.

"New emotions, he's still feeling his way," Samiel went on. "He knows he has a thing for demons, and Lux is fucking *hot*. I'd do him."

Samiel wasn't helping. "Mikhail isn't like that." He ground his teeth. Mikhail wouldn't turn around and do that to Severn. He wasn't made that way. But Lux... the smallest hint of doubt in Mikhail, and Lux would find it, latch on to it, twist it. When it came to desire, Luxen could talk Mikhail around in circles.

Samiel's reflection filled the space in the window behind Severn. "You said he's been brainwashed not to love all his life, and now, suddenly, he's had his eyes opened to all the wonderful possibilities," Samiel said. "He barely understands desire, and Lux knows desire like the back of his hand. Just sayin', seems strange he hasn't broken out of wherever Lux is keeping him, that's all."

Samiel slithered away and set his drink aside on a cabinet and propped a hip against it, folding his arms. His heated gaze drew Severn's eye. He looked pleased with himself, and why wouldn't he? Here he was, all cozy with Severn in his den, a few convenient bottles of Severn's favorite vodka on hand.

Severn's reflection smiled back at him, but there was no warmth in his grin. "You think I don't know what you're doing?" He crossed the floor to Samiel and tried to read his face, but his friend just half smiled back. "Don't try and fucking manipulate me, Sam."

"I wasn't—"

"Bullshit. You forget who you're fucking talking to."

"And who is that exactly?" Samiel straightened. "A brooding, self-pitying demon who might have been someone once but is now just a washed-up excuse for a concubi who still thinks he's half angel? You were everything once. I look at you now and you're just a sad shadow of a lord."

The words should have rolled right off him. Maybe it was the vodka, or the lack of ether, but Samiel's words hooked into his doubts and yanked them to the surface. Gods, he shouldn't have drunk so much. This was a mistake. He turned away from Samiel, ignoring the smaller demon's snarl.

"Go on, run away to your angel lovers. That is why you're going back to this Solo, right? You can't have Mikhail, so you're going to get yourself another angel-ass to fuck—"

Severn had Samiel pinned to the wall, a hand around his throat, before he could finish his sentence. His golden eyes widened. His sharp nails dug into Severn's hold. He shoved at Severn's shoulder and tried to kick. Ether born of violence and fear rippled off his skin and licked over Severn's. Severn pressed in, smothering every inch of Samiel's smaller demon body. "You don't pick a fucking fight with a bigger demon unless you have the balls to back it." Samiel struggled pathetically, trying to shove and writhe free. Ether beat off him in waves, teasing Severn with the promise of more. And he was so fucking *starved*.

Fuck, no. He shook his head clear. Or tried to, but the ether licked at him, and after so long abstaining, it tasted divine.

Samiel's lips ticked, his writhing ceased, and the ether

throbbed, turning thicker, heavier—switching from prickly violence to seductive honey—its source no longer violence, but the more potent desire.

"You starve yourself for angel," Samiel wheezed around the choke hold. "You're pathetic."

Severn tightened his grip, sealing off the words and the air Samiel needed to speak. But Samiel's smile stayed, and the hand that had been shoving against Severn rested on his shirt instead, over his heart.

All he had to do was surrender to the need and fuck Samiel into the wall. He couldn't, but gods, he needed it. There was too much at stake.

He had to find the madam, find Solo. There might be news of Mikhail, and for all that to happen, he needed to be strong. Every day he hadn't fed made him weaker, physically and in the eyes of demons who watched and waited for him to fail. They'd smell weakness on him, and Red Manor wasn't fucking weak.

Severn brushed his cheek against Samiel's and breathed in, sucking ether into his lungs. Pleasure rippled, trying to empty out Severn's thoughts. He eased his grip on Samiel's throat, freeing Samiel's panting.

His chest heaved against Severn, his heart pounded—Severn could hear it. "You're starving yourself for an angel who is right now fucking Luxen."

Mikhail wouldn't. Severn knew that, but... Ether made his nerves sing and his body burn. Samiel's fingers skimmed down his chest, over his waist, and found his hard cock—evidence of his incubi need.

"Hate fuck me if you like," Samiel whispered. His palm pressed in, grinding against Severn's cock. "You're as weak as a pup. You need this."

Severn still had him by the throat loosely, but Samiel had stopped trying to fight. The hand at Severn's cock rubbed some more, fingers kneading low. Samiel's demon body blazed with ether. Severn could take him in all ways, fucking his body and mind and drink him down. The temptation, the need, he couldn't fight this. He had to feed. And Mikhail was somewhere else, with Luxen, willingly or not. Severn couldn't change that, not while weak.

"Fuck me." Samiel growled against Severn's neck, and some time in all of this, he'd grabbed Severn around the waist, holding him close instead of pushing him away. "Fuck me hard, like you used to," he said breathlessly, golden eyes lifting to Severn's face. His hand rubbed and stroked, sending shudders through Severn. He was an open invitation, a feast for Severn to gorge on. "Make me come over and over."

Mikhail would never forgive him. He'd never forgive himself.

He grabbed Samiel's jaw so hard his nails drew pinpricks of blood from his cheek. *"If I fucked you now, I'd kill you."* He ripped himself free of Samiel's body and fled for the door.

"Fucking coward!" Samiel's yell followed him into the hallway, up the stairwell, and onto the roof.

Severn ran for the edge, toward the twinkling city lights, spread his wings, and leaped into the air. The wind caught him, teased him, lured him higher, and it was all he could do to soar wherever the wind could carry him.

He needed Mikhail back, and if he didn't find him soon, there would be nothing left of Severn for Mikhail to love.

CHAPTER 11

ikhail

SUNLIGHT POURED in through the windows and sparkled off glass and steel. It seemed important that he get up, but he couldn't imagine why. The door opened and the familiar click of Luxen's polished shoes announced his arrival, followed by the thud of a second pair of boots.

Mikhail drew his wings in, having spread them over much of the bed, and braced an arm under him to get a look at the lord and his companion. The second demon was named Samiel. Heavier than Luxen, but shorter, built for battle, not... whatever Luxen was built for. Samiel pulled up short and stared, his lips slightly parted and eyes big, as though waiting for Mikhail to say something. He couldn't imagine what.

Samiel was an irritating nuisance that buzzed around

Luxen, demanding attention. Attention Mikhail would have preferred the demon lord gave him.

Luxen cleared his throat, drawing Samiel's eye. "You were saying?"

Samiel closed his mouth and glanced at Luxen, then back to Mikhail. "I was, er... He's, er..."

"It's all right," Luxen assured, "you can say anything in front of Mikhail." The High Lord draped all of his suave self into his favorite armchair and crossed his legs.

Samiel lingered in the middle of the room, apparently speechless.

Mikhail blinked at him, wishing he'd hurry up and say his piece, then leave. He preferred to spend the mornings with Luxen. The demon had a way of soothing him, especially after the dreams.

"He's going back to the angels," Samiel finally said.

"Again?" Luxen snorted. "He never gives up. What for this time?"

"He knows one called... Solomon who he says can help."

They both looked over at Mikhail, though why, he couldn't imagine. Was he supposed to know this angel, Solomon? Luxen had reminded Mikhail how the angels had forsaken him and the demons wanted him dead. Luxen was his only sanctuary now, this room his safe haven. He was safe here. Protected.

"All right," Luxen said after a few moments' thought. "Have our nephilim contacts warn the angels. With any luck, they'll deal with him properly this time."

Samiel nodded. "Oh, and there's these." He handed some small squares of paper over to Luxen. Luxen's brow pinched as he studied whatever was depicted on them.

"Good. These will be *useful*." He looked up to find Samiel staring at Mikhail. "Was there anything else?" Luxen prompted.

"I just... He's weak. He's, er... not feeding."

The smile that spread on Luxen's face was entirely predatory. "He's sampled angel. No demon will satisfy him. He wants what we all want. You've done well, Samiel. Soon Severn won't be a problem any longer. The war will be ours to win, and angels will bow to us."

"I don't think it's just that he fancies himself some angel-ass, High Lord. I was... very persuasive. As you know, concubi struggle to resist ether. But he did resist. I think... I think he does love him." A skitter of some unpleasant feeling trickled down Mikhail's back. They both looked at him, again expecting a reaction. But none of what they'd said meant anything to him.

"Well, it seems love to angels is entirely malleable." Luxen waved the lesser demon away. "Oh, and what of the young one? The pup?"

"Dealt with."

"Excellent." Luxen grinned.

"High Lord, our kin haven't seen you in days. They're beginning to question if you have a plan to defend against Remiel. Djall has built a rank—"

Luxen lifted a hand, cutting the other demon off. "I'm clearly working on it," he said, pointedly staring at Mikhail. "Now leave."

Samiel cast one final look at Mikhail and left, closing the door behind him. Mikhail's gaze quickly returned to the demon in the chair. Luxen leaned forward. Behind him, his high-arched wings shimmered into sight. The twin horns were revealed next, and with the grand unveiling of his demon attributes came the demon's soothing presence.

He pushed to his feet and strode to the end of the bed. "You really do look good enough to eat."

Mikhail raised his chin. There was a hunger in Luxen. Even the fool Samiel would have been able to see it. But Luxen hadn't acted on it. Though in what way he might, Mikhail couldn't be sure. The demon had only ever been accommodating. He listened, asked about angels, asked about Mikhail. His company was comforting. Without it, Mikhail feared he'd be alone in a world that clearly despised him.

Luxen came around the side of the bed and settled on the edge, where a shaft of sunlight warmed. "How do you feel today?"

"I had the dreams again." The dreams were of a different Mikhail. A cruel vision of himself butchering demons and raining death from the skies.

"Hm..." Luxen leaned in and touched Mikhail's forehead. The sensations of clarity and calm washed through him, stealing a small sigh from his lips. Luxen's knuckles stroked Mikhail's cheek. Mikhail opened his eyes to find Luxen so close, his heady scent tingled on his tongue, and also tingled parts of him elsewhere.

"You really are quite beautiful." His fingers skimmed Mikhail's jaw and trailed down his neck, over his collarbone.

His heart hastened its beat. He didn't want to be that angel again. Luxen was helping him change. And Mikhail wanted to please him, to thank him for all he'd done. Luxen pulled away, and Mikhail surprised himself by catching his wrist. They both looked at his hand on

Luxen's wrist like it meant something more, and when Luxen flicked his eyes up, the tingling in Mikhail became something far more needful.

Luxen laughed suddenly and moved away. "The more I have you, the more I feel the old stories might have been true."

"Stories?"

"Never mind." Luxen looked again at Mikhail, but this time the hunger had been replaced by something far sharper in his eyes. "Stand for me, Mikhail. Let me see you."

Mikhail threw off the sheet, placed his feet on the floor, and stood. He wore only loose cotton pants low on his hips, and as he emerged from the side of the bed, Luxen's throat bobbed as he swallowed hard.

"Show me *all* of you."

His voice trembled some, which Mikhail took to be a good sign. He sighed out, rolled his shoulders, and spread his wings. Luxen looked almost distraught for a moment, and Mikhail almost retracted the wings. He didn't want to hurt him. But then Luxen smiled, and everything was right again.

"Are they pleasing?" Mikhail asked.

Luxen swallowed before replying. "Very." His voice quivered. "Now, rest. You have a big day coming up. You'll need your strength."

Mikhail lowered his chin, and in doing so, illusioned the additional wings away, shutting off the power with their absence. When he looked up, Luxen was gone, and Mikhail was alone again, making him want to run after the demon and pull him back. But he'd be back. He always returned. Mikhail trusted him.

CHAPTER 12

evern

THROUGH THE MADAM'S network of overeager nephilim, it became clear that Solo had been seen regularly visiting a house in Whitechapel. It was unlikely he'd moved into a human home, so he probably visited someone or something there. Most of Remiel's flights were in Aerie, rebuilding and training for the battle to come, not in Whitechapel. With Aerie habitable, there was no reason for angels to continue to inhabit the human area of Whitechapel, leaving the area unguarded. Solo's daily visits to the area were a stroke of luck Severn sorely needed.

A sword was too cumbersome and would slow him down. The idea was to get in and out of Whitechapel without being seen. He attached two daggers to the light leather armor and flew in as far as he dared after sundown and under the cover of heavy rain. He walked the streets along the final stretch. Angels hated staying at street level. He just had to avoid long lines of sight and nosy nephilim.

As he approached the address, it became clear Solo's house was the same dwelling Mikhail had adopted. Severn climbed a fire escape to a nearby rooftop and watched the large sash windows from behind a neighboring chimney stack. The lights were on, and after a few minutes of observing, a figure moved behind the ground-floor drapes. The rooftop door would be open—the same rooftop Severn had stood alongside Mikhail and admired London's skyline. Mikhail had wept at his healed wings and used them to shield Severn from the rain.

He had no feathered wings to keep the rain off now. It relentlessly tapped on his wings and leather-clad shoulders. At least angels wouldn't be flying tonight.

Keeping low, he traversed the roofs and took a risky running leap from one side of the street to the other, using his wings to glide in silently. A cat yowled somewhere in the dark, but nothing stirred. The rain and its shadows made the perfect hiding place.

He reached for the door handle and hesitated. Solo would react badly to having a demon suddenly appear. They had been friends before. Even after the lies had been revealed, Solo hadn't completely given up on him. Their last conversation hadn't exactly been a happy one. He'd warned Solo about Remiel, and Solo had told him to back the fuck off. Which was fair, given the circumstances. Maybe he'd mellowed? There was only one way to know for sure.

He hid his wings, flicked a dagger free, opened the door, and ventured quietly inside. Water dripped from his clothes, leaving bootprints on every step. He'd fallen down these steps before, right into Mikhail, who'd had that slightly startled look of someone mildly pissed off but also concerned. A painful twinge squeezed his heart. Couldn't think about Mikhail. This wasn't about him, this was about finding a way for the angels to see the truth of Remiel and hopefully turn against him.

A black-and-white cat skittered from a doorway and darted down the stairs, jolting Severn to a stop with his heart in his throat. He didn't hear any voices or see any movement. But the ground-floor lights had been on. Solo was definitely inside. Somewhere.

A step on the stairs creaked under his boot. He paused. Listened. Rain lashed against the house's sash windows. He crept down the final steps to the ground-floor hallway. The rooms to the right were empty, their lights off. Light slid under the door of the room to his left. Severn reconsidered the dagger in his hand and tucked it away. Anyone would fight a demon with a dagger. He was trying to avoid startling him.

He pressed a hand to the internal door, swallowed, turned the handle, and eased the door open. The crack of light grew. "Solo, before you do anything, just listen—"

A flash of golden hair—not red—a vicious snarl, and white-feathered wings. *Not Solo!* Severn reached for his dagger. A cold hand grabbed his horn and yanked, hauling him suddenly off-balance. He scrabbled for the dagger a second time. If he could just—A boot hit him square in the chest. He flew back, weightless, heard the old windows shatter. Glass rained like falling stars, and among those stars, an angel's snarling face loomed —*Remiel.* Severn's back struck the street, punching all the air from his lungs. Cold rain dashed his face. Hard glass glinted. He blinked into both and brought an arm up.

Not Solo...

Remiel.

A knee slammed into his chest, landing like a sledge-hammer. Severn bucked, the blows coming too fast to block. A fist almost tore his jaw clean off, rocking his head to the side. Blood wet his tongue. He spat onto the wet road and saw a blurred line of angels marching toward him.

They'd been waiting...

They'd been warned.

A punch landed in his side, involuntarily curling him around the sudden agony. Then the hand was at his throat, the air was under him, and he flew. The wall he hit didn't give as much as the window. He collapsed to his knees. Spat blood. Gods... he should have fed. He could not fight a guardian, not weak like this.

This was how it ended. Surrounded by angels. Just not the one he wanted to see. Damn them... damn them all to fucking Haven and back. They would not take him on his knees!

Remiel strode through the rain, coming at him like a predator homing in on his prey's final moments. Rain soaked his pretty white feathers, turning them gray, and plastered his blond hair to his hard face. He looked as mean as they came, and by Aerius, his face wouldn't be the last thing Severn saw.

Severn snapped his wings open and launched off his back foot, tackling Remiel in the gut. The angel buckled around him. They both tumbled to the ground, wings flapping, feathers ripped free. Severn pinned Remiel—his weight his only advantage—and smashed Remiel's face against the wet road. Remiel thrashed, somehow got a knee between them. He kicked and pulled at the same damn time, and before Severn could think to counter, he was thrown up and over, landing with a hard thump on his back. The terraced houses all tilted. The road tipped. Remiel's roar came at him. He rolled, more from instinct than skill, snatched his daggers, and flipped to his feet. "Come at me then!" He beckoned with his blade.

Remiel's right wing looked a little bent, but otherwise he was so far mostly unharmed from the brawl.

"Demon," Remiel growled.

Severn rolled his eyes at the angel's lack of imagination and pointed the dagger at Remiel's face. "You've had this coming since you put me in that cell."

It took him a moment, and then his blue eyes widened. "Konstantin! What a pleasure it will be to finally kill you."

He scanned the angels surrounding them. All mute, all watching. A flash of scarlet among their pristine whiteness marked Solo from the rest. Red hair braided down one side to keep it from his glaring green eyes, armor shining, angelblade in hand. Severn's heart stuttered. What had he truly expected? Angels only saw what they were shown, not the truth beneath it. Solo saw the demon Konstantin. They all saw demon.

"Seraphim did not want this!" he tried to sound confident, raising his voice over the pounding rain, but the angels had him beat. "The war is a lie, fed to you by *him*."

Remiel suddenly rushed him. He slammed into Severn, straight into another wall. Something brittle snapped in Severn's right wing. He gritted his teeth, smothered in angel. Remiel raised his blade. And Severn did the only thing he could think of that was guaranteed to repel him.

He grabbed his face in both hands and kissed him hard on the lips, spilling what little ether he could afford into soothing the angel's rage. Remiel tasted of mineral bitterness, like cold, hard glass.

Remiel tore himself free and staggered back. He wiped his hand across his lips and spat to the side. "Foul creature!"

Severn grinned. He could deny it all he liked. "Oh, but you liked it." He pushed from the wall, not liking the way his wing ticked and twitched. He wouldn't be flying out of here. "I know you liked it..." He staggered, trying to keep his battered body upright, but it was clear to everyone here that Remiel had him beat. "I see it in your ether. Ether doesn't lie, Remiel." The angels still stood back, like fucking statues guarding old human churches. "You're all hypocritical bastards too blind to see what's right in front of you!" He found Solo in their midst. "Open your eyes. Open your hearts. Your guardians are lying to you."

Remiel held out a hand. A helpful angel from the crowd tossed him a sword. "This ends now, Konstantin."

"Fine by me." He chuckled darkly, tasting blood. "But the truth is coming for you, guardian. You can't outrun it, and you can't bury it. You know it, you *fear* it."

Remiel bared his teeth and lunged. Severn ducked the sloppy swipe of his sword, ducked his wing too, and spun, rising behind Remiel's expanse of pretty wings. If he'd had a blade, he could have severed one of those appendages. Instead, as Remiel began to twist, Severn roundhouse kicked the bastard in the back, sending him sprawling into the same wall Severn had cracked. The wall gave. Remiel fell through the crumbling bricks, and the rest of it collapsed on top of him. It was too much to hope he'd been crushed.

Solo ran at him, blade raised. Severn thrust his wings downward, creating enough lift to launch himself up and over Solo's head—his damaged wing barked a retort—but he came down behind Solo, between his red-feathered arches, and looped an arm around his neck, jerking the smaller angel against his chest like a shield. His dagger's blade sat snugly against the angel's throat. "Do not fucking move, or I will slit your throat, Solo. You've left me with no choice." Solo's wings twitched, his back shifted, muscles readying for flight. He could launch, taking Severn with him, and then this really would get messy. "Do that and you won't see the dawn."

Angels closed in.

"Back up!" Severn turned Solo, let his flight see how he'd gladly spill their friend's blood in the street for them. Not that they'd give any fucks. None of them cared anyway. "Back the fuck up or he dies." Some hesitated, glancing at their companions.

Remiel staggered free of the rubble, shaking out his wings. Feathers stuck out at odd angles. A few had snapped off, leaving bloody trails. "There's nowhere for you to go. This is over."

Solo breathed hard, making his wings and shoulders heave in Severn's grip. Any second now, he'd try something and it'd damn well get him killed. Severn hadn't come here to hurt him. That was the last thing he wanted. If Solo'd been the only one in that house, this would have all gone very differently.

Severn could only hope there was a shred of friendship left in him. "Solo," he whispered, "I came for you, to talk.

If our friendship was worth anything to you, don't fight me, please."

The angels moved closer. There were too many. He needed Solo's help to get out of this or neither of them would see the dawn.

Solo couldn't answer with a blade at his throat, and Severn wasn't about to ease off to see if he was game. Solo was strong enough to turn on him and fast enough to fill him full of angelblade-shaped holes.

He glanced behind him for a way out. The Whitechapel church loomed in the rain. Behind it, Severn remembered how an alley led deeper into Whitechapel's narrow backstreets. He could lose the angels with their heavy armor in that maze of alleys. "Back off!" he warned again, catching them creeping closer. "I fucking mean it. I will cut him."

Remiel tossed his hair and flicked out his wings. "You're surrounded. Let him go and I'll kill you quickly. It's the only mercy I can offer."

"I don't want your fucking mercy, asshole." He continued to back down the street, dragging Solo with him. "I want you to tell them what you told me right before you tried to murder Mikhail. Because that was what happened. You shoved him off the edge of Aerie—"

"Where *is* the traitor Mikhail?"

"He's no traitor," Solo hissed, finding his voice.

A ripple of unease flowed through the rank of angels. Solo wasn't the only one who believed Mikhail's innocence, it seemed. A little flutter of fucking relief lifted Severn's heart. Not all was lost. He tucked his chin into Solo's neck and whispered, "If you care for Mikhail, follow my lead. I need you, Solo. Mikhail needs you. We were brothers for ten years. Not all of it was a lie."

It was a risk, but it was all he had left. The church was close now, its alleyway unlit. The angels kept coming, but slower than before. Remiel stood in front of them, his wings wide, so he didn't see how they hesitated. Rain weighed all their wings down. None would be flying far.

"Destiny is coming for you, Remiel." Severn smiled. "And it looks a whole lot like a six-winged angel."

Remiel's confident stride tripped.

Severn whirled, dragged Solo with him, and shoved him forward. "Go!" By some miracle, he ran. Severn raced down the alley behind him. Solo took a jagged left and leaped down a set of steps.

"Hide the wings!"

Solo's red feathers vanished.

Severn sprinted by him, his own wings hidden. Solo's green eyes widened— probably remembering how he was absconding with a demon. Severn grabbed him by the arm and hauled him along before he got any ideas about backing out. "Don't think, just run. For Mikhail."

The alley dumped them out near an old section of road. Severn dashed under the shelter of a bridge, taking Solo with him, and slammed into a steel door, knocking it open. They spilled into a stairwell leading down, below street level and into some sort of old pedestrian service tunnel. Orange lights flickered high up on the walls, illuminating Solo's wide-eyed, distraught expression. The tunnel tilted downward, eventually leading to a disused tube station currently shelter for half a dozen cambion—likely evicted from the damaged cauldron. They eyed Solo like he was their Sunday roast.

Solo made it up the steps and into the station's ground-level entrance, where old ticket booths and gates had rusted in place, and that's where he lost his nerve.

"I can't do this." He headed straight for the exit. Rain poured over the open archway, spilling from gutters like a waterfall.

"Solo, wait."

"No." He kept walking.

"Stop." Severn jogged up behind him.

The angelblade was suddenly out and pointed at Severn's throat, freezing him mid-stride. He lifted his hands. Shit. He was fucking fast.

Solo glared down its length, green eyes set with determination. But that determination began to fade as he studied Severn's face. His gaze darted, likely taking in the horns and the differences.

Severn swallowed. "I'm still Severn."

"You're Konstantin."

"No. I'm Severn. Konstantin is gone. I'm the same person you fought alongside. The same person you dragged from the mud. The same who has blocked a blade from finding its home in your lovely neck too many times to count." Solo stroked his neck, frowning. "And I need your help. I can't do this without you. Mikhail can't do this without you."

"Do *what* exactly?" The question echoed about the empty station. He lowered the angelblade to his side. "What can a demon possibly want from me?"

Severn slowly lowered his hands, careful not to make any sudden movements. "I mean... it's kinda a lot, so maybe we could find somewhere—"

"Start talking or I'm gone!" His blunt white teeth

shone behind a tight snarl.

"Luxen has Mikhail." That hadn't been entirely what he'd planned to say first, but as Solo had made it clear he still cared, it was the most important thing to lead with. "I can't find him. The demons are... shit, we're barely clinging together, and we know Remiel has a force ten times ours. We're all going to die, Solo."

"Good." He turned away but stopped at the archway, keeping back from the waterfall of rain.

"You don't mean that." Severn approached slowly. Carefully. He'd get one chance at talking Solo around. "I know you don't. Because you care. You care like angels are *supposed* to care. I see it in your eyes. You're so damn tired. You're like Mikhail was, like he is now."

Solo sighed, resigning himself to listening. "Who is Luxen?"

"Our High Lord. And a dick."

Solo pressed his lips together and side-eyed Severn. "You lied to all of us, to Mikhail and to me. You lied for years, and then you..."

"I know. I'm an asshole."

"No, well yes, but no. That's not what I was going to say. You lied, but you saved Mikhail. I saw what happened. You dove over the edge after Mikhail, doing the one thing I should have done—we all should have done, but nobody did. I see it over and over. Remiel stabbed him, and you didn't hesitate. You were wingless, and you threw yourself into death. *You* saved Mikhail. *Konstantin* saved Mikhail."

His throat suddenly dry, Severn swallowed. "I love him, Solo. I love him like"—he wet his lips, unsure how to express love in a way an angel would understand—"like he's a part of me, like he's my wings. And I have to save him again."

"From Luxen?" Water droplets had gathered on Solo's auburn lashes. He blinked them away.

Severn nodded, afraid his voice might not hold. A wave of tiredness fell over him and all the aches returned. His jaw throbbed, his wing sizzled, and somewhere around his middle he was fairly certain Remiel had pummeled a rib to dust. "But that's not all of it. We have to end this war. It's not right, any of it. And if I'm right, you don't need me to tell you any of this. You've already begun to see it."

"Maybe. I heard the things you said to Mikhail that day, and I've... felt things." He bowed his head. "Things are different without Mikhail. I'm different. And I don't trust Remiel."

"You shouldn't."

"You know things... about Remiel?"

Severn nodded. "There are angels in Haven who care. They know the truth too. We can get them out."

"We?" Solo arched an eyebrow and raked his gaze over Severn. "You won't get anywhere near Haven. You'll be lucky to get out of here without being seen." He stared at the falling wall of water again, contemplating leaving. "Are you really still Severn in all *that*?"

He was finally yielding and believing. Severn couldn't contain his smile at possibly having his friend back. "Will you hear me out?"

"All right. I'll listen. For Mikhail."

CHAPTER 13

*S*evern

THE OUTER AREAS of the cauldron—what had been London's financial districts long ago—had survived the collapse of Aerie's disks. All the shiny glass and steel had dirtied up with age and neglect, but the crisscross pathways beneath the towering high-rises provided ample shelter for the displaced cambions.

Severn walked its narrow streets, keeping an eye on Solo trailing behind him. His pale skin, mocha freckles, and heavily lashed eyes marked him as angel, even with his wings stowed. His hastily knotted bun of red hair was a sign to every cambion and nephilim that an angel walked among them. That and the angelblade strapped to his hip, plus highly polished armor. To see him wide-eyed, trying not to step in the oily puddles, would have been amusing if his being here weren't so risky.

113

The madam's Infinity sex club was long gone, but other places had clung to their trade in the rubble. One of them being the bar on the corner. It had no name, just a sheet hanging over the door, and no sign outside, but the cambion had gathered here, and some enterprising guy had decided to sell them alcohol, and so it became the bar on the corner—at least, that's how the madam described it when Severn had asked for places on the down-low where he might talk with Solo without local tongues flapping.

Severn pulled the sheet aside and ventured into the warmth. Thumping music played from somewhere near the back of the low-ceilinged room. He caught Solo's shudder at the sight of the closely packed customers, gas fires spewing fumes, and general gloom and grinned. A nod to the owner and Severn managed to get Solo tucked away in a hidden corner so they didn't have the cambion falling over themselves to get a look at an angel.

"I'm beginning to regret this," Solo grumbled, perching on the chair like it might swallow him. "Why did you bring me here? Aren't there other, *cleaner* places we can talk?"

"Well, there's Dagenham, but you won't get far there looking like you do. This is about as neutral ground as you can get 'round here. If any angels or correctioners show up, we'll get wind of it long before they get here. This is the safest place for us. Trust me." He waved over one of the cambion servers and ordered two drinks. By the looks of him, Solo could do with something strong enough to smooth out his nerves, and Severn needed something to numb the aches and bruises Remiel had left him. The beating had dented his ego some too and left him drained and wretched. But having Solo here was a win. He just had to convince the stalwart battle angel who had spent his entire life fighting demons to switch sides.

The drinks were delivered, and Solo glared at the grubby glass with its golden liquid like someone had handed him a shot of piss.

"Relax. We're just talking." Severn's own heart was rattling its cage. Having Solo on their side was *everything*. He needed this angel to listen and to agree.

"You used to come here, as angel?" He raised his hard angel-gaze, and the tension of Severn's past lies simmered between them.

"No, this place is new to me, but there are lots like it dotted around these parts of old London, and I did use one of those to... satisfy my demon needs."

Solo scanned the cambion crowd again, emerald eyes absorbing the sight of half humans, half demons mingling. "Are angels so terrible that you had to resort to *this*?"

"Yes. This is *real*. It's honest—" Solo swung a cutting glare his way, prompting Severn to flinch. "What you have in Aerie"—Severn pointed a thumb toward the ceiling, indicating *up*—"is sterilized."

"What happened to you, Severn? I mean, clearly you're *you* now. But where have you been since Aerie?"

He told him about Haven, about Mikhail, and how they'd grown closer since he'd caught Mikhail from his fall from Aerie. Told him how the guardians had tried to force Mikhail to give up half of himself, and of how he'd lit up the skies over Haven like he had at Tower Bridge.

Solo's eyes grew wider with every word. "The Haven flights said Seraphim had returned and attacked them."

"It wasn't Seraphim. It was Mikhail, *boosted*. He saw

what was happening in Haven and reacted... like Mikhail does."

Solo smiled. "Yes, he does have a tendency to go to extremes. But how does he have those wings?" Solo leaned in closer. "How does he do the things we've seen? The truth, you owe me that."

"There's a demon, goes by the name of Amii." He told Solo all about Amii. Told him *everything*. More than he'd told anyone, more than he probably should have told an enemy, maybe more than even Mikhail knew. Solo gradually grew more restless, shifting in his chair, then picked up his drink and finished it off in a few gulps with surprising ease. Pressing the back of his hand to his mouth, he wheezed around the burn. When he looked up, his eyes were glassy, their pupils wide. All things considered, he was taking the whole *you've been lied to your entire life* pretty well. "You want me to go to Haven?" he asked.

"There are angels there who care. If they don't fall in line, the guardians lock them up or kill them. The truth of that place, and the guardians' part in it, must be exposed for this war to end."

He shook his head, dislodging a few locks of red hair. "I can't go to Haven. I don't know how to love. They won't let me in."

"Just tell them you've been having... *urges*."

He winced. "I can't..." What little conviction there was in his voice faded when he next asked, "What kind of urges?"

"You know..." Severn waved a hand. "Needs." He must know *something*. He'd kissed Mikhail. But his face was blank.

"Needs?"

Severn leaned in. "The kiss. Right? With Mikhail?"

"Oh, that." Solo's freckles suddenly hid behind a flush. He quickly looked down and picked up his empty glass, intensely studying it.

"Don't tell me you haven't thought about what comes after?"

"I don't think I have," he denied, looking everywhere but at Severn's face.

Severn snorted. "Oh c'mon, when I looked like Remiel, you were eye-fucking me the whole time. You talked to my nipples more than my face. Angels strut around Aerie half naked, and none of you have a clue how homoerotic you all are? You kissed Mikhail and you felt no stirring in your loins? Seriously?"

"Homo what?" He did look genuinely confused, and Severn reminded himself to reel it in. Solo wasn't just suddenly going to accept everything he'd been told, even that which he knew to be true inside. He needed to experience it—like the kiss—to fully believe.

"You're fucking adorable. If we had time, I'd take you to a willing nephilim and really open your eyes..." He trailed off. Now there was an idea. Solo needed a convincing reason to get into Haven, he clearly knew he had urges and would benefit from exploring those, and Severn needed ether. It didn't have to be a lot, just a little more than a kiss. "What if you could explore your urges some more?" Severn asked softly. "You'd be able to get into Haven without lying, and you'll have a whole new set of skills."

Solo pursed his lips, and with his shoulders slumped, hair loose, and lips a little pouty, he looked entirely bedraggled. "I can't believe I'm talking to a demon about this."

"A *concubi* demon, and I hope... still a friend. I'm uniquely qualified to help." He grinned, and finally Solo's true, bright smile returned.

"How do I explore such things?" he asked, puffing out his cheeks and resigning with a sigh.

"Do you have tokens?"

"Some."

A little... detour. A few hours. It had to be quick, but in the right hands, Severn could have Solo fully on board in a matter of hours. "Order another round of drinks. I'll be right back." He didn't have to go far to find information on what they both needed. The madam wasn't the only one who saw to the sexual needs of those in the cauldron. A cambion was a stretch too far. Solo would never go for it. But a soft, nonthreatening nephilim would gently ease Solo into exploring those urges of his.

Collecting Solo, they left the bar and entered a typical terraced house a few doors down, taking the narrow stairs to the top floor. There were no signs, but the place was clean and well-lit.

"I'm not sure this is a good idea," Solo muttered, arriving behind Severn at a desk halfway down a narrow, high-ceilinged hallway. The sign said to press the bell and wait.

Severn pressed the bell. "It'll be fine. Just keep your head down and look inconspicuous."

Solo gulped, folded his arms, and leaned against the wall. "I'm following a demon into some kind of deviant den on some whim of his to explore forbidden urges," he grumbled. "This is not how angels do things. I don't recognize myself right now."

"I'd help you out myself, but you're not ready for a demon to go down on you."

Solo's eyes widened, but before he could splutter, a cheery voice said, "Ah, sirs." A bright young cambion female appeared, dressed impeccably in a cream pantsuit. More human than demon, her only telltale hint of demon was the daisy-yellow tint to her eyes. "A room for the both of you, or some company?"

"Company," Severn said.

"Male, female, non-gender, or all of the above?" She beamed but must have seen something in Solo because her demon eyes suddenly widened. "Wait... He's an angel?"

Damn. "Yes."

Solo frowned. "Is that a problem?" he asked in his mightier-than-thou voice.

"He can't be here." The cambion's brows dug in. Like maybe she had a shotgun stashed beneath her desk and wasn't afraid to use it.

Severn laughed the tension off. "He's harmless... Look at him."

Solo didn't look harmless, especially in his armor and with the demon-killing sword at his hip. He looked one step away from raiding the place and raining holy righteousness down on them all.

"Oh, *no-no-no*." She backed away from her desk and them. "I run a respectable business. I can't have angels here!"

Severn hopped around the side of the desk and slipped an arm around her shoulders. "He's not going to hurt anyone. He just needs some *company*."

She flicked her attention between Solo, now frowning and second-guessing his life choices, and Severn. "But angels don't have sex," she whispered, eyes pleading.

Severn glanced back to find Solo eyeing the exit. If he left now, Severn would never get him back. "Look, I'm not exaggerating when I say all our lives rely on him getting laid."

"Really?"

Solo blinked and chewed on his thumbnail.

"Male," Severn told the assistant. "Nephilim. Someone gentle and thoughtful. Please. There's a lot more riding on this than you can imagine. If he were going to shut you down, he wouldn't just stand there, would he?"

The assistant warily returned to the desk and ran through some ground rules, all of which were reassuring, unless you happened to be a first-time angel. Solo looked about ready to spread his wings and leap from the nearest window. As the assistant disappeared to ready their company, Severn squeezed Solo's shoulder and pulled him closer. "She already covered it, but we're gonna talk about consent. If you don't want this, you can stop at any time. Understand? Any time at all." His ether would reveal his feelings, but control for an angel like Solo would be everything. "I'll find another way into Haven. You really don't have to do this."

"I was eye-fucking Remiel," he blurted. "Er—you, I mean, when you were Remiel." The confession clearly worried him. His pale face had drained of even more color. "Since Mikhail... since we... I've been confused."

Severn grinned. "You're gonna love this."

The assistant returned to collect them. "The company has a right to refuse you if they wish. Just because you're an angel, don't expect to have your way. If your company declines, you listen." She led them down a hallway to a closed door. "Your room. Have fun." She smiled tightly and hurried away, leaving Solo chewing on his lip outside the door.

The angel's face crumpled a little, all of his new emotions playing out in every crease and line around his eyes and mouth.

"What you're feeling is shame," Severn said. "That shame isn't your fault. Nothing happening here is wrong. Seraphim wouldn't have given you all cocks if he didn't want you using them."

Solo winced and slumped against the hallway wall. He rubbed at his forehead and swept loose locks away from his eyes. "Are you coming in?"

"Do you want me to?" *Please say yes.* He needed the ether hit.

Solo chewed on his lip, then nodded.

"You know what I am?" He had to be sure Solo understood what was happening here. No more lies. He was demon, and not just any demon. What went on behind that door would deliver him the ether he needed to be strong, to get Mikhail back.

Solo snorted. "I can hardly forget when you look as you do. But yes, you're a concubi incubus. You need this as much as I do. Correct?"

Good, he understood. And seemed to be taking it remarkably well. "Is that a problem?"

"I have no idea, honestly. I don't even know what I'm doing, or how this... goes. Just that I have this need... inside me, eating me up, and these thoughts, and... I have to know."

Severn wrapped his fingers around the door handle. "You've got this."

The nephilim inside was a mid-twenties honey-blond male with typical angel-blue eyes and sweeping lashes. His slip of a gown was as transparent as dragonfly wings and fell like water around his slim body, pouring over narrow hips while obscuring his cock enough to be tantalizing.

The nephilim looked over Severn's shoulder to Solo. His blue eyes widened. "Shit, you're really an angel? I mean—I don't—sorry, Your Grace. I just—I haven't..." He did a strange little half curtsy, saw Severn's frown, and rapidly straightened again. "It's just I've never fucked an—"

Solo groaned and turned toward the door. "I can't."

"That's okay. We can leave right now."

But Solo didn't move from his spot and didn't go through that door, despite nothing stopping him. He dipped his chin and chewed on his bottom lip some more. He wanted this. He'd probably wanted it since Mikhail had kissed him, maybe even secretly before that. But there was his old uptight angel-self, and the new Solo, who was beginning to see things differently, and right now, those two parts warred inside him.

Severn waited, giving him time to think it through. His shoulders rose and fell, and the hands at his side clenched. His struggle was the guardians doing. If they hadn't screwed with angels since killing Seraphim, the world would be a very different place.

Severn took a step to the side and tilted his head, hooking Solo's shy gaze. "For what it's worth, Mikhail experienced the same confusion. I can't exactly say he handled it well, but once he allowed himself to experience feelings... I can't explain it. It's one of those things you just have to do. Or not. It's up to you."

Solo turned on his heel and strode to the nephilim, stopping so close the blond blinked his doe eyes up at him. "Are you happy to do this with me?" Solo asked. "No coercion. You're free to say no."

The nephilim puffed out a breath. "Gods, yes."

Solo swept in like he'd been unleashed from a tether and kissed the nephilim hard on the mouth.

The sudden rush of ether had Severn grabbing a nearby chair to stop himself falling to his knees. By the time he'd poured his tingling body into the seat, Solo's bloodred wings were unfurling, filling the room from wall to wall. From Severn's angle, just out of Solo's peripheral vision, he could see how Solo had the nephilim's cheek cradled in his hand and kissed him like he was the most precious thing in the world, not a man he'd just met for a fuck. That right there was exactly why this had to happen. Solo needed this. They all needed this.

The nephilim's hand had made fast work of Solo's armor, loosening it off to give him access to the part Solo had hidden away for years. Ether beat from Solo in heady waves, twitching Severn's lust alive. The room spun, the air rich and swollen with ether. The nephilim must have touched something sensitive of Solo's because ether swelled, making Severn's head throb and his body hum.

Gods, Severn gritted his teeth. He'd been unprepared for a sudden deluge. All that sexual need dammed up for decades behind Solo's conditioning was ready to blow. If Severn didn't get a handle on it, the overdose would knock him out cold like a pup reeling from his first hit.

The nephilim's soft mouth was working at Solo's neck

now, his fingers in the angel's hair. Solo had his head tilted back, his lips parted. The rapturous look on his face finally told the truth.

Severn squeezed his eyes closed. Watching felt too much like betraying his promise to Mikhail. Besides, this was Solo's moment. Severn dropped his head back, ignored his pounding erection, and concentrated on filtering the ether deep inside, where his concubi hollowness devoured it quickly. The pain from Remiel's beating soon faded, leaving only the ever-present ache for Mikhail. He wished he were here and not far away with Luxen somewhere, maybe receiving the same treatment Solo was now.

Gods, he couldn't think on that. He dug his fingers into the arm of the chair and thought of his angel on his knees—Mikhail's tight, wet mouth sealed around his cock, the beautiful eyes looking up at him from between his knees.

Ether lapped over Severn to the sounds of an angel and a nephilim panting and the beat of Severn's own frantic heart. With Solo's flood of ether, he might finally be strong enough to root out Luxen and see to it he never touched Mikhail again.

CHAPTER 14

*M*ikhail

"You are going to make it right," Luxen said.

Mikhail looked up from his knelt position. "I am." Mikhail had been a monster. But now, with Luxen's help, he'd rise up and be better, be worthy of the High Lord's trust. He wanted to please him. To thank him for everything he'd done in giving Mikhail a new place in the world. Giving him a second chance.

Luxen took Mikhail's hand and lifted him to his feet. They stood eye-to-eye. Angel to demon. He felt... something for this demon. Gratitude, surely. But something else too. Something *powerful*. Luxen's gaze softened.

"There is one last test." His voice quivered in a way Mikhail hadn't heard from him before. The demon's dark pupils dilated. The sensation of calm and peace had Mikhail lifting his wings. He stretched their tips wide,

125

drawing the demon's gaze in a way Mikhail knew pleased him.

Luxen's fingertips trailed up Mikhail's jaw. "I've never known temptation like you," he whispered. Though Mikhail couldn't imagine what was so awe-inspiring about himself. Still, Luxen's words coupled with his touch added to the medley of strange sensations running through Mikhail's body.

Luxen suddenly turned away and crossed the room, clearing his throat. "These images." He opened a dresser drawer and from inside took the squares of paper the other demon had given him. "Who do you see?"

Luxen held out the prints—photographs, Mikhail realized now he could see them.

He studied them. The images featured two demons, one of which was clearly the irritating Samiel. The other demon held Samiel against a wall. Even though the images were still, the promise of violence between the two demons was very real. Yet, Samiel smiled and had a hand pressed to the other demon's chest, perhaps to push him back. No, that hand was there for another reason. Samiel wasn't in distress. He was *aroused*.

"*Who* do you see?" Luxen asked.

"Samiel."

"And the other?"

He knew him but couldn't be sure from where. The large, striking demon had his wings hidden, but Mikhail remembered how they looked when spread—*glorious*. No, wait. He frowned. Something wasn't right with the photographs. "I know him," he said softly. "But I..." The memory flitted away, frustratingly out of reach.

"Do you recall a name?" Luxen pressed. His tone suggested this test was important.

He'd seen this demon smiling, seen him on his knees. Mikhail touched his lips with his fingers. A tingling, a distant memory of touch.

"Konstantin," Luxen prompted, growing impatient. "Do you remember him now?"

Konstantin. His enemy from *before*. Mikhail had done terrible things to him. But he wasn't that angel any longer. "They're lovers? Samiel and Konstantin?"

"They are. How does that make you feel, Mikhail?"

He looked up. What any of this had to do with him, he wasn't sure, but Luxen had rarely appeared this agitated. "That's... good."

"Yes, I think so." Luxen's grin lightened his whole face, and Mikhail sighed in relief. He didn't want to fail him.

Luxen tossed the photographs back into the drawer. "You passed the test. Well done, Mikhail. Meanwhile, dress in those." He gestured at the clothing laid out on the bed. Not dissimilar to the Lord's own lightweight leather armor. Finally, Mikhail would be useful. That was all he wanted. To do good, to help, to make amends for the sins of his past.

Luxen approached. His two fingers tilted Mikhail's chin up. "A gift." The demon's lips brushed his own, and with the featherlight kiss came a sudden rush of *need*. Mikhail's sharp inhale had Luxen chuckling as he left the room. The laughter lingered long after he'd left, swirling around and around Mikhail's head like water down a drain. The floor tipped, his sanity going with it. He reached for the wall, missed, and fell against one of the windows.

Images shattered inside his head, flashing so brightly,

and then exploded apart, each one breaking some part of him he hadn't known existed. A kiss. A demon. Not Luxen.

Luxen's laughter rolled on and on as the kiss sizzled on his lips, burning like acid.

He tried to swipe at the sensation, to brush it off, but it *burned* hotter, like the startling evidence of a crime he hadn't known he'd committed. Luxen tasted like wrongness. But that couldn't be right. Luxen was trying to help him...

His blurred vision fell to the dresser and the top drawer. Stumbling forward, he tugged it open. The photos lay inside. He reached for them but stopped, fingers hovering over them. Samiel and Konstantin.

Konstantin.

Samiel was Konstantin's lover. Had *always* been Konstantin's lover. Hate burned the back of his throat. The photographs were a lie.

Mikhail snatched up the photos and crushed them in his hand. The paper turned to ash and fell as dust between his clenched fingers.

This room. The bed. Luxen. Something was very wrong here.

He gripped the dresser, needing its solidity to anchor him. His wings fell open, their feathers shimmering black, blacker than the darkest night. His twisting reflection in the mirror snarled at him. His eyes—their sharp crystal blue told a truth just out of reach.

This was all wrong... but what part of it? The old or the new? The past or the present? His heart pounded, beating like the drums of war. *Lies.* They were everywhere. But whose? He slammed his fist into the mirror. Glass exploded, shattering his reflection into a thousand pieces.

A thousand faces snarled back at him in judgment. *You are not this compliant thing*, a voice said, perhaps his voice. *You are a guardian. A god. You do not kneel.*

The urge to pick up the dresser and toss it into the windows made his finger twitch. There was more happening here, more his fractured mind struggled to unravel. He could break the windows and fly, but he'd be leaving the answers behind. No... the world he occupied was wrong, and he needed to know why.

He leveled his breathing, counting down through the swirling, maddening memories—fragments of a past full of burning wings and blood on blades. Hate and vengeance simmered in his veins, vengeance on them all.

He turned and regarded the bedchamber with its large, sumptuous bed, white cotton sheets, and the dark splash of demon armor laid out for him to wear.

There was another way to deal with this. A better way to deal with *them*.

He buckled himself into the leather, threw a sheet over the broken mirror, and waited at the windows for Luxen's return. London's sky churned gray and thunderous around Aerie's distant pillared foundations. He raised a hand and pressed it to the cool glass.

He did not belong among those angels, of that he was certain. But he did not belong among demons either. He was a fractured thing, broken apart from everything he knew.

"Mikhail?"

The High Lord had returned. He stood a few strides into the room, eyebrow arched at the sheet thrown over the mirror. Sparkling bits of glass lay on the floor between them.

"Is everything all right?"

He glanced at the glass, as though only now seeing it. "Yes. The dresser fell."

Luxen studied Mikhail. His wings framed his tall figure. Their arches had tightened since entering. He sensed a threat in the air. Mikhail's memory ticked: A crone scowling at him. The shrill caw of a rayvern. *"Luxen is a problem,"* they'd said.

Concubi could smell emotion. Mikhail must master his or this demon would know he was faltering.

He rolled his shoulders and flicked out his wings, shaking off their stiffness and his anger. He had to be in control, despite the mess in his head. This demon was not a friend, but right now, Mikhail wasn't himself either. Better to continue this charade until he uncovered the answers. "I am ready to obey."

"Good." Luxen stepped aside and gestured toward the door. "Your audience awaits."

CHAPTER 15

evern

HE MADE it back to Dagenham just as a storm broke. Fat raindrops drummed on the warehouse roof.

"Anyone home?" he called, shaking water from his coat and wings. Nobody was. When he'd flown in, he'd seen demons making their way toward the meeting hall. If Ernas was back, he'd probably be there. He really did need to catch up with the pup for any news on Mikhail's or Luxen's whereabouts.

Solo's sexual revelation had been quite the ether dump. Severn's skin simmered with power, and his wings were flushed with heat. He hadn't been so thoroughly topped up since laying with Mikhail. Solo had more than enjoyed his encounter with a nephilim too, but afterward, once the sexual high had worn off and they'd left the nephilim dozing lightly, he'd withdrawn into his angel-shell.

He'd needed time. They'd meet again in a day in the bar on the corner to discuss Solo's imminent visit to Haven. If he didn't join Severn, then Solo had made his choice. He could only hope Solo made the right call and didn't let a lifetime of conditioning convince him he was wrong.

"You're back?" Samiel stopped in the doorway. A look of disappointment crossed his face, but as quickly as it had come, he shrugged it off and smiled, so Severn wondered if he'd seen it at all.

"You seem surprised."

Samiel sauntered into the warehouse. "No, I just—I didn't expect you back from Whitechapel so soon. I thought I saw you fly in though. There's a meeting in the hall. We should probably head over... Represent Red Manor."

"Any sign of Ernas?" Severn asked, trying to catch Samiel's eye, but he kept shifting his gaze away. There was something different about Samiel's stride combined with his shallow smile. A tightness in his stance. He didn't want to be here, probably because of their last argument.

Samiel waved a hand. "Ernas? Right. He's around somewhere. Luxen wants us at the hall. Apparently, he has a surprise—"

"Finally the coward comes out of hiding." The desire for vengeance simmered through Severn's veins, stoking his anger. He'd take that bastard down in front of everyone and beat him to a bloody pulp to get to Mikhail.

Shoving by Samiel, he flicked his coat collar up and left the warehouse, stepping into sheets of driving rain.

"Wait, Stantin. What are you gonna do?" Samiel jogged after him, his boots splashing through puddles.

"You don't wanna know." Luxen wasn't leaving that hall until he gave up Mikhail's location, and Severn was so fucking full of power, the High Lord would have to back down or get his skinny ass kicked.

Samiel fell into step alongside him. "You seem different?"

Severn glanced over, and right on cue, Samiel glanced away. "So do you." Why was he so nervous?

"How did Whitechapel go?"

"I got what I wanted."

"Oh? That's good."

Samiel was giving off a whole array of weirdness. Severn didn't even need to stretch his concubi senses to read him. As tense as a scaffold pole and as jumpy as an angel in a brothel. Something had him spooked. Samiel's attempt to seduce him still hung like a black cloud between them, but that didn't explain Samiel's nerves.

"Hey." Severn stopped. Other demons filed around them, hurrying to get out of the rain. "You okay?"

"What? Yeah. Sure."

"Look, I get it. This has been tough on us all. Everything is different. But we're still friends, right?"

Finally, he looked him in the eye, but instead of smiling or laughing all this off, like he would have in the past, he scowled. "You've fed, haven't you? Fed from angels?"

Oh, okay. That's what this was about. Severn started forward again, jaw clenched. He didn't like the sound of accusation in Samiel's tone. Where he sourced ether was none of Samiel's fucking business. They weren't *together*.

The huge hall building dominated the other side of the street. Demons funneled in from side streets and flew in from above, some glancing at Severn and veering away at the last moment, just in case they caught the urge to fuck an angel off him. Or maybe they were picking up on the fact he buzzed with power and he was fucking pissed off. Again.

The demons closed in, funneling them toward the meeting hall's high doors. The crowd left little room for Samiel to back off, and as the bodies closed in, Samiel flinched—either afraid to touch Severn or disgusted to.

Whatever nonsense this was, Severn was done with it. He grabbed Samiel by the arm and yanked him out of the flow of demons. Water dripped from Samiel's hair and horns, streaming down his face and clinging to his dark lashes.

"What's going on with you?"

"Nothing. It's nothing."

Clearly, it was something because he reeked of guilt. "Try answering again."

Samiel had pulled Severn from the rubble of Tower Bridge. Samiel had waited for him for ten years. Samiel loved him, but loving someone didn't mean they couldn't hurt you.

Shit...

"You told Luxen I was going to Whitechapel?"

"No!" But even as he denied it, he looked at the demons streaming through the warehouse doors, and a muscle ticked in his cheek.

"You can't even fucking look me in the eye. *You told him*."

"Stantin... I told you. Luxen is our High Lord—"

Severn grabbed him by the collar and slammed him into the wall, sending the nearby demons scattering. "He's not *my* fucking High Lord. And you nearly got me killed!

Luxen told the angels! Remiel was waiting. He kicked the shit out of me thanks to you! He almost killed me, Samiel. Why did you tell Luxen my shit? Because I wouldn't fuck you?"

Samiel lifted his chin. "Did you fuck him?"

Severn recoiled, the words landing like a slap. "What the fuck?"

"You like *angel* so much. You're brimming with power. I can taste it on you. So you fucked him, right? Because that's who you are now, Konstantin Angelfucker."

Samiel was his friend. They had their differences, they fought, but he'd always been his friend, before and forever. Severn pushed away before he did something he'd regret, like punch that horrible smile off Samiel's face. "What the fuck has gotten into you?"

"I watched you fight that day, ten years ago." He shrugged his coat back into line and flicked out his wings, stepping forward—coming in like he wanted to fight. "I was there, right beside you."

Why was he bringing ancient history up now? "What does that have to do with anything?"

"You don't remember what happened next because you threw the memory away to make yourself a fucking angel."

"Samiel, what—"

Another step. Samiel's wings stretched in a threat. "I saw Mikhail that day. I sought him out in the blood and shit of that godsforsaken hellhole. He almost killed me. He would have. He attacked, I only barely held him off, and then I told him where to find the Great Konstantin, Concubi Lord of Red Manor." He said it all with such manic glee that Severn heard the words but didn't understand where they were coming from because Samiel wouldn't ever surrender him to their enemy.

No... that wasn't what happened. Samiel hadn't been there. Samiel hadn't returned from battle. He remembered it now. He'd been on his knees... Wait. The memory stuttered and shifted. He'd been on his knees because Mikhail had cut the tendons in his ankles. Severn had grasped a handful of feathers from Mikhail's wings as his angelblade had cut the air, coming down to cleave Severn's wings from his back.

"I led him to you." Samiel shoved a finger into Severn's chest, rocking him back. "I watched as Mikhail cut your legs, so you couldn't run, and then, when you were on your knees in the mud, he sliced your wings clean from your body. I saw it all. The blood, the wings fall in the mud. Saw him pick them up and carry them off."

Severn's wings reflexively contracted. "You weren't there," he said again, as though the more he said it, the more it would become true. But the memory he'd lost, the memory so powerful it had helped turn him angel, reemerged now, summoned by Samiel's terrible truth.

"He was supposed to kill you"—Samiel's teeth flashed —"but he left you there. I thought you'd come after me, so I ran."

A thudding sickness swirled in Severn's guts. "Why are you saying this? You weren't there."

"Because Luxen is and has always been *my High Lord*. And he wanted you gone that day. You and the dregs of the pathetic Red Manor."

Severn staggered from the weight of it all. Luxen had gotten his claws into Samiel too, years ago, long before all this. Luxen had always wanted Konstantin gone, he'd said as much. *"And I didn't have to lift a finger to see it done."*

Samiel shoved at Severn's chest. "You're a disgrace. The best thing you can do for all demonkind is go back to the angels you love so much."

The demons filing into the hall had stopped to stare, and all of their gazes accused. He was despised. He was a traitor. "We don't need you, Konstantin." Samiel snarled, then shoved through the gawking demons and disappeared inside.

A painful, choking knot clogged Severn's throat. The betrayal of it all made his eyes sting and his heart shrink. *Fuck.* He'd been so blind. So *trusting.* The old Konstantin had *loved* Samiel, and Severn still cared. Even now. This was fucking Luxen's doing. All of it—from the day he'd lost his wings to turning Samiel against him. It was all Luxen's fault.

Severn fought through the demons and into the hall—the same hall where he'd been tried for defection. It was just as packed now as it had been then. Demons gathered on stacks of pallets and filled the space from wall to wall, filled the galleries above too. Wings rustled among hundreds of murmured voices. He scanned the crowd for Samiel and caught sight of his curled horns near the raised stage area.

Luxen was already on the staging area, lit by spotlights, adorned in armor, talking about winning the war with angels as he soaked up the attention of his devoted audience.

Severn shoved through the throng, but the crowd was too closely packed. He'd never make it to Samiel inside or the stage to pull Luxen down. Better to wait until Luxen's ridiculous self-absorbed show was over.

"We will use their own kind against them," Luxen was saying. The High Lord glowed under the play of bright lights and against a backdrop of a floor-to-ceiling crimson curtain. As concubi, he was made to be admired. And that's what this was, Severn realized. The demons right and left of him looked up to Luxen like he was some fucking god—like the angels admired their sacrosanct guardians. Severn hadn't seen the comparison before. Hadn't cared to because he'd had ten years away. Ten years in which Luxen had meticulously woven his incubus allure through all the demons. He had them all bespelled.

Thunder rumbled, shaking the warehouse roof and walls.

"We will win this war, and we don't need thousands to die, to succeed, when their most powerful guardian belongs to me." Luxen swept a hand, and the crimson curtain fell.

An angel in demon armor stood behind Luxen. Vast black wings spread from one side of the stage to the other. Silken black hair framed his cold, hard face. Mikhail.

Oh shit. A nervous whispering hissed through the hundreds of gathered demons. Luxen smiled, his eyes glittering with pride, but the demons surrounding Severn weren't as joyous. Their combined ether switched from excitement to bitter fear. And they were right to be afraid.

Severn knew the look on Mikhail's face.

He was about to raze the place to the ground, with everyone in it.

CHAPTER 16

ikhail

HIS BLOOD RAN SO cold it burned through his body.

Countless demon eyes scored the very depths of his soul, and Mikhail knew only one thing. Every single demon here would kill him given the chance. He did not intend to give them that chance.

Luxen's grin cracked some when he turned to look at *his* angel.

Mikhail lowered his hands to his sides and spread his fingers. All his available power bloomed, sizzling from deep inside and bubbling to the surface. A further two pairs of wings unfurled behind him, their weight comforting. Light poured from him, destroying shadows, leaving nowhere for demons to hide. Thunder shook the air and walls.

He knew only one thing. His enemies surrounded him.

"Mikhail—"

Mikhail grabbed the High Lord around the throat and threw him into the crowd. *That* demon still had an obscure and slippery power over him. Mikhail could not allow him purchase in his mind. Demons screamed. The crowd boiled, suddenly in motion, pouring through exits and out broken windows. Those that came for him, Mikhail knocked aside, instantly healing the cuts from their small blades.

"Mikhail—stop!"

The demon who clambered on stage was the same one from the photograph. *Konstantin.* He held up an arm, shielding his face from Mikhail's light, and held out his empty hand as though he could hold Mikhail back with determination alone.

"If you do this, we will *never* end this war," he spoke through gritted teeth. His wings were poised, not open, not closed. He wasn't attacking.

"Mikhail? It's me. You don't know me, do you...?" A strange kind of hurt showed on the demon's face.

Konstantin lowered his hand. "Easy." His voice trembled. He ducked lower, subjugating himself. "Let's talk, all right? Just talk. Nothing else." His dark hair lay in wet locks around his horns and clung to his face. But his eyes, Mikhail *knew* those eyes.

A shot rang out. Pain snapped through Mikhail's upper right wing. He snarled and found the shooter reloading his rifle on the gallery.

"No—Mikhail!"

Mikhail spread his wings, pulled power into his veins, and thrust out a hand. Lightning tore from the skies, snapped whip-like through a broken window, over the heads of startled demons, and ricocheted off Mikhail's hand, snarling its way to the shooter. Only, another demon was suddenly in the air, in the lightning's path, his wings spread, shielding his kin. The jagged golden strike grabbed hold of Konstantin like a giant hand and crushed him in its fingers. Power spasmed through his body and wings, lighting him up. He fell from the air and hit the floor with a sickening thud—and lay motionless among fleeing demons.

Thunder shook the world. Mikhail barely heard it. A terrible dread choked off his air, freezing his lungs. *Don't turn me away. I can't lose you.* Severn's voice from another place, another time. *Just you and me in this crazy moment.* Said by an angel, *his* angel, his demon too.

His Severn. His Konstantin.

He touched his fingers to his lips and remembered. He'd kissed a demon in a starlit field... and the lies had crumbled to dust. Like they did now. So many, all twisted and barbed, but they fell away, and the truth came rushing back. All of it. Haven, Tien's drug, Amii, and Severn... Severn as demon, so vulnerable in that bizarre moment.

Mikhail's knees struck the stage. His light stuttered and blinked out, taking the abundance of power with it. What had he done?

A shimmer of light caught his eye. Mikhail thrust out a hand, grabbed the metal bar, abruptly jarring its swing to a halt, and growled at the demon on the end. *Luxen.* The High Lord tugged on the bar, trying to free it so he might make a second attempt at taking Mikhail's head off.

"Your mistake, *demon*, was letting me live." Mikhail yanked it from his hands, threw it away, and roared his fury. An immortal rage fueled him now. The rage of a love lost. Luxen and all these demons would pay for their deceit!

Samiel ran through the fleeing demons—toward Severn's motionless body. A dagger flashed in his hand. Samiel: the traitor. Samiel: the demon who had orchestrated Konstantin's fall ten years ago.

Mikhail flung open his wings, leaped from the stage, and landed straight in the traitor's path. Samiel skidded and rapidly reeled backward, wings flapping to haul him out of reach.

There were no words for this treacherous one.

Samiel glanced to his High Lord for help, but when none came, he glared at Mikhail. "So much for love. You killed him anyway."

Killed Severn? The demons forgotten, he reached for Severn's motionless body, afraid to touch but needing to. Severn's new wings lay limp around him. No. He wasn't dead. He couldn't be. He hadn't meant for this at all. He'd been confused. So confused.

Brushing Severn's wet hair behind a horn revealed his smooth cheek and defined jaw. His eyes were closed, lips apart. Mikhail trembled too much to see if he breathed. He dug his hands under Severn's body and rolled him into his arms. He was bigger than before, so much bigger, but it didn't matter. Standing, he staggered, hesitating. Not all the demons had gone. Some had returned, some moved in now.

He knew how it looked. An angel, taking his kill. He'd ruined everything before they'd had a chance to make it right.

Spreading six wings, he launched into the air, plowed through the brittle roof, and hefted Severn's limp body higher into the swirling clouds and jagged lightning, where no demon would dare follow.

HE WASN'T sure where the storm spat him out. The land was flat and stretched for miles without a hill to break it. A house jutted from a field. He entered through an unlocked balcony, not caring if anyone happened to be home.

He laid Severn on the neatly made bed, careful to avoid tangling his wings, and felt for a pulse at his neck.

The heavy thudding rhythm pulled a sob from Mikhail. He lived...

A heavy wave of emotion slammed into him. Fear, disgust at himself, pain, horror at his actions. He stumbled back, hit a wall, and slid to the floor. Pulling his knees up, he hugged them to his chest and squeezed his eyes closed. That angel hadn't been him. It hadn't. He wasn't that guardian anymore. He'd changed. He'd changed for the better. He felt, and he hurt, and he wished he'd been stronger. He should have resisted Luxen. Should have fought him.

What if Severn woke and hated him all over again? What if he didn't wake at all?

Seraphim, it hurts.

Everything hurt. His head. His heart.

Severn *should* hate him. If he woke and drove his daggers through Mikhail's heart, he'd welcome it. It would be justice. It would be right.

 evern

His BODY FELT like he'd been run over by a truck. No part
of him was spared the dull, thudding ache. He groaned and
buried his face in a pillow. The faint smell of human soap
tickled his nose and sweetened the less pleasant odors of
burnt flesh. Birds twittered outside the window. There
weren't many birds left in Dagenham. Mostly just angel
sirens to warn of an incoming attack.

A clock ticked.

He turned his head and frowned at the framed photo
on the bedside table of a human family he'd never met.
Whose bed was this? Shoving onto his hands revealed
more of the bed he'd never seen before and a room that
wasn't his, and an angel sitting on the floor, staring out a
window.

"Mikhail?"

He didn't reply or move or acknowledge him at all.

Severn swung his legs off the side of the bed, waited for the room to stop spinning, slid to his knees, and crawled the short distance to Mikhail, avoiding his drooped wings. Only a pair, not three. "Mikhail? Hey?"

Nothing.

Severn rested a hand on his knee. Mikhail jerked and stared at Severn, his face wrought. Dried tears had left tracks on his cheeks. "I have made things much worse."

Well, worse was relative. Everything had been pretty shitty before. He slumped to the floor beside Mikhail, his own wings like deadweights pulling on his back. He lacked the strength to illusion them away. Had he not been brimming with angel-ether, he might not have survived the attack.

"I'm sorry," Mikhail said quietly. "Sorry for everything. I didn't mean to hurt you. I wasn't in control."

"Yeah, I got that." Severn shuffled closer, folded his wings out of the way, and tucked a shoulder against Mikhail's arm. After a few moments, a fan of black feathers lay over his legs like a blanket. At least Mikhail didn't pull away. Though trying to fry him with lightning wasn't the best of signs that they were in any way okay. He said he didn't mean it, but maybe the angel part of him saw demon and figured *kill it*. A stupid thought. For all his faults, Mikhail was honest. If he'd wanted Severn dead, he wouldn't lay a wing over or sit close with him now. Severn had to believe that or he might weep, and he couldn't fall apart now he'd gotten Mikhail back.

"I'm sorry for more than that," Mikhail said in a small voice. "Luxen showed me who I really am. I'm sorry for it

all, Severn. Truly sorry. And I do not know"—he gulped—
"how to make it right."

That fucking bastard. Severn slipped an arm around
Mikhail's waist and pulled him in tight. He trembled
dammit. Luxen had a lot to answer for. "Luxen—everyone
—they look at us and they see who we were, not who we
are. We've both changed. You are not the guardian who
killed my kin, and I am not the demon who lied to you for
ten years. I look at you now, Mikhail, and I see an angel
who desperately cares. I hope you look at me and you see...
I don't know... maybe a demon who gets it wrong more
than he gets it right, but who loves you with all his heart?"

"I see someone who is brave and honorable." Mikhail's
lips tucked into his cheek. "Someone I want to better
myself *for*."

Oh gods. He didn't need to be better for Severn. If he
wanted to be better, it had to be for himself. "We began
again, you and me. Remember? We were together in a
field—"

"You revealed the truth. I kissed you."

Hm. That was a nice memory. One of the better ones.
They needed more of those. Severn rested his head over
Mikhail's shoulder, careful to keep the horns out of the
way. Mikhail's shoulder felt a whole lot smaller against
Severn's than he remembered. In fact, all of him felt fragile, like Severn could bundle him up, feathers and all, and
fold him close. Protect him from the Luxens of the world
who would use his self-doubt against him.

The clock ticked some more.

None of this was their fault. Djall had ruined a
perfectly good kiss, and Luxen had twisted all the good

into knots. If people would just leave them the fuck alone, they'd be fine.

"You okay?" Severn asked.

"I don't think so, no."

"No, me neither. Samiel fucked me over years ago and only told me yesterday."

"I remembered him." His sorrowful eyes found Severn's. "I almost killed your Samiel that day, during the battle. He pleaded for his life and betrayed your location. He led me to you with wicked intent."

"Yeah. Yeah, he did. And I trusted him, back then, and now. It fucking hurts." He sighed and bowed his head. What he felt inside, that twisting, choking sensation, Mikhail must have felt the same when his friend of ten years turned out to be his enemy.

"*Everything* hurts," Mikhail whispered. Head bowed, his black hair hid much of his face, but not the soft quiver of his lips. Before his fear got the better of him, Severn tucked that curtain of hair back, revealing Mikhail's face. When he was soft, like this, he was someone else entirely. Someone vulnerable and riddled with doubt. Someone only Severn saw.

The sound of a car rumbled closer. Wheels crunched on gravel outside. Severn withdrew his touch. The returning homeowner might not be too pleased to find an angel and a demon in their bedroom.

"Are you well enough to fly?" Mikhail unfolded his wing from over Severn and got to his feet.

Every one of Severn's muscles protested the moment he tried to stand. "Probably. Not sure how far though." Mikhail offered his hand, his face back to its passive guardian mask. Severn grabbed his hand and headed for the balcony doors. "Any idea where we are?" The long horizon and flat land suggested Norfolk somewhere.

"The storm carried us north."

That tallied up with a few hours' flight north of London.

The human was leaving his car and headed into the house. Keys rattled in the lock. Time to leave. "Follow me. There's someone we both need to meet." Severn leaped from the balcony, snapping his wings open wide to catch the air. The human yelped, then yelled an expletive.

Severn signaled for Mikhail to follow and climbed hard until an updraft caught him. Once the rising thermals took the work out of flying, he breathed easier. A glance back revealed Mikhail gliding slightly on the thermals behind him, looking even more magnificent now he was windswept, brooding, and rough around the edges. He noticed Severn's gaze and mustered a tiny smile—enough to warm Severn through and make his heartache lessen. Mikhail was hurting. And he had every right to. Luxen had done a number on him.

Severn wouldn't blame him if he called the whole thing off. Whatever he needed—space, time—he'd get it. War be damned. He was just grateful to have Mikhail back with him.

ROAD SIGNS POINTED the way back to familiar territory. They couldn't risk going too far south or too deep into London. Demons would be looking for Mikhail. A good thing then that Severn had already planned to rendezvous with an angel.

Daylight had begun to wane by the time they alighted on a church's conveniently high-pitched roof.

Mikhail knelt on the ridge tiles, looking suitably dramatic against the backdrop of jagged steeple. He wasn't saying a whole lot, but then, what was there to say? *Oh hey, Severn, your High Lord held me captive for a few weeks, using his incubi allure to keep me subdued and alter my thoughts—oh, and aren't you an incubus too? So there's two reasons the whole love thing was a terrible mistake.* Wonderful.

"Wait here. I'll be right back." Ignoring his own mental attempts to sabotage them, he quickly glided over the street and landed at the bar on the corner. The plastic sheet flapped as before, and a couple stumbled from inside, laughing in each other's arms.

Severn braced against a wall, catching a few breaths. All the power he'd consumed was gone. Mikhail was right when he'd said everything hurt. And even though he'd been clear in that he hadn't meant to hurt anyone, Severn saw the look on Mikhail's face when he'd unleashed his power. He'd have killed everyone in that warehouse, starting with him. But that wasn't the real Mikhail. He believed that. That was the guardian in him. The part he was trying to shake off. Still fucking hurt though.

Inside the bar, Solo had tucked himself into a corner in a doomed attempt to blend in. Even beneath a hooded cloak, there was no mistaking his svelte frame and a few errant locks of red hair.

"Hey," Severn croaked.

Solo looked up. "You're late. I was just about to leave —" His eyes widened. "By Haven, what happened to you? You look terrible!"

"Mikhail is here."

He shot to his feet, almost toppling the table. "He is? Where?"

"Yeah, but honestly, we're both fried. We need a place to stay. Do you have more tokens I can use to get us a—"

"Take me to him." His tone left no room for discussion.

Severn led the way. If Solo had tokens, Severn could rent a room for a few nights in some nearby mediocre hotel. They needed rest, needed to regroup, and Mikhail needed to know he was safe. He had to get into Haven and intended to bring down Remiel, but those things could wait.

Mikhail's instantly recognizable silhouette interrupted the profile of the church roof. Solo darted ahead and landed on the ridge tiles, practically running at Mikhail, his red wings flailing behind him. As Severn landed, Solo fell to a knee in front of Mikhail. "Your Grace, forgive me."

Mikhail briefly lifted his gaze to Severn, silently asking why the angel was here.

"It's complicated."

Mikhail rested his hand on Solo's bowed head. "Solomon. Please, rise. There's no need for this. What am I forgiving?"

He didn't rise and kept his head down. "*Everything*. I didn't believe you. I didn't protect you. I should have. Remiel tried to kill you. Severn said... he said Remiel would. I didn't listen. And then he... And then, when you fell, I understood too late." He lifted his face. "I understood it all."

Mikhail's wings sagged, probably from relief but maybe from a little sadness too. The sympathy in his eyes had

Severn gritting his teeth and looking away before he went to his knee too.

"It's all right," Mikhail said, so damn softly.

"No, no, it's not. It's all *wrong*. You were persecuted for *love*," Solo whined. "It's wrong. Everything is wrong. The angels. Haven. All of it! All these years we've lived a lie. It's *unthinkable*."

"Yes," Mikhail said. "But we're trying to rectify that, and I'd—Severn and I would appreciate your help, I think. I assume that's why you're here?"

"Of course." Solo thumped his right fist to his left shoulder. "My blade is yours, Your Grace."

"Thank you, Solomon. Your allegiance means more than you can know."

Severn cleared his throat, interrupting their moment before Solo did something emotional and spontaneous like kiss Mikhail. "Let's get out of the open."

THE ENFIELD TRAVELODGE was a dull concrete box built sometime in the '80s. Thick coats of white paint and plastic-framed windows had done nothing to add to its charm. The inside was just as unimaginative, but it was clean, dry, and quiet, and so nondescript that their chances of being found were slim.

Twin single beds dominated the small room they'd been given. An old radiator hummed beneath a window. Severn closed the blinds and flicked on the bedside lamp, poorly illuminating two angels, one still wrapped in demon armor, the other scowling at the room like he'd rather bunk in the killing fields. Both had their wings hidden.

Two angels were a squeeze, two angels and a demon barely fit at all. "It's the best I could come up with."

"It's fine." Mikhail began to pry open his leather coat's buckles. He shrugged the coat off his shoulders, revealing a snug gray undervest, and laid it on the bed, then stared at it like it was the first time he'd seen it.

Solo glanced at Severn, brow pinched in a worried frown.

"Haven..." Severn began, pulling out the chair from the tiny desk and flopping into it. "What did you discover, Solo?"

"It's largely in disarray after Serap—after you both broke out. Remiel sent Vearn to oversee its repair and organize the angels you terrified. Remiel has made Vearn Haven's guardian."

"A good choice," Mikhail commented in a tone that suggested he was only half listening. He continued to stare at the coat.

It was a terrible choice. Vearn was a hard-ass and fucking great at her job. Which also made her their enemy. Vearn wouldn't hesitate to kill them both.

"I can get in, but I don't know if I can get out again," Solo added.

"Mikhail," Severn said. He looked up, but emotion had his gaze glassy. He couldn't handle much more of this. "Do you agree that there are likely to be angels in Haven who feel, like you and Solo, and they're in the process of having their emotions corrected?"

Mikhail's gaze had drifted behind Severn to the closed blinds.

"Mikhail?"

"Yes?" He blinked slowly.

Solo glanced again at Severn. It was clear to both of them that Mikhail wasn't in the room. Severn's fingers twitched. He'd peel Luxen's fucking skin off his bones the next time he saw him. But until then, they needed Mikhail functioning. He needed time, that much was clear, but Remiel wasn't going to back off anytime soon.

Severn shoved from the chair and guided Solo toward the door. "Can you stay close and maybe grab some clothes he'll be more comfortable in? We'll talk some more tomorrow."

Solo nodded. "Is he going to be all right?" he whispered.

"Yeah. He'll be fine."

Solo chewed on his bottom lip, like he always did when worried, and left. Severn checked the hallway, found it quiet and empty, and after closing the door, snicked the lock over. Not that it would stop a demon, but they didn't need housekeeping walking in on them.

"Do you want to get cleaned up, maybe take a shower?"

Mikhail lifted his head, and for a moment, his face betrayed complete confusion. He blinked, and recognition sharpened his focus.

His gaze wandered over Severn, but whatever conclusion he'd come to, it didn't ease the deep furrows in his forehead. "Luxen was able to take a sample of my blood and discover the drug Tien had used to try and subdue me and no doubt other angels like me. I fought it, at first, and then... Then I stopped fighting."

"You didn't stand a chance, not with a drug combined with Luxen's allure."

"Didn't I?"

"Mikhail..." Severn reached for him.

"I'll take that shower." He quickly headed into the bathroom, where water hissed moments later.

Severn sank to the edge of the bed. He was losing him. It was all too much. The war, Haven, seeing Severn as demon. Then having Luxen do whatever he'd done... confirming every nightmare Mikhail knew about demons.

And now Severn clearly was demon. No longer angel with blond hair, blue eyes, and a lithe body to match. His skin glossy black, his body very different, with horns and dark eyes and featherless wings. Amii had said love wasn't fed with the eyes, but he wasn't sure he believed them. Mikhail had feelings, but those were for Severn-the-angel.

He dragged a hand down his face and glanced at the open bathroom door. Splashing sounded from within, water falling from Mikhail's body. He wanted to go to him, to touch him, remind him what they'd had and how it wasn't so different now, just strange. But how could he cross that gulf between them?

Gods, everything was a fucking disaster. Ever since they'd broken out of Haven. Ever since he'd lost his angel-skin.

He could get it back...

He gripped his thighs and sighed. No. No more lies. There was no going back. It had to be like this, and if it meant they couldn't be together, then he'd respect Mikhail's choice.

"Fuck," Severn muttered.

He didn't know how to help him and for once actually wished Amii were here. Amii had steered them on this path and then apparently abandoned them on it and fucked off wherever they went when shit got hard. But they would have the answers.

Bowing his head, he grabbed a horn and closed his eyes. Not since losing his wings had he felt so lost as this.

"Severn?"

Severn shot to his feet and entered the bathroom, stopping in the doorway. Steam and condensation blurred the glass surrounding the shower. Mikhail's tantalizing outline drew Severn's gaze down his chest, over his ass, and down powerful thighs.

Mikhail swiped condensation from the glass. Blue eyes speared into Severn's chest, stopping his heart.

"Join me?"

Severn's battered heart leaped. He tried to keep the grin off his face and probably failed. "It's pretty tight in there." He tugged off his coat and dropped it at his feet. Holy shit, Mikhail was asking for this. Though, given his intense glare through the shower door, it wasn't so much an ask as an order.

He discarded his boots, and the rest of his clothing in a few steps, stripping off in record time, and stood naked under the angel's heated gaze. Climbing inside the shower with Mikhail would be interesting. There was barely enough room for two normal-sized humans. Mikhail wasn't small, and Severn, well. He wasn't an angel anymore.

Mikhail slid open the shower door, letting out a blast of hot, wet air. His heavy gaze demanded this, but for the first time in forever, Severn held himself back, unsure. What was he asking? Comfort? Sex? He was about to have a whole lot of demon pressed against him and there was no avoiding it. There wouldn't be much room to avoid Severn's stiffening cock either.

"Unless you don't want to?" Mikhail asked, still holding the door open.

Severn didn't have to be told twice. He stepped into the warmth behind Mikhail and immediately brushed against Mikhail's warm, slippery ass. Long black hair spilled down Mikhail's back, as silky as rayvern wings. Severn had its length in his hands without thinking and swept it aside. With the beautiful curve of Mikhail's back revealed, he skimmed his knuckles down Mikhail's spine.

Mikhail shuddered, and given how close they stood, his tremor shivered through Severn too. Severn's stiff cock had become impossible to ignore. It currently rested against Mikhail's hip, pretty fucking obvious in its persistence. The damn thing throbbed with want.

Mikhail braced a hand against the tiles, tilting his shoulders forward and his ass back, fitting his backside neatly against Severn's upper thighs. Gods, he was warm and smooth and soft. Severn swallowed, trying to slicken his suddenly dry throat, and stroked both hands down the stunning pale canvas of Mikhail's back to where the twin peaks of his ass rose to meet Severn's palms.

"Mikhail." Shit, his voice had dropped a note. "I'm not a fucking saint."

"I am aware."

Heart thudding in his throat, he dug his thumbs into Mikhail's ass cheeks, kneading its supple flexibility. He just fucking hoped Mikhail knew what he was asking because now his cock was in the game, its base tucked precisely into the valley of Mikhail's ass, the swollen head riding up Mikhail's lower back.

Water ran in twitching rivulets down his back, pooling toward and around Severn's cock. Severn lost his thoughts somewhere in the sight of his hands on Mikhail's hips, his cock against his back.

Mikhail suddenly arched his spine, keeping his ass down but bringing his shoulders close enough to bite if Severn just bowed forward. Water rained over his hair, pouring its blackness down Mikhail's back like spilled ink. Either he'd been holding back on Severn, or he truly had no idea how much of a fucking tease he was.

Severn ached from the tips of his invisible wings to his toes to explore Mikhail all over again, to rediscover every inch of him beneath demon nails. To taste Mikhail with his true tongue, to bite at his supple skin with demon teeth. To have his angel surrender to him beneath his real hands, his true self. He hadn't realized until now how much he'd wanted this and how much he'd feared it would never happen.

"You're so beautiful."

The sound of Mikhail's chuckle sent a dart of lust straight to Severn's cock, making it twitch as it sought any kind of tightness to slip into. Severn bent forward, trapping his cock between them, and slid his hand around Mikhail's waist, running his fingers over the ripple of abs, up his warm, slick chest. Finding a hard nipple, he teased it between his finger and thumb and nuzzled Mikhail's neck, breathing in the sweet scent of angel. He tasted exactly as Severn remembered. Like sunshine and long summer evenings. Like good memories.

Mikhail gasped, shoulders back, his neck Severn's to lick and tease. "I lost you," Mikhail spoke, and Severn couldn't be sure if the noise of the shower made the sound of his voice tremble or if Mikhail's own tremors did. "I can't lose you again."

Severn's mouth hovered over the curve of Mikhail's

neck. He should reply, but he didn't know what words to speak that could ease his pain.

Mikhail's hand grasped Severn's on his chest. "I need to feel you. I cannot... I can't be alone, Severn. I feel everything, and alone, it eats at me, but with you... with you, I breathe again."

There was a time for words, but this was not one of them. Instead of replying and probably screwing this up by saying the wrong thing, Severn gently eased Mikhail's shoulders forward, making him brace against the tiles to present the luscious curve of his back and rise of his ass to Severn.

With his cock stroking the top of Mikhail's pert ass, he spread both hands up Mikhail's back. *Demon hands on angel-skin.* Ether cloyed the air, all of it for Severn. Fuck, it was enough to have Severn salivating and his cock leaking strings of precum. With his angel surrendered in his hands, he kissed and swirled his tongue between Mikhail's shoulders. Mikhail shifted his ass, deliberately grinding against Severn.

He'd have liked nothing more than to spread his ass and fill him deep, but that would take a lot more prep than they'd needed before, and if Mikhail kept rubbing his ass down Severn's cock like he was, he'd be halfway to coming before long anyway.

Mikhail straightened, his wet skin slippery in Severn's hands. Water beat against them both as Severn trailed kisses up Mikhail's neck and sucked his earlobe between his teeth. Mikhail's ass cheeks clenched, holding Severn's cock captive, while his neck a meal for Severn's mouth, and if he didn't quit being so damn accommodating, Severn was going to have to pace himself.

He stroked down Mikhail's taut chest, skimming his hip, and found Mikhail's jutting erection. The thick cock fit eagerly in Severn's fist. Mikhail gasped and bucked, thrusting his cock through Severn's grip, making it clear exactly what he needed.

"You have no idea how crazy you're making me," Severn growled into his ear. He was going to make him come so fucking hard they risked shattering the glass with his wings. It'd be worth it.

Mikhail's dark, wicked chuckle was a rare treat, and it undid all the ties around Severn's heart, banishing everything he'd feared. Severn pumped his rigid, slick cock, kissed and bit at Mikhail's shoulder, alternating between hard and soft to the sounds of Mikhail's short, ragged gasps, and reveled in every twitch and shudder of Mikhail's ass against his cock.

"Come for me, Your Grace. Come all over those fucking tiles, like I know you want to." Mikhail pumped harder, meeting Severn's strokes, his body writhing in Severn's hold. With his head thrown back and teeth gritted, he was a vision of lust on an angel who deserved to *feel* everything.

The roughness of Severn's grip on the most sensitive part of him, the hard press of Severn's cock riding against his ass, the pierce of Severn's teeth in his beautiful angel-skin. It was a fucking crime all these wonders had been kept from him. *"Yes, Mikhail."* He gripped Mikhail's hip with his free hand. Mikhail had found his rhythm. He was lost to the building ecstasy, lost in Severn's hands, his grunts coming as fast as he pumped his cock. Growls sawed through Mikhail's teeth, the sound more demon than angel. And fuck, Severn's own release threatened, tingling its way down his spine and pooling there, pressure building.

Mikhail's relentless thrusting stuttered. He cried out. Warm seed creamed Severn's dark fingers and dashed the tiles in spurts.

His release tipped Severn's over the edge. The building climax was suddenly on him, stealing his breath and his thoughts. He clutched Mikhail hard against him, hips jerking, grinding his unloading cock against Mikhail's back. Fuck, he hadn't expected to lose control so soon.

The pummeling water quickly washed Mikhail's back clean. The angel slumped in Severn's arms. Severn greedily folded him close, breathing him in and loving him with his body and heart. Heady relief lifted all the aches, pains, and emotional hurt away. When demons mated, they'd spend hours entwined afterward, kissing, stroking, all night sometimes. He wanted that soft, precious time with Mikhail, but he'd been through too much to ask. Just being close was enough.

After everything they'd been through, every battle they'd fought, every enemy who had tried to tear them apart, they were here, together, and that meant everything.

ikhail

A KNOCK at the hotel door roused Mikhail from a bless-edly dreamless sleep. Severn was by the door, peering through the peephole, his bulk blocking the view. Severn. He could still feel his hands in all the most intimate of places, still recall the delicious thrum from the bites and the tingle from his impossible kisses. His body sang at the memories, and his member roused all over again, seeking Severn's deft hand.

"It's Solo, you, er—should maybe..." Severn glanced back and arched an eyebrow. "Never mind. It'll be fine." He opened the door.

Solo entered with a bundle of clothes in his arms, made it two steps inside the room, and stopped dead. His mouth fell open, and a flush heated his pale skin.

Mikhail groggily sat up, letting the sheet slip to his

waist, and brushed his hair from his face. They'd pushed the beds together last night to accommodate their bodies and expanse of wings. Mikhail's feathers had knocked a lamp over, while Severn's had taken up all the space between the beds and the window. It had quickly become clear they didn't really fit in the room, but there had been comfort in Severn's closeness and in seeing *all of him*. They'd spent hours dozing, tangled together as one, Severn's fingers stroking his. Mikhail had sorely needed him, surprising himself by how much their union had settled both his heart and head.

Solo continued to stare.

Severn tutted a small laugh, took the bundle of clothes from Solo's arms, and handing them over to Mikhail, he whispered, "Solo has a crush on you."

A crush? It sounded painful.

Mikhail threw back the sheet and rose to his feet, illusioning his wings away to prevent them from scraping the ceiling.

Solo spun on his heel and stared at the door. *"God."*

"Solomon, are you well?"

"Fine." His voice cracked, and he cleared his throat. "It's just, I recently had something of an *awakening*, and your appearance is quite stimulating. In multiple ways."

His appearance was alarming? Mikhail looked down at his torso, waist, and legs. Nothing about him had changed. Severn was the one who'd undergone a dramatic physical change.

Severn smirked, enjoying himself far too much.

Oh… wait. Ah, yes. Mikhail was naked and semihard.

"He means you're hot and he's horny," Severn translated with a wolfish grin.

Mikhail tossed him an irritated look, earning a bigger grin from Severn, and quickly stepped into the fresh pair of cotton slacks and tied them off. "Apologies, Solomon. I hadn't realized you were *aware* in that way. Let's discuss Haven and our best means of securing a flight of angels to our cause?"

"Just... give me a few moments to calm myself, Your Grace."

Severn leaned against the wall, looking exceedingly pleased with himself. He'd clearly had something to do with Solomon's recent awakening. "What did you do to Solomon?"

"Me?" He fluttered his lashes. "Nothing he didn't want."

Had Severn been intimate with Solomon? The thought summoned an ugly bite of jealousy. "Did you and he—"

"No. Not that." Severn was suddenly in front of him, his fingers running along Mikhail's jaw, his mouth tantalizingly close. "But I did consume his ether while a nephilim popped his angelic cherry. I was half-starved and had little choice. Forgive me, Mikhail?"

A gamut of emotions ran through Mikhail, but they all vanished when Severn looked at him like he wanted to strip him naked and rut like they had in the shower last night. Had Severn been weak, he might not have been able to mend the power Mikhail had burned through him.

Mikhail's smile replied for him. "Perhaps you can make it up to me later?"

Solo's shoulders stiffened. "If you'd like me to stay, please stop flirting."

"Of course, Solomon." Mikhail playfully batted Severn's hand away and received a silent, teasing snarl that promised more wonderful apologies later. "Please, both of you, tell me everything I've missed."

As Mikhail dressed, Severn told of how Luxen had squirreled Mikhail away, and went on to explain how he'd tried to locate Mikhail, and when his efforts had failed, he'd attempted to rebuild something of Red Manor, recruiting the madam, Samiel, and Ernas. The madam had eventually led him to the site of the Whitechapel house, which Solo apparently visited, and where Remiel had sprung a trap—with Luxen's aid—leading to Solo's eventual defection. It was quite remarkable, but of course, so was Severn. Far from being idle, he'd made great strides in furthering their cause.

"Did your Ernas return?" Mikhail asked carefully, all too aware of how Luxen had threatened the young pup in his presence.

"Haven't seen him in weeks," Severn said. He'd casually propped himself against the wall. "My guess is he stumbled on something and—"

"He discovered me, during my... procedure. Samiel was ordered to deal with him. I fear he might not have survived."

Severn's stillness betrayed the effort it took to keep his feelings from his face. His "I'm going to kill him," was said like a fact, not a threat.

Whether he meant to kill Samiel or Luxen wasn't clear. But their demise wouldn't stop Remiel, and his threat was far greater. "Have you been back to the house, Solomon, since Remiel discovered Severn there?" Mikhail asked.

Once Solomon had his urges back under control, he'd taken a chair by the door and listened intently to Severn's recollection of events. "I have, yes, but I was careful. I wasn't followed."

"You should abandon the dwelling for now. Remiel may take an interest in your activities given how you've recently come into contact with Konstantin. He'll be watching you."

Solomon leaned back in the chair but gripped the arms tightly. "Oh, I think he's too busy gathering more angels to Aerie to notice me."

"All the same, it's unusual for an angel to adopt a human home. Remiel will be watching for changes in behavior among his flights."

"I..." Solomon swallowed. "I have to go back."

"Why?"

"I have a cat."

"A what?"

"Well, more than one, actually. I'm not entirely sure how it happened. I took pity on the creature after I was charged to guard the house should either of you return. Frankly, I believe Remiel knew I was close to you, so he stationed me there to keep me out of the way. Anyway, a white cat came to the door one night. I offered it salmon, which seemed to satisfy it. And then, the next night, there were two cats. A multicolored one with half its tail missing had joined the first. I couldn't feed one and not its friend, and so she also had some salmon, and... well"—he shrugged a little sheepishly—"there are six now."

Severn had hidden his face beneath his hand, but the soft lift of his shoulders suggested he was laughing.

"Oh." Mikhail had never known an angel to keep a pet and couldn't really comment on whether such a thing was necessary. But like love, he supposed, it seemed a bond could form between animal and angel. Humans bonded with pets all the time.

"Do they have names?" Severn asked, pinching his lips together.

"Oh yes." Solomon grinned. "One to six."

"Wait. One, two, and six?" Severn pressed.

"No, one to six. One, Two, Three, Four, Five—"

"Yes, thank you," Mikhail interrupted before Solomon could hurt himself. "Perhaps stop feeding them salmon and they'll go away," Mikhail said.

"I..." His grin fell away, and his face fell like he'd lost a battle, not six cats. "I suppose I could ask someone else to feed them."

"Good. Your comings and goings are far more helpful in Aerie." This all seemed reasonable, so why then did Mikhail feel like he'd wronged Solomon. It was the angel's stricken face. Mikhail frowned at him, or himself, or this whole situation.

"You can't ask him to abandon his cats," Severn said.

And now Severn had that sorry look too, like this was some emotional ambush. "Fine... Return to your cats, Solomon. Just be careful. Keeping pets is not an angel trait. Should Remiel discover your companions, his treatment of you and the animals will not be kind."

"Of course." Solomon rose from the chair. "I would never risk their lives. Or yours, of course, Your Grace."

"You can probably feed them tinned cat food though," Severn added, eyes sparkling with humor. "Keep feeding them salmon and you'll have all of London's strays on your doorstep."

"They really do get very excited for salmon. They're

everywhere. All over the countertop, with the purring and the fluffy tails and the big eyes."

Mikhail aimed a severe look at Severn. He was surely encouraging Solomon. "Can we perhaps get back to the imminent war and how exactly we're going to infiltrate Haven to free the angels and retrieve the evidence we need to topple Remiel?"

Severn's posture immediately straightened now they were back on the topic of war. "We aren't going to infiltrate Haven. We're going to *take* it. Their defenses are limited to a few jittery angels who believe their god Seraphim kicked their asses, and one competent guardian. Mikhail, if you can summon the light like you did for Luxen, then we'll have the Haven angels bowing to you in no time. Easy."

That was all well and good, but the power was temperamental, and using it to subjugate others felt... wrong. "I do not want them to bow to me."

"No, but... you know what I mean." Severn waved a hand. "Just scare them a little."

"Doesn't frightening them reinforce the very wrongs we're trying to right?"

Annoyance tightened Severn's lips. "It's only initially, then once they're ready to listen, you can tone down the godly aspects."

The very idea made Mikhail go cold. "You want me to lie to them and pretend I'm Seraphim?"

"Well, I mean..." Severn gestured between them. "What is this if not history repeating? Aerius and Seraphim, only this time we win."

"Seraphim died. Aerius vanished, with some myths having him turn into a rayvern," Mikhail reminded him.

"Aerius turned into a rayvern?" Solomon asked.

"No," Severn denied, lifting a finger. He faced Mikhail again. "Why did Amii give you the wings if not to use them?"

"Like cocks," Solo said.

"What?" Severn snapped.

"'Why did Seraphim give angels cocks if he didn't want you using them,' you asked me. I was making a comparison." He winced. "Was it a terrible comparison? I admit, I really don't understand cocks."

"Solo, just...for a second, please stop trying to help."

"No. He's right." Mikhail thought back to the moment the crone—Amii—had caught him and lathered his wings in the salve. Amii had changed him, of that there was no doubt. And Amii had been alongside them at every turn, guiding, or steering him and Severn toward an outcome neither truly understood. Amii, with their rayvern always by their side. Amii with a power like no other demon on this earth. "Amii is Aerius."

"What?" Severn's shrill laugh cut the idea off at the root. "Have you both lost your damn minds? First, Solo with his cats, and now you're claiming a wretched cambion is the first demon? Can we just focus on Haven and what needs to be done to stop Remiel from killing every last demon?"

Severn was clearly concerned, and rightly so. But still... Amii was powerful in ways that no demon should be, and they clearly had an interest in Severn and Mikhail that went beyond meddling. Mikhail had been changed on the inside too. The power he'd experienced and continued to summon, that wasn't a guardian's power but something bigger than them all.

"Mikhail, what else are your wings for, if not to help stop angels and demons from killing one another?" Severn pressed. "Not utilizing their gift is foolish."

"I understand why you think lying is the only way to attack angels, but you should also know that such things rarely result in the preferred outcome."

Severn laughed, but it held no humor. "For what it's worth, you and I wouldn't be here without my lies."

"Your lies almost killed us both."

"And the guardians are so much better because they lie to you while the sun shines out of their perfect angel asses?" Severn shoved from the wall. "Mikhail, I lied because I was manipulated by a demon I trusted when he handed me over *to you* on the battlefield. I lied because there was no other way to save demons." Sharp demon teeth flashed. "I lied because demons are dying by the hundreds every damn week. I lied because there is nothing left for demonkind. No way out. So if you want to waltz back into Haven as Mikhail the Angel Traitor and watch them try and kill you a second time, be my fucking guest. But we can make a difference here. You can make a difference by using those extra wings for some good, instead of trying to kill everything in sight every time you sprout six wings and lose your shit."

The quiet returned, disturbed only by the humming radiator.

"Are you finished?" Mikhail asked.

Severn winced and hung his head. "Fuck. I didn't mean—"

"Seraphim is dead. He died protecting Aerius from his guardians. I am not Seraphim, but I will do everything in my power to protect the innocence in this war, angels and

171

demons alike. Even those who rightly despise me. But I refuse to pretend to be someone I am not."

"Like me?" Severn lifted his face and, with a grimace, pushed by Solo and left the room.

Mikhail hadn't meant to argue and wasn't even sure where the fervor had come from. With a sigh, he ran a hand through his hair. Navigating these feelings was proving far harder than he could have imagined. Solomon still stood to attention, likely caught between his duty to stay and the urge to flee. The corner of Solomon's mouth tucked into his cheek in sympathy.

"I did not mean for that to happen," Mikhail admitted.

"He cares deeply for his people."

"As I care deeply for ours."

"Then... it seems you both want the same thing. You'll find a compromise."

"I wish it were that simple." There was no escaping how different they were, more so now Severn was demon. The truth hit Mikhail anew every time he looked at him. Not in a bad way, just... unbalancing. Their intimacy in the shower had been a revelation. Severn's touch had been the same confident strokes as before, the same whispered filthy words that Mikhail longed to hear. But tangled with him after, their fingers interlaced, Mikhail had studied their hands so closely, marveling at their differences, feeling his heart flutter with the strange lick of fear. "I sometimes wonder if the guardians were right and perhaps love is too destructive to be set free."

Solo's russet eyebrows pinched. "But they've lied to keep us all controlled? That cannot be right."

"These emotions, I am a slave to them. I care that angels are free to make choices, that the truth is revealed, and I care that they are no longer thrown into an unnecessary war. But these feelings inside"—he pressed a fist to his heart—"they're so powerful. I fear they will consume me. Before, without them, I functioned as Aerie's guardian without flaws. Now I am riddled with doubt."

Solo approached the bed. "May I?" he asked, gesturing at the spot beside him.

"Please, you do not need to ask my permission, Solomon. I am no longer your guardian. You are free to do as you please."

He perched on the edge of the bed, angled toward Mikhail, and looked him in the eyes. "What we had before, it wasn't living. It was sterile. Going from day to day, focused on the war. A war that is a lie. For some time, I have been experiencing emotion. Long before you, well... that thing that happened on the rooftop? Long before that. I cared for you, in a way that went beyond an angel's duty, and I cared for others around me. I'd return from battle and..." He moistened his lips, and his gaze briefly skipped away before darting back with renewed intensity. "I would weep alone in my chamber, for fear the others might see how the deaths of so many tortured me. There was no allyanse, no reason for me to feel so deeply about such things. I cried for the dead. I thought I was failing, and the more the horrors of war had me on my knees, the more I tortured myself for my weakness, for this madness I should not have been experiencing. Had you not kissed me, had Severn not revealed the truth, I suspect that during the next battle, I would have deliberately sought an end to the torture." He paused, face troubled. "How many others have already sought an end to their torture by the point of a demon's blade?"

Angels taking their own lives because of the weight of their forbidden emotions? The thought struck like a blow to Mikhail's heart. He hadn't considered how fear could fester within an angel. The guardians had more blood on their hands than those they'd tried and failed to correct. "Angels must be saved before it comes to that."

"Severn showed me these emotions are not shameful. What is shameful is how they've been kept from us, and how we cannot be seen to feel for fear of being shut away in Haven, for fear of being seen as weak, as wrong, as failures. For all the messiness of emotion, I would never wish to return to the cold, hard thing I was before."

"Nor I."

"Then we will navigate these feelings and learn to harness them, and that will make us *more* powerful, Your Grace, not less. Severn is right in that we should take Haven. We should free those who every day fear their feelings are shameful and wrong. And with them behind you, you cannot fail to bring Remiel down. It is the right course of action."

Solo's faith was admirable, but his strength of feeling was exactly what Luxen had been able to manipulate in Mikhail. Feelings left him vulnerable and exposed. Harnessing them felt like an impossible task. But perhaps a worthy one. "You are wise, Solomon."

He smiled somewhat shyly. "I learned from the best."

They were two angels out of thousands waiting to be freed. All the others needed was a demon like Severn to help them see the light. He had clearly had an influence on Solomon, and his impact on Mikhail's life was immeasurable. For their differences and faults, Mikhail's love for

Severn grew with each new revelation. "I should find Severn."

"You are both hurting. Perhaps my finding him will be less confrontational?"

"Thank you, Solo." Mikhail smiled. "For everything."

A blush warmed his cheeks. "You're welcome, Your Grace."

CHAPTER 19

 evern

HALFWAY UP one side of the Travelodge and out a window lay a bowed, flat roof. Pools of rainwater collected in the dips. Severn sat cross-legged on a rounded bump, staying away from the edge of the roof to avoid being seen, and watched the misty breeze tease across the puddles. Drizzle cooled his sagging wings and dampened his face. The dreary weather suited his mood.

He should probably go back inside and apologize. Mikhail was right. Pretending to be Seraphim was a dick move and clearly not something Mikhail would ever do. But the last comment had stung the most. He'd dug the knife in with that one. Severn deserved it.

He was trying not to screw this up. And failing. Sulking seemed like a perfectly good way to handle the clusterfuck that had become his life.

Solo emerged from the same window Severn had kicked open earlier and shook out his wings. He then frowned at the damp air. Mikhail clearly hadn't wanted to come himself.

"I know," Severn grumbled. "I'll go back. Just give me a minute."

Solo crouched beside him, arms resting over his knees. His red feathers draped in the puddles.

"Your wings are getting wet."

Solo glanced behind him and shrugged. "Mikhail is sorry."

"I'm the one who should be sorry. I lost it back there." They had an opportunity to end hundreds of years of slaughter for demons and angels. But Severn had been no better than Lux by suggesting they use Mikhail to end it. "I saw what Lux did to him and then I'm right there doing the same."

"It's not the same though because he had a choice and he chose not to." Solo fell quiet and watched the drizzle swirl around them. "How do we take Haven?" he asked.

"Are the glass domes still broken?"

"They sealed those first."

"Too afraid their emotional angels would escape." When he'd stayed in Haven, a thread of uncertainty already ran through the population of angels. Having a Seraphim-like guardian apparently rescuing a demon-winged angel would have shaken them all. Haven was a powder keg waiting to blow, and Mikhail would surely be the match to ignite it, if he chose to.

"A few flights patrol it," Severn added, "but it wasn't heavily guarded. There are no threats there, just angels living out their happily ever after. We should be able to break in fairly easily. Once inside, we'll need to convince Vearn to listen to us—and I can't do that. She hated me when I was angel. She'll try and kill me now."

"And if Mikhail can't convince her?"

That was probably the part where Severn came in. "There will probably be casualties." Solo's troubled expression did nothing to ease Severn's concerns. "There will be *more* casualties if we don't recruit a flight of angels large enough to stop Remiel's next attack," he added. "We can't get near Aerie and don't have the time to root out angels there who may or may not be sympathetic to our cause."

"What about demons?"

"What about them?"

"Will they fight for us? For you, as Konstantin?"

It was a nice idea, but demons didn't work like that. "I doubt it. I'm not my kins' favorite person. They don't yet see the bigger picture. Angels have been attacking us forever. Generations of slaughter won't just go away because angels have suddenly become touchy-feely."

"No, I suppose not. But they'll see you and Mikhail side by side, and that must count for something?"

"We'll have to hope so." Their forbidden love hadn't changed Samiel's mind, or Luxen's. The more Severn considered it, the more he feared demons might prove more difficult to convince than angels. Djall had listened, although she still had her doubts and would kill him at the first sign of fucking up. Samiel had burned whatever existed between them, if any part of it had ever been real. The madam was reasonable but understandably despised Mikhail since he shredded her wings.

Fuck, the task ahead felt like climbing a vertical cliff without wings to catch them if they fell.

And what had they succeeded at so far? They'd survived, that was all, and lost people for nothing. Like Ernas. The pup had trusted him and paid for that trust with his life.

Solo's expression had softened. He looked at Severn in a way no angel looked at demons, ever. So perhaps he'd achieved something; if just one angel could care about all this, then so could others. Solo was enough, for now.

Severn got to his feet and illusioned his wings from sight. "Let's go in before Mikhail thinks we've abandoned him."

Back inside, Mikhail opened the door at their knock and stood with his wings hidden, clad in his demon armor. Solo must have blinked at him because Mikhail huffed. "It feels right that I should wear this."

Severn wasn't about to argue. All those sculpted muscles hugged by supple leather, held in place by straps and buckles. He looked like an anti-angel. Solo must have been so confused.

"All right, here's what we're going to do." He ran through the same ideas with Mikhail as he'd mentioned to Solo, deliberately leaving out the whole six-wings-avenging-angel-wrath plan B. If Mikhail decided to use those aspects of him, then it would be his choice and nothing to do with Severn.

"We should leave immediately," Mikhail suggested, suddenly in motion, striding down the hallway. "It will take a few days to fly to Haven, and if we're to fly high where the air is thin to avoid being seen, it will be arduous. Solomon, can you secure us weapons from Aerie?"

"Yes, I think so—this way, Your Grace." Solo guided him to the window. "I have full access to Aerie's armory."

Severn followed behind Mikhail and Solo. The pair had fallen back into their soldiering ways, where they were both most comfortable. It almost felt like old times, with Severn among them, plotting the next battle ahead.

"Meet Severn and I where the human's fast roads intersect. The junction resembles a star from the air. It's a few miles east of Haven," Mikhail said.

"He means where the M4 and M5 meet," Severn clarified, but the clarification only further confused Solo. Severn rolled his eyes. They each climbed through the window and back out onto the roof. The two angels freed their wings within a few steps. Severn shook his own wings out and frowned at the grim weather. The mist would clear higher up. "Just keep flying west," he told Solo. "Use the motorway as a guide, and you can't miss the junction. Meet us there in two days?" Two days didn't leave much time for error or bad weather, but time wasn't something they had a surplus of.

Mikhail and Solo made it to the edge of the roof.

"How long do you think this insurrection will take?" Solo asked.

"It's difficult to know. Even if we succeed, the Haven angels will take some time to mobilize. A couple of weeks? Hopefully less."

"Oh." The absolute patchwork of emotions playing over Solo's face had Severn grinning. Like Mikhail, he'd make a terrible liar.

"Why?" Mikhail asked.

"It's just, the cats need me..."

"They'll be fine," Mikhail dismissed, turning his face toward the rolling mist. "Find a human to feed them. Humans like cats. Or so I've heard. But be discreet."

Solo nodded his agreement and thumped a fist to his chest. "Two days, Your Grace." He spread his wings, stepped from the edge, and was gone in a swirl of gray.

Severn stepped to the edge and peered down. Mist swirled, obscuring the street below and everything else nearby. He slid a glance Mikhail's way and caught the angel side-eyeing him. The strange look on his face had Severn's heart skipping. "What?"

"You saved Solomon's life."

The heart flutter strengthened. "I just told him the truth. He's the one who took a leap of faith."

"We will stop this war." His tone left no room for doubt. "We'll stop what was begun long ago, and we'll make it right."

"Yes," Severn heard himself say, and he believed it. This had to be right, didn't it? It felt like nothing could stop them, not when they were together like this. Angel and demon. As it was always supposed to be.

Mikhail's lips tilted into a small sideways smile. "Fly with me." He pitched forward, spread his wings, and was gone.

Severn stared into the swirling mist after him. *Fly with me.* He spread his wings, stepped to the edge, and dove into the gray. Mist swirled, wetting his lashes and blurring the world, but as he beat his wings and rose above the thick soupy wetness, blue sky gradually opened, its vast canvas stretching all around, and there were Mikhail's broad, dark wings sweeping that canvas.

Joy lifted an unknown burden off his back. He beat the air harder, chasing after the magnificent swirl of black feathers. Mikhail made flight look effortless, as though he were born on the wing. He reached a point high above the ocean of clouds and arched his wings wide. Sunlight blazed behind him, painting his body in a dark silhouette, and it was all Severn could do not to just hover and stare.

He'd never dreamed he'd fly again, and he'd never dreamed he'd fly with an angel. With *his* angel. Miracles must be real, because this was one.

Mikhail suddenly tucked his wings in, pivoted, and dropped like a spinning arrow toward the bubbling clouds.

Instinct had Severn diving after him. His approaching angle was lower. He'd never catch him before he vanished inside the clouds, and then Mikhail's wings flared and he swooped upward, dramatically slowing again—like a roller coaster riding invisible peaks and troughs. Severn was suddenly alongside him, wings spread, his right almost touching the edge of Mikhail's leading feathers.

It was quiet on top of the world, the only sound his racing heart. Mikhail nodded, and together they flew westward.

Mikhail's blue eyes bespelled, his smile was the new, rare kind. The smile of an angel free to live, free to love, and in that moment, it had all been worth it—the lies, the heartache, spilled blood, and betrayal. It was all worth it. Just for this, for him.

Mikhail tipped, folded his right wing under him, and rolled onto his back, falling away as his gaze pulled Severn with him. Severn fell with him, seeing only Mikhail, and when Mikhail spiraled, Severn mirrored his dive, so they spiraled together, falling as one, angel and demon, light and dark, different but the same. And as they danced in the sky, nobody and nothing could stop them.

CHAPTER 20

$\mathcal{M}$ikhail

HE LANDED breathless in a field of waist-high, golden grass. Flying so high, for so long, left his body abuzz and his wings tingling. Or perhaps that was Severn's gaze making them shiver because the moment Mikhail turned and tucked his wings in to keep the feathers from collecting grass pollen, Severn carved through the grass toward him. His hair was mussed about his horns, tangled from the wind, and desire set his gaze ablaze. He'd come at Mikhail like this before, on a battlefield long ago, but this time he didn't have a blade in his hand, and a different kind of need blazed in his eyes.

Mikhail would never have believed the sight of a demon would make his body sing and his heart race for reasons that had nothing to do with battle and everything to do with needing to pull that demon close. The taste of

Severn sizzling on Mikhail's tongue, the touch of his hands, the sound of his name on Severn's lips. These things were a strange kind of addiction.

Severn's hand came up, slipped around the back of Mikhail's neck, and his mouth was suddenly upon Mikhail's, tongue sweeping, thrusting, answering Mikhail's. The kiss was hard and fast and over too soon. Severn pressed his cheek to Mikhail's. He smelled of warmth and demon. His breaths raced, making his chest beat against Mikhail's. Severn was everywhere suddenly, all around and inside Mikhail's head, the taste of him, the feel of him. Mikhail wanted more in ways that continued to terrify him. His love was a living, breathing thing inside him. He could feel it in every beat of his heart, every breath he took. He could not describe such things with words, but perhaps another way.

He reached up and cupped his demon's face, then brushed his mouth against Severn's, gently teasing Severn's open with his tongue, and kissed him as though he were an unobtainable dream, as though this kiss meant more than a meeting of lips and bodies but was instead a meeting of eternal souls.

Severn's arm came around, under his wing, and hauled him close.

Love was not a curse but a miracle. It was the reason this war had to end, the reason they could not fail. Love was everything.

"I want you, here in this grass..." Severn panted against Mikhail's ear.

He clutched at Severn's coat, then plunged his hand down his back, cupping his firm rear. He wasn't sure what he wanted, to drop to his knees and take Severn between his lips, or to have Severn take him. The need was blinding, muddling his thoughts.

Severn's teeth nipped at Mikhail's throat, then skimmed down the curve of his neck. By Haven, Mikhail pulled him so close he couldn't tell where he ended and Severn began. He'd lusted after him when Severn was an angel, but now that lust had turned into a raging inferno.

They sank to their knees, hidden among the grass— just their wing tips visible. Acting on pure instinct, Mikhail shoved Severn down into a pillow of grass. He grunted, desire pooling in his eyes, then grabbed Mikhail's waist and pulled him over him. Straddling the demon, Mikhail leaned forward and kissed him hard, then tore at his coat and the shirt beneath, riding it up to slide his hands over Severn's hot chest. He wanted to explore every inch, but there was one part of him he needed the most.

Mikhail sank his fingers behind Severn's belt, yanked it open, and slipped his hand inside.

Severn threw his head back with a moan.

Mikhail massaged the thick, warm rod, struggling a little at first to get his fingers around its length. He gave it a few strokes. Severn bucked and made a guttural sound at the back of his throat.

Mikhail tore the remaining buttons open with his free hand and bowed forward, spreading his wings as he sealed his lips around Severn's substantial member.

"Ugh... fuck." Severn grabbed for him, then his fingers hooked into Mikhail's hair.

His spicy demon taste warmed Mikhail to the tips of his wings. He beat his wings a little, in time with riding his lips around Severn's need, meeting Severn's restrained thrusts. Severn wanted more—need strummed through him—but he was being careful. Mikhail lifted off, switching his mouth with his hand, and half-mindless, he quickly opened the buckles trapping his desperate erection. His member jutted free, and Severn sat up suddenly, eye-to-eye, trapping their needs between them.

"Touch us," Mikhail breathed. "Together."

Severn eased Mikhail back, making him brace on both arms, allowing Severn to reach between them and encircle both erections in his demon hand. He rippled his fingers, and the need that had been burning Mikhail up inside suddenly flared, like a wildfire in his veins. He tilted his head back. Like this, straddled over Severn's thighs, back arched, his member was utterly at Severn's mercy. And Severn clearly had none because he began to stroke faster, stoking Mikhail's lust, burning it brighter and hotter still, until he lost all sense of everything but Severn's hand and his member.

"Shit, I'm gonna come."

Severn's words sent Mikhail's thoughts reeling and snapped the rising pressure, freeing a jolt of pleasure down his spine. He lost his control, his mind, and his seed all at once and jerked sporadically, spilling over Severn's hand. Severn spat a curse, his hand juddered, and his member freed its cream. They came back down together, chests heaving.

Severn's salacious gaze met Mikhail's. "You're so fucking hot when you come."

But Mikhail knew Severn was the one who shone in those rapturous moments. Even his wings shimmered and twitched when he climaxed, and it had to be one of the most wonderful sights an angel could witness. But no other angel would ever see Severn that way. He belonged to Mikhail, now and forever.

As the sun set far in the west, Mikhail tucked himself against Severn, his demon heart thudding its steady, reassuring beat in Mikhail's ear. Exhaustion numbed all but the warmth and weight of demon, and Mikhail knew why Seraphim had paid the ultimate price to protect Aerius. He had died to protect his love. Mikhail wouldn't hesitate to do the same.

ON THE EVENING of the second day, Solo's distinctive red wings in the skies over Bristol were the signal they'd been watching for. Mikhail promptly took to the air and led Solo back to the empty industrial lock-up he and Severn had used as shelter for the day.

Solo handed over a pair of angelblades and multiple daggers.

"Any trouble?" Severn asked, clipping a blade to his belt, then slotting a dagger into an ankle sheath. The act of arming himself was clearly a familiar one, even given his change in physique.

Mikhail slung his blade's sheath over his shoulder, resting the blade against his back, between his wings. He'd be less inclined to draw it from that position.

"None." Solo's tone alluded to bad news. "Largely because Aerie is empty. But the skies around it are thick with angels. Remiel's flights are vast. Whatever number we liberate from Haven, I fear it will not be enough."

That's what Mikhail had feared. But they did not intend to fight Remiel blade to blade. Such a tactic would lose them the battle before it had begun. They needed to sway Remiel's angels. Severn's concerned gaze found Mikhail, looking for reassurance.

Severn applied daggers to his hips, arming himself should Mikhail's discussions with Vearn turn deadly. Beside Severn, Solomon was the very picture of a devastating battle angel. Side by side, they were very different, but also similar in their passions to make right the wrongs. Did Seraphim see the beauty in both his creations? Did he dream of their accomplishments, or did he fear the chaos they would unleash in their pursuit to kill one another? Perhaps in creating demons, Seraphim had hoped love would save them all.

"Are we ready?" Mikhail asked.

Solo bowed his head. "Always, Your Grace."

Severn grinned. The tips of his sharp teeth glinted in the fading light. Teeth that had pricked Mikhail's shoulder during their lovemaking. He spared his demon a knowing smile and took to the sky, with Severn and Solo flying in formation behind.

The setting sun stained the horizon and glinted off Haven's glass domes.

Mikhail climbed higher than angels usually dared fly, where the air was thin and tight, making his wings work harder. Clear skies stretched for miles all around, and as the sun sank out of sight and the stars appeared in the blackness above, he spiraled downward directly above Haven's distinctive bubbled domes.

As they spiraled down, Mikhail spotted only three pairs of angels patrolling far outside Haven's immediate area. With the fading light and their steep angle of descent, they dove by unnoticed and landed among brambles on the windswept estuary side of Haven's domes. The unpredictable wind currents here would keep the patrols from gliding too close, and the ground cover provided ample camouflage.

Haven's domes were a formidable barrier. Two skinned and braced with steel pentagons, they'd been designed to keep angels *in*, not out.

"I got this." Severn shoved through the brambles, twitching his wings to keep them from snagging on thorns.

He rolled his shoulders and lined himself up with the center of a glass pentagon. After drawing a fist back, he threw all his weight into a punch. A fracture sparked outward, but the glass held.

"Fuck," Severn spat.

"Or you could use this?" Solo held up a strange lever-looking device with a rubber cup on one end and grinned. "Humans have lots of highly useful tools, like this one for cutting glass. They're very ingenious."

Severn scowled. "Dammit, Solo." He shook out his fist and grabbed the cutter. "Why didn't you say you had this?"

"And miss you flexing your demon muscles? There's a great deal of strength in your shoulders, probably from carrying the weight of those wings—"

Severn grumbled something about Solo having hidden the cutter *"up his ass."*

Solo snorted, then caught Mikhail's glare and pressed his lips together.

Severn did have an impressive right hook that was entirely admirable, at the right time. But breaking into Haven was not that time. "May we focus on infiltrating the secure angel facility and not Severn's physique?" Mikhail suggested.

Severn applied the cutter's suction cup to the glass. "Admire away, but you're not fooling an incubus Solo, so don't try and tell me you're ogling my ass for science."

"That wasn't…" Solomon stuttered, face flushed. "I-I wasn't looking there, Your Grace," he said to Mikhail.

"Now you are." Severn circled the cutter, neatly scoring a line in the glass.

Solomon rapidly looked away, catching Mikhail's smile. The angel rolled his eyes and laughed.

Mikhail allowed himself a moment to admire Severn's broad back and the muscle at play across his shoulders. He'd chosen not to wear armor and simply wore a leather three-fourths-length coat over dark clothes. The coat obscured his ass, and from their tumble in the field, Mikhail did know it was perfectly formed.

The cutter popped a neat circle from the glass, large enough for them to crawl through and give Severn access to the second layer. Severn made quick work of the inner glass layer and set the last section aside. With their wings illusioned away, they crawled inside and grouped up among Haven's shrubs. The neatly trimmed bushes ended a few meters ahead at the edge of a meandering path, one of many paths that snaked through Haven in an effort to convince angels they were free to roam in their glass cage.

Mikhail frowned at his thoughts and then at the lanterns illuminating Haven's perfectly manicured grounds. He'd been a fool when they'd arrived in Haven the first time and almost lost Severn in that mistake. He knew better now.

"Vearn will be in the main administration building," Mikhail said. All the illuminated paths terminated at the admin building. They'd need to cross the well-lit gardens and ornamental ponds to reach it. "There are levels below ground, where I suspect they're keeping angels requiring correcting." Those levels had surely been where Mikhail had been destined once Tien's drug had fully taken effect.

"I'm too conspicuous," Severn said. "I'll sit this out until you two raise the alarm," Severn said.

"If the guards do see you, Severn—"

He grinned. "They won't find me as nice this time around."

That was what Mikhail feared. He caught Severn's keen gaze.

"Don't worry," Severn said. "I'm not going to taunt them. Just hurry up and find Vearn, then come get me when you need some muscle. And Mikhail... no ideas about surrendering your emotions this time, okay?" Reflected light shone in his dark eyes. There was humor there, but a shimmer of anxiety too.

Mikhail resisted the urge to kiss him for the sake of Solomon's easily distracted focus. "There is no risk of that, demon," he grumbled low, relieved when he smiled back.

A quick glance to check the paths were clear, and Mikhail emerged from the grass, with Solomon falling into step alongside him. Other than being aggressively armed, Solomon looked as though he belonged. Mikhail's armor, however, would take some imaginative explaining should he be challenged.

"We're just going to walk right in and ask for Vearn, huh?" Solomon asked.

"I am, yes. I need you to stay outside. If anything should go wrong, return to Severn and abandon the plan."

"Leave?"

"You can't fight all the guards. If I don't return, retreat and regroup."

"Well, yes, you're right, in theory. But in practice, no. I'm not leaving you here, and if you think Severn would, then you don't know him as well as I thought you did."

"This is an order, Solomon. I will not be responsible for any further harm coming to those I care for."

"Yes, Your Grace." Solomon hesitated a beat. "But you also relinquished your leadership over to me. Remember?"

"I do remember that, yes."

Solomon smirked. "I'm a free angel. I follow you because I choose to. And that means I won't be abandoning you, and neither will Severn."

If Mikhail had his wings displayed, he'd have ruffled them. He couldn't decide if he admired Solomon for his emotional progress, or if he preferred the angel have his epiphany after they'd taken Haven. Solomon's smile was all too familiar. Severn had more influence than the demon probably realized.

The path carried them over a small bridge and past a trickling stream. The admin building loomed ahead. A few guards stood illuminated at the top of its steps, far enough away for them not to yet notice their approach. "You have twenty minutes to find Vearn," Solomon said. "If I haven't heard anything, I'm coming after you. And I suspect, if we take any longer, Severn will come for us both."

"Yes. Fine. Thank you, Solomon." He softened his tone by adding a glance and caught Solomon's knowing twitch of the lips.

The guards began to descend the steps, marching to meet them. This would be interesting. Severn as an angel would have talked his way around these two with ease.

Mikhail feared the imminent conversation would not end well for them.

"Brothers!" Solomon jogged ahead to greet them before they could get too close a look at Mikhail's armor. "We were just coming to find you!" Solomon breathed, as though rushed. "While we were patrolling, we happened to notice something unusual. Come and take a look?" He drew them down a side path and neither thought to give Mikhail more than a passing glance.

The door leading into the admin building effortlessly swung open, revealing a single angel seated behind a sweeping glass desk far larger than she could possibly require. The last time Mikhail had entered the admin building, he'd left parts of it in ruin. They'd clearly fixed the foyer, making sure to polish out the cracks. Appearances were everything to angels.

"Hello, it's rather late to be..." She trailed off, clearly noticing his armor, and then, as her eyes widened, she'd probably noticed the weapons.

"Vearn?" Mikhail said.

The angel gaped.

"She is here, yes?"

"She is."

"Then summon her." After imagining Severn's scolding him for his lack of tact, he added, "Please."

"And *you* are?"

"Mikhail. She'll know the name."

"Oh." The angel's eyes darted toward the phone on her desk, but she didn't reach for it. She'd stilled. Which probably meant she was about to do something foolish.

"Take me to her." He couldn't risk her alerting more guards.

"It's late, as I said. You can come back tom—"

He placed both hands on her shiny desk and peered into her eyes.

"—orrow morning?" she finished.

"Tomorrow morning will not work for me."

"Goodness, you're quite rude, aren't you?" Emerging from behind her desk, she glanced nervously back at him. "Then follow me, please." Her wings unfolded behind her, either as a threat or from nerves. Mikhail allowed his to shimmer into sight too, for the sake of appearances. This was Haven, after all. His trailing feathers skimmed the wall and floor, leaving little room to maneuver. Perhaps that was the point, to keep angels restrained in neat little boxes.

Something bitter burned his throat. The last time he'd walked these halls, he'd come to surrender his love in some misplaced hope that without love he'd be stronger. He knew that to be a lie. This building was a lie—the shiny façade on an ugly wound.

As he followed the angel's petite frame, he considered how much he had begun to hate Haven. The moment they'd broken through the glass, Haven's oppressive atmosphere had fallen over him, making his wings itch. This was likely the same sensation Severn had experienced the first time they'd stayed—a prickly sense of unease and wrongness.

The receptionist suddenly whirled. A blade flashed in her hand, slicing toward Mikhail's throat. He batted her arm aside, snatched the knife from her fingers, grabbed her neck, and slammed her into the wall. *That was a mistake.*

"I know who you are," she wheezed, trying to pick at his grip.

"Then you know you will not survive this fight."

"You are Mikhail, the Fallen One. Banished from Aerie! And you will not prevail!"

So, he'd been given a new name to suit Remiel's narrative. "What is it you believe I seek?"

"To end all angelkind *for demons!*"

He sighed. And so the lies continued, fed to her by Remiel. "You could not be more wrong." He leaned in, ensuring she looked into his eyes and nowhere else. "Take me to Vearn, listen to my words, and choose your own fate, not the one guardians designed for you." Dropping her, he backed off, reversed his grip on her knife, and held it out for her to retrieve.

She snatched the knife back and eyed him cautiously.

"I do not intend to harm your guardian," he added. "I simply wish to speak with her. I protected Aerie and Haven as your guardian for decades. Have I not earned the right to speak?"

After a few moments of consideration, she jerked her chin. "Top floor, third door on the right. She knows you're coming."

CHAPTER 21

evern

THE PAIR of guards strode closer, and any hope they might take another path vanished at the last junction. Now they were almost on him. He couldn't retreat without disturbing the long grass. The only real option was to deal with them the demon way, but Mikhail would be pissed if he returned to find two dead angels at Severn's feet, and all the progress he'd made with Solo would be for nothing. Maybe he could talk his way out of a fight?

The left-most guard, a tall male with close-cropped hair, freed his angelblade and glared into the gloom. "Who's there?"

Well fuck.

Lifting his empty hands to his sides, Severn slowly straightened. Even in the shadows and without his wings on display, they'd have to be idiots not to see he was demon. He probably could have hidden the horns, but the rest of him wasn't going anywhere.

The other guard fumbled for his angelblade, a look of comical surprise on his face.

"I know what this looks like." Gods, Mikhail was going to lose it. "I guess a demon in your bushes is probably the most excitement you've both had in years—"

Buzzcut roared and lunged, blade thrust out in some blind attempt to stab him. The move was sloppy, more noise than skill. Severn twisted, grabbed Buzzcut's extended arm, twisted it behind him, and shoved him face-down in the dirt with his arm twisted behind his back and locked there. He'd executed the entire move in less than a blink. With one angel pinned, Severn grabbed his angel-blade and pointed the tip toward Buzzcut's twitchy pal. "Easy there..." Twitchy looked about ready to launch himself skyward and alert the entirety of Haven of the demon in their midst. "It doesn't have to go down like this. I don't want to hurt you."

Severn freed Buzzcut from the armlock and backed up, letting the angel scrabble back to his feet, as Twitchy watched.

"See?" He showed them his hands again, albeit still holding a blade—he wasn't a fucking idiot. "I'm not fighting."

Buzzcut sprang off his back foot, using the downward lift of his wings to come at Severn from a higher angle. Severn thrust up his blade, blocking the strike to the sound of singing steel, then danced aside again, avoiding a sweeping low slash of a dagger he hadn't previously seen in Buzzcut's free hand. He was quick, this angel, and sneaky.

Severn might have admired him more if he wasn't hell-bent on murdering him.

Hunched, hands out, Severn backed into the grass. "Look, I'm trying to be reasonable here. My angel boyfriend is gonna be real pissed if I kick your asses. He's kind of a big deal. You should probably put down your weapons—"

Twitchy came at him like a lightning strike. There was no mistaking the murderous gleam in his blue eyes. No compassion, just cold, hard, killer instinct. Severn ducked the first stroke of the blade, but the second came fast, slashing the air so damn close to Severn's face, he felt its whisper up his cheek. Ducking, he thrust the angelblade up, meeting his target. Twitchy grunted, skewered on the blade. His moment's hesitation bought him a fist in the face. Twitchy staggered and dropped somewhere near the edge of the path.

Buzzcut flew in like a bull, tackling Severn off his feet. His shoulder hit the dirt, then all he knew was angel all over him, wings spread, hands around his throat, blunt white teeth bared in a vicious snarl.

Severn punched the prick in the waist, dislodging his weight, and twisted, flipping Buzzcut over, reversing their positions so now Severn had the flapping asshole pinned. *I was trying to be fucking nice!* He pinned a knee on the angel's wrist, holding his blade-hand down, and captured the flailing other hand—the one with the dagger—and managed to get that pinned too, leaving Severn with one hand around Buzzcut's throat.

He gurgled something, maybe a plea, possibly a curse, but slowly his struggling ceased and his wings finally quit their flapping.

Buzzcut's pulse still beat. He wasn't dead. They were hard to kill, but it had been a while since Severn had thrown down with an angel, and he had a whole lot of demon muscle behind him.

He slumped off the unconscious angel. Twitchy was sprawled halfway across the path, in dramatic angel fashion. Severn grabbed him by the wrists and dragged him into the long grass next to Buzzcut. Maybe they'd wake up next to each other and declare their lifelong love for the other. He could hope.

Crouched beside the angels, he watched the skies for any incoming guards who might have heard or seen the scuffle. Nothing appeared to move in the dark above—no shining angel wings or armor. He might have gotten away with it. But these two wouldn't stay out for long, and they clearly weren't going to believe Severn had good intentions. If he moved to another spot and left them here, they'd wake and alert the rest of Haven. Dammit. The clock had just started ticking.

"C'mon, Mikhail. Do your thing."

The grounds around the distant admin building were still quiet. The kind of quiet that held its breath. Solo had left with two other guards. Severn had seen them head off toward the recreational areas, but for all Solo's enthusiasm, he was shit at lying. How long before those guards realized something was off?

"This is taking too damn long."

Buzzcut groaned.

Killing him and Twitchy was the obvious solution. A blade to the throat, another in the heart. That would end them.

"It's your lucky night, sleeping beauties." Keeping low,

Severn cut through the grass, hugging the interior glass dome, creating some distance between him and his two new best angel friends. With a bit of luck, Mikhail would say his piece in a few minutes, Vearn would agree, and they'd all live happily ever after.

A siren wailed—the type designed to wake a city—screaming so damn loud, Severn felt it in his back teeth.

Floodlights blasted on from high above, like a dozen suns, turning night to day and chasing away all the shadows Severn had hidden in.

He hunkered down behind a mound of brambles, for all the good it did him. The sleeping angels would now be easy to spot from the sky.

Angels flocked into the sky—sixteen smudges against the blinding lights. All of them would be armed and on the hunt.

Something had spooked them. Severn could only hope it wasn't Mikhail.

CHAPTER 22

ikhail

VEARN'S OFFICE occupied a top-floor space. Impenetrable
if not for the wall of sliding doors leading out onto a large
balcony, designed to allow angels to alight without having
to traipse through tight corridors.

Mikhail's gaze skipped to the windows first, noting a
possible quick exit should he need it, and then back to
Vearn seated at her sweeping steel-and-glass desk. She
wore a gray pantsuit, had her wings hidden, and appeared
to be in the middle of signing documents when Mikhail
had walked in without knocking.

"Alissandra?" Vearn queried, apparently addressing the
angel with the dagger standing behind Mikhail.

"He wants to talk, Your Grace." Alissandra made her
way around Mikhail, cautiously watching him, and stood

on guard at Vearn's side. The pair of them would make a formidable force.

"Mikhail." Vearn's smile danced through her expression like a crack through glass. "What a wonderful surprise." Her cool gaze took in his demon armor, her disapproving thoughts becoming clearer in the pinch of her brow.

"Hands on the desk please, Vearn. There's no need to alert your flights."

She folded her arms on the desktop. "Let me be frank, Mikhail. Recent intelligence suggested you're working with High Lord Luxen, so your insistence that you're here to talk while clad in demon armor and armed to the teeth is not reassuring."

He stopped a few strides from her desk. "I'm not working with Luxen, and I'm armed for defense, not attack."

Her smile was flattening off, its pretense of friendship not enough to hold it up for long. "The last time you were in these premises, you killed Tien. Explain to me how that is not an act of aggression?"

"My being here is bigger than one guardian's death. All our fates and the future of both angel and demonkind rests on what I have to say. Will you hear my words?"

"Hear the lunacy of a mad angel?" She sighed. "I truly wanted to help you, Mikhail. I both admired and revered you."

"By watching Remiel stab me and shove me from my home?"

"You fell from Aerie while trying to save your demon lover."

How simple, the lie. "Is that how Remiel framed it? For an angel, he has a demonic skill for lies."

"Surrender, Mikhail. Nothing you say here will change the sins of your past."

"You're wrong." He closed the distance and pressed both hands to her desk. "The past is wrong. The narrative we've been taught our entire lives is a lie fed to us by the old guardians. Remiel, I suspect, among them. He was likely there when Seraphim fell—"

"Mikhail—"

He slammed his hands into the desk, making it groan. "If I am to be condemned as a traitor by the very people I love, then the least you can do is hear me speak!"

"Very well, Mikhail." Her thin cheeks flickered. "Speak."

"We're taught from the moment we open our eyes that Seraphim was a force of good, but we're also taught how he was imperfect. His rage was well-documented. He was a terrifying force to behold. Do you deny it?"

"That is true, but he created angels without those flaws so that we might protect the human race without such distractions."

"Isn't it true, if he was susceptible to one emotion, then he experienced other emotions? Isn't it true he could also experience love?"

Vearn leaned back in her chair, making it creak. "In theory, yes."

"Seraphim created Aerius, the first demon, to temper the mistakes made by his early guardians."

"Seraphim—our revered god—made mistakes."

"Yes, he did. And angels are his mistake. Not demons."

She dipped her chin and lifted her lashes. "Be very careful, Mikhail."

"He made demons to hold angels to account. To

balance out the bad with the good. And it worked. It worked so well that Seraphim fell in love with a demon—the Rayvern Lord Aerius."

"Mikhail, do not waste this—"

"Guardians saw how Seraphim loved his demon and feared his love would take Seraphim from them. Jealous and confused, guardians lashed out, blamed demons, fought them. The war began, and on the eve of the Battle of a Thousand Stars, guardians attempted to murder Aerius—"

"Fantasy!" She shot to her feet.

"Seraphim stopped them, but at the greatest of costs. Guardians killed Seraphim, and Aerius survived—"

"Enough!" Heat flushed her face. Her lips trembled around a sneer. "You come to Haven, the most sacred of places, and you spout foul rhetoric. What happened to you, Mikhail? I would have followed you to the ends of this earth. I admired your strength, your honor. You were the finest of guardians. A pillar of everything an angel could attain." She clutched a fist to her chest in an echo of Solomon's gesture of allegiance. "Where did it go so wrong?" A single tear fell from Vearn's eye.

Mikhail lifted his chin and pushed away from the desk. All the evidence he needed was in that single tear. For an angel to cry, they must care. "You volunteered for Haven."

Vearn blinked and shook her head. "I... did, yes."

"Your Grace?" Alissandra gestured at her cheek. "You're crying?"

Vearn swiped the tear from her face and looked down at the glistening wetness on her fingertips.

"You volunteered to oversee Haven because you *feel*, just like all angels. There is no shame in it. It's how we were made. Guardians took it from us. Here, inside these very domes. They've been taking our emotions for generations, turning us into the weapons of their jealously time and time again. Killing demons in a pointless war that serves only to reinforce their lies. It's all a lie, Vearn. All of it."

Her face crumbled in a way he'd never seen from her. Vearn had always been level, reliable, stalwart in her duty. But the angel who had served Mikhail hadn't been the real her. No angel truly knew who they were until they were free of the lies. Perhaps his falling from Aerie had made her experience feelings. Or perhaps she'd felt emotions before that, like Solomon had. If Vearn could feel, and Solomon had realized the wrongness of it all, then there *would* be others.

"Get out!" she screamed.

"Vearn, listen... Remiel is about to attack the demons. He cannot—"

Her wings snapped open so fast they cracked like thunder. She reached beneath her desk and retrieved an angel-blade. *"Leave!"*

Sirens blared through the fabric of the building. Light flooded through the balcony doors. The alarm was raised.

Vearn's twitching snarl left no room for negotiation, but neither did the stream of tears wetting her face.

Mikhail lifted his hands. "I did not come here to fight!" he yelled over the sirens.

"It's too late for that." She emerged from behind her desk, wings stretching. The balcony doors were the only way out. He backed toward them, and Vearn stalked forward. "You are a traitor, Mikhail. You wear demon armor and lay with demons. Your wicked sins have infected all those who

were close to you. You are a sickness *that must be cured*!" She raised her blade, bared her teeth, and charged.

"Wait!" A wall of brown wings suddenly blocked Vearn's route to Mikhail.

"No!"

Alissandra's body arched, her wings twitched, and the point of a blade sprouted from her back and then vanished as Vearn yanked it free. She staggered and turned toward Mikhail, her face full of confusion and loss. Her bloody hands trembled.

Vearn raised her angelblade a second time, its shimmer dulled by Alissandra's blood.

When Mikhail had been sworn in as a guardian, he'd vowed to protect all angels. He'd devoted his life to the cause, to Aerie, to the hundreds of flights who had fought and died alongside him. He loved them all. And would never stop fighting for them, for their truth.

He was still their guardian.

This was his life, his duty.

Alissandra slumped against a wall, her face pale.

Vearn ignored her and stalked toward Mikhail. The rage on her face mirrored Mikhail's own. "You feel lost," he said. "You're afraid. I understand."

"Get out of Haven or so help me Seraphim, I will kill you where you stand!"

Mikhail pulled his blade from its back sheath. "Seraphim wouldn't want this, Vearn."

"Seraphim abandoned us!"

"Seraphim died, Vearn. He died for love. You know it. You feel the truth inside, just like I do. Do not continue to make the same mistakes we've made for centuries. We *must* break this circle of lies. Hear my words, feel them. Trust me, Vearn, to save you."

"Angels don't need saving. What they need is this rot out of their hearts."

"Vearn—wait," Alissandra staggered from the wall. "Listen to—"

Vearn's blade struck Alissandra in the chest, plunging through her heart. The guardian cruelly kicked her back. Alissandra sprawled to the floor and twitched where she lay, her heart pumping the last of its immortal beat. She died with tears in her eyes.

"Damn you, Vearn!" Mikhail lunged.

Vearn pivoted, blocked high, and kicked out. Her heel struck his chest, driving him backward, wings flexing. Glass shattered, and he reeled. Light flooded from above. He stumbled another step, and the solid balcony vanished under him.

 evern

SEVERN DIDN'T HEAR the sound of glass breaking beneath the ungodly sirens but saw the sparkle around Mikhail as he teetered on the edge of the admin building's balcony. His dark hair waved like a black flag, and then he was falling. Black wings exploded outward—their enormous span so beautiful under the blinding lights that all Severn could think was how that glorious angel was his.

Then the winged bastards hovering above shot toward Mikhail like arrows intent on tearing into him.

"Oh no you don't!" Severn sprinted into the open, flung open his wings, and was airborne. He rose hard and fast through the air, demon wings pumping.

Angels plunged toward Mikhail, bodies and wings streamlined. Six, seven, maybe more hidden in the blinding lights. Mikhail didn't see them—he had his own problem as Vearn dove from the balcony.

Any shout from Severn would be lost to the deafening sirens. *Harder*, he willed his wings. *Higher!* He had to reach the leading angels before they knocked Mikhail out of the sky.

His muscles burned, back and shoulders on fire. But the wings held, and each stroke hauled him higher.

Vearn took a swing at Mikhail. Mikhail dodged, and then Severn was above him, facing three leading angels tearing down on top of them. They were never going to be able to pull up in time, not without gravity yanking out their consciousness. They didn't plan to. Severn flung open his wings with a roar. The foremost angel banked hard, veering wildly to the right, but the second plowed into Severn. The impact drove Severn *down*, his wings uselessly trying to grab the air while the angel who had struck him suddenly found himself tangled in demon. He shrieked, pulled a blade from somewhere, and tried to ram it into Severn's side. The force of the wind snatched the blade from the angel's grasp and sent it spinning away. The angel's pretty eyes widened in horror. His white wings shot out, trying to slow their rapid plummet, but his wings buckled, too delicate to hold both angel and demon aloft.

Think. Think. If he didn't get control of their descent, they'd both be eating dirt in the afterlife. Severn thrust out his right wing, flipping him over the angel. That put the struggling angel beneath him. The ground rushed up damn fast. *Oh fuck.* He threw out his aching wings, forcing them wide, like kites fighting a gale. He should drop the damn angel, halving his weight, allowing him to soar. But the angel—on his back—would never right himself in time.

He'd shatter against the ground. Severn clung on, ignoring the angel's screams.

Pain rode down his back, and he might have screamed too, but the sirens and the agony drumming through his skull drowned everything out but the beat of his heart and the desire to *live*. His gut swooped, the horrible descent leveled off, and Severn dropped the angel. The fool hit the ground in a roll, sending feathers flying, but he'd live.

Not that his friends would notice.

More angels poured in from all sides.

Severn banked a hard left and beat his shuddering wings higher, catching sight of Mikhail and Vearn locked in an aerial battle. Mikhail had avoided the diving angels, but they were regrouping, about to swoop in and rip him out of the air. Mikhail couldn't fight them all and Vearn. Why wasn't he pulling the six-winged angel shit? Perhaps the same reason why Severn hadn't yet killed any of the angels that had attacked them. They'd come here to save lives, not end them.

Severn would keep the angels off Mikhail.

He climbed hard again. Four peeled off from hunting Mikhail, their sights now firmly locked on demon.

Four on one. Severn grinned. *Just like old times.*

He met the first with a fist to his pretty face, relieving him of a few perfect teeth. Angels often forget they had fists when they preferred blades. Severn kicked the wounded one away.

A snap of pain in his right wing alerted him to a second angel playing dirty by grabbing his wing. He flicked them off, tore a dagger from his ankle, and flung it into the angel's wing, ripping out a bunch of feathers and sending him spiraling downward.

A blow to the back alerted him to the third. Then a face-full of feathers blinded him. Severn flapped aimlessly. The new weight on his back unbalanced him. Cold steel suddenly kissed his throat. He gasped, rolled forward, and tucked his wings in, flicking the angel over his head. The kiss of metal vanished as the angel tumbled away, trying to find his balance.

An angel snagged Severn's horn and had the balls to grin in Severn's face.

"I like you." Severn thrust an uppercut into the angel's chin, snapping his jaw shut and sending the angel cartwheeling back. "But not that much."

They were still coming, more and more of them, above, below, all around. A flicker of fear quickened Severn's heart. He could do no more to slow them. Looking up, he fixed Mikhail's darting black-winged form in his sights and began to climb to meet him.

Mikhail artfully parried Vearn's attack. He could easily wipe her out but had clearly opted for an attempt at peacemaking. Talking with her had failed. If she kept up this shit, she'd find herself on the wrong end of Mikhail's blades, and that'd be a damn shame. Vearn could be stubborn, but she'd make a powerful ally. Still, if she mussed up a single one of Mikhail's feathers, Severn would gladly take the bitch out.

The sirens blessedly cut off, leaving their throb in Severn's ears.

"Demon!" Vearn predictably snarled on seeing him. The crazed look on her face wasn't a good sign.

He beat his wings, treading air to hover beside a breathless Mikhail, who wore his own semi-crazed look.

Diplomacy had failed.

Six angels hovered behind Vearn, waiting for her command. Another six approached from below. All armored. The only way out of this was for Mikhail to unleash the wings and god-like powers.

Vearn hung back, breathing hard. At least the blood on Vearn's blade didn't appear to be Mikhail's.

"Solo?" Mikhail asked.

Shit. In the panic to reach Mikhail, he'd forgotten about him. Scanning the air and grounds revealed only more incoming angels. "No idea."

"Mikhail killed Alissandra!" Vearn proclaimed. "Hold them!"

Who the fuck was Alissandra? Severn glanced at Mikhail. He shook his head. The lying bitch.

Her flight of six immediately started forward in a flurry of wings.

"Vearn, hold up," Severn butted in. "Mikhail can rip you out of the air and down every one of your flight, but he's barely—"

"Demon!"

"You said that already." It appeared Vearn was more than just a little upset, like maybe she was feeling some of those emotions they all so adamantly denied existed. Pointing that out to her would probably result in her blade finding a new home between Severn's eyes.

Vearn's angels finally surrounded them. Mikhail sheathed his blade against his back in a gesture Severn could only assume was surrender.

"Mikhail?" he queried.

He nodded solemnly.

Severn huffed. Giving up without a fight? Mikhail

clearly had a reason, but as the angels closed in, it didn't feel like the greatest of plans.

"Land them," Vearn ordered. "Everyone shall witness the Fallen One and his demon before they're both dealt with. Permanently."

An angel dared grab Severn's arm. He shook him off with a snarl. "Touch me again and I'll knock that pretty off your face, angel."

The flights hung back, letting them descend without being molested. Outnumbered and out-weaponed, their only hope had to be Mikhail letting loose with his *gift*, but while he didn't appear to be concerned, he wasn't raging either. And the power usually came from his rage.

Severn had barely set a boot down on the manicured lawn when an angel dashed from the group, blade flashing, a glint of murder in his eyes.

There was no thought, just action. Severn met the angel's lunge at the tip of his own blade, the sharp point pressed to the angel's chin. "Unless you're about to kneel and lay that blade at Mikhail's feet, back the fuck off."

All around, feathers ruffled and steel sighed free of countless sheaths, surprisingly loud. Severn had thirty or more pairs of angel eyes on him, and none of them were friendly. More were arriving. Some still hovered above, covering the exits. His heartbeat thumped at the back of his throat. If Mikhail had a plan, he'd better spring it damn soon.

"Drop the weapon, demon." Vearn landed effortlessly inside the circle of angels, her sweeping wings silently stroking the air. Severn hadn't heard her approach and made a mental note to watch for her stealth in the future —if they had a future. She folded her wings but kept them visible. In her Haven-inspired pantsuit, she had the look of a human, one of the ones who liked to play with numbers and spreadsheets.

A guard snatched Severn's blade from his grip. Two more grabbed both his arms, twisted them behind his back, and drove him to his knees. "Well, fuck, boys, if you wanted to get frisky, you just had to ask."

Mikhail's dark eyes had narrowed, a prelude to his world-ending anger.

"Quiet, demon!" Vearn snapped.

A growl bubbled through Severn's clenched teeth. "I have a fucking name!"

"And what is your name today?" Vearn approached and looked down at him as though he were something foul to be kicked in the gutter. They'd never been close, but the strength of her disgust was so thick he could taste it. "You change it so regularly, it's hard to know who you really are."

"Who *I* am?" He snorted a laugh. "Have any of you looked at yourselves lately?" Gods, if Mikhail didn't do his thing soon, Severn was going to take matters into his own hands and permanently silence these pricks.

Vearn stood over him. "You're concubi. You're the root of all these lies." She had a blade in her hand again, the same blade coated in angel blood. Whatever had happened in the admin building, an angel had died, and Mikhail wouldn't have killed his own kind. If she could kill an angel, she could certainly kill Severn. "You have Mikhail under your control," she went on. "If we kill you, Mikhail will be free."

"Mikhail is already free—" A guard's rough hand grabbed his horn, tilting his head to the side, exposing his neck. Shit. This was going too far.

"Vearn," Mikhail finally growled. "Let him go."

But Vearn wasn't listening. She hadn't been listening for some time. Severn flicked his eyes right—to Mikhail. *Any time now—with the wings, Mikhail.* His eyes met Severn's, and holy shit, he was afraid. Severn tried to convey that it'd be okay, he wouldn't lose control if he just unpacked those fancy wings of his and gave them all a fight. Mikhail wouldn't kill them all. He was better than that. But clearly something ate at him, some niggling fear that had him hesitating to unleash all his power. This was fucking Luxen's fault. The bastard had undermined all Mikhail's work in figuring himself out.

"Mikhail?" The grip on Severn's horn tightened. He yanked back. Growls resonated through his chest. He wasn't damn well on his knees because a bunch of angels thought themselves better than demons. He was here because he trusted Mikhail. "Look at me."

Mikhail did, and the internal struggle played out in the lines around his eyes and mouth, the tightening of his lips.

"I love you," Severn said, ignoring the gasps from their crowd of emotionally stunted angels. "You've got this."

Vearn howled her rage like some wild creature. She flew at Severn, her teeth gritted and face twisted in her mad desire to kill.

Six wings suddenly spread behind her like a never-ending wall of darkness. The angels holding Severn tried to recoil simultaneously, stumbling over each other in their haste to retreat, half dragging Severn by the horn before dropping him in the damp grass.

Mikhail must have struck Vearn because all Severn saw was her smaller body fly backward across the lawn. Her wings flashed outward, and she landed in a controlled crouch instead of tumbling, but at least she was farther away and not about to skewer Severn. And then Mikhail was between them. Up close, there was no denying who or what he was. His shining armor—pulled from wherever his blast of power came from—overlaid his demon leather. The shimmer in his eyes spoke of something *other* too—sharpened by vengeance.

The fine hairs on Severn's arms rose. Shivers danced down his back. The angel who had toppled Tower Bridge and Haven had finally revealed himself. There was no denying they were in the presence of something—*someone*—divine.

Maybe he was Seraphim? Severn had dismissed it before, because... well... Mikhail was Mikhail, but the creature who stood before him now radiated energy and ether and glowed like one of those unreachable stars, his six wings the night between them.

Severn staggered to his feet. Angels scattered, some took to the skies, others just ran, not realizing there was no safe distance from Mikhail once he flipped.

The last time Severn had seen him like this, he'd shot him out of the air with a blast of raw power. He had no wish to experience that again.

"Mikhail?"

Mikhail looked at him, and just like he had after Luxen had poisoned him, with no recognition on his face. Between one second and the next, something cold and ancient stared back from behind Mikhail's eyes. Then, in a blink, the cold creature vanished, and Mikhail's softness returned in a small lift of his lips and the slight widening of his black-lashed eyes.

A quick scan of the grounds for any immediate threats

confirmed the angels hadn't gone. They still watched from afar, wings and faces illuminated by Mikhail's light.

"We're good?" Severn asked, stepping toward Mikhail. Power throbbed off him in waves.

"We are." Mikhail slowly bowed his head.

Okay, this was probably going to be a terrible idea, but... Severn unfurled his wings, shaking off sprigs of grass, and stepped right up close to his terrible angel. The thin space between them shimmered with heat. His shining armor reflected Severn's dark outline.

Severn used two fingers to tip Mikhail's face up, checking it was Mikhail behind those beautiful blue eyes.

Mikhail's tentative smile spoke of the fragility only Severn could see. Joy lifted Severn's heart. He loved his angel with everything he had in him. Mikhail closed the small distance between them. His head tilted and his eyes questioned, asking permission. Severn delicately brushed Mikhail's lips with his, answering that ask. There would be no denying it now, no backing out, no pretending this hadn't happened. Mikhail's soft lips parted. His tongue sought Severn's, and the kiss deepened. Severn's heart soared. He kissed Mikhail, in the heart of Haven, surrounded by angels. This was everything, this was magnificent, this was *them*. How it should be. And damn anyone who dared deny it.

CHAPTER 24

*M*ikhail

Severn tasted of spicy heat, of love and safety, of a home he hadn't known he'd been searching for. He wanted to drop to his knees and disappear inside his embrace. But this moment was more important than them.

Angels watched, and for the first time, angels *saw* love.

"Kill them!"

Vearn's screech from close behind him shattered everything. Mikhail turned and looked into the eyes of the guardian who would try and take his demon. He'd never let that happen. He'd kill her to protect Severn, *kill them all*. Vearn lifted her blade for the kill. A wild sneer cut across her face. The heady lust for vengeance summoned power from the endless reservoir.

Then Severn was suddenly in front of him. His savage right hook drove Vearn to her knees. "Stay down, bitch!"

He kicked her blade free of her grip and struck her a second time, knocking her sprawling into the grass.

The thunderous furor of a thousand wings filled Haven's domes. Severn pivoted. "Holy shit, Solo!"

Columns of angels poured from the admin building and formed a tornado of multicolored feathers. Solo's distinctive red wings marked him out as the angel breaking away from the others. Angels flooded the sky, surging toward the floodlights. One of the lights blew in a shower of sparks. A second exploded. And like flocks of birds evading a predator, the angels swooped and dipped, avoiding falling glass. Mikhail's heart skittered in his chest —so many angels, so beautiful. They carried a tightness in their flight, movements jagged and sharp. Their display wasn't the dance of normal angels. They wore no armor and carried no weapons, but they were warriors all the same.

Solo's scarlet wings drew Mikhail's eye. He soared in, alighting in a jog. "There you are. I found some friends under admin, just like you said." Breathless, he skipped backward, watching the angels zig and zag in the sky. "They're rather flighty. And very angry. So who do we have to fight to take this place?"

Severn spun. "Shit, Vearn…"

The grass where she'd lain was flattened, but the angel herself was gone. A number of the guards that had observed had fled too, but many more loitered in the gardens, still watching. Waiting… for Mikhail?

"Mikhail," Severn muttered, "I think maybe… now would be a good time to do your thing."

He stepped back from Severn and Solo, if only to give his multi-wings room. "I am not the god you believe me to

224

be, but I will tell you Seraphim's truth. The truth that has been kept from you." He caught Severn's half smile and took a leveling breath. "It began with a demon..."

THE RELENTLESS STREAM of questions continued throughout the day and into the evening. So many angels, so many afraid of him, of what he represented, and of themselves. Mikhail tried to ease them into the idea of choosing their own fates, while at the same time offering what comfort he could. The strength of those who had been trapped beneath Haven surprised him the most. The lucky ones had survived, while any others who had persisted in feeling emotions had been put to death. Mikhail had only narrowly escaped such a fate after he'd foolishly handed himself in.

It was a travesty, and it had been happening for as long as Haven had existed.

Mikhail had half a mind to put a flame to the place and burn it to ash, but even though Haven's gates had been thrown open, few angels left. Haven was still their home.

He stared into the ponds, still hearing the angels' pleas to help them, to save them, and from some, to avenge them.

"Excuse me, have you seen a badass angel around these parts? Big guy, black hair and wings. Permanently brooding. You can't miss him." Severn's smiling reflection rippled in the water next to his.

He'd been so consumed by guiding the angels, the day had gotten away from him. He hadn't seen Severn since the kiss on the lawn, but seeing him now had all of him wanting to reach for him and pull him close. He settled for folding his wing around him, which Severn took as an invite to lean into him.

"They still need advice." Mikhail lifted his gaze from the pond. Angels silently soared above their heads, beneath Haven's glass ceiling.

"They'll be needing advice for the rest of their lives. Meanwhile, I need you to regroup with Solo and help figure out what comes next for us."

That was true. Mikhail had been consumed with being available for the angels, he'd almost neglected everything else. This was a victory, but it was also just the beginning.

He followed Severn to the eatery area, where a few angels huddled close in small groups. Severn's passing drew their eye, but there didn't appear to be any malicious intent in their gazes. Just curiosity. Solo waited outdoors on the veranda, red wings tucked against his back. Ponds stretched around the deck. Colorful fish glimmered in the water, and crickets chirped in the grass. An occasional bark of laughter sailed through the quiet, like a sudden, startling reminder of why they'd taken Haven.

Mikhail opted to stand beside Solo's table while Severn casually slumped into a seat. "Here's how it stands," he began, wasting no time. "We have a shit ton of angels who would love to get their hands on any lying guardian. Solo? You've been speaking with them. What's their mood like?"

Solo frowned and shifted uneasily in the chair. "Passionate. Angry. They're not entirely sure about either of you. Half are curious. Half still have some *issues* with demons."

"But they'll fight for the truth?"

Solo lifted a shoulder in half agreement. "They'll be

difficult to control. Most of them are out for vengeance. We may have to rein them in a bit."

"Vengeance is good. We're going to need it. If we can harness them, our forces will number perhaps a thousand..."

Mikhail watched the big koi carp swirl and glide through the water. Far away, someone was humming. The tune drifted over him, its rise and fall like those of the angels above, somehow melancholy.

"Mikhail?"

"Hm?" He looked over and found Severn and Solomon watching him. "I'm sorry, you were saying?"

Severn frowned. "Have you slept at all since yesterday?"

He waved his concern away. "It's fine. Continue."

They exchanged a look, which was fast becoming a theme with the two of them. Clearly, they both knew him too well. "All right." Mikhail sighed. "I'm tired, but I'm listening. Continue."

Severn got to his feet, ignored Mikhail, and said to Solo, "We'll do this tomorrow."

The sudden glance from Severn cut Mikhail's protest off before the words could leave his lips.

"Make sure there are loyal guards at the exits, Solo. We're assuming Vearn has left, but we don't know for certain. You"—he pointed at Mikhail—"with me."

Solo dismissed himself and took to the air, probably to check the guards. He was a fine warrior. Thoughtful, strong, and intelligent. And he'd managed his own personal revelations well.

"Eyes this way, big guy." Severn jerked his head, urging Mikhail to walk with him. Referring to him as Big Guy was somewhat erroneous, as Severn was now the bigger of them.

"You feel that?" Severn asked a while after they'd walked the paths back to the habitats. Severn had sunk his hands into his pockets and allowed his wings to show. The soft glow from Haven's pathway licked down his horns and wings, highlighting their intricate swirls and subtle golden and hazel tones.

Severn caught Mikhail looking over his wings and tossed him a sly smile. "Haven feels different, lighter."

"It does." Or perhaps they felt different. He could never have hoped they'd free so many angels. Though there were clearly issues to deal with. Having a disgraced angel tell them everything they knew was a lie would take some adjustment. Many would leave, find their own paths. Which was good. Just so long as none ran into any guardians.

"Hey." Severn leaned against their habitat's porch, half in shadow. "Are you okay?"

He didn't feel in the least okay. "Just thinking."

Severn studied his face, probably reading the things Mikhail had no idea how to say. "If nothing comes of this," he said, "if we crash and burn, we did a good thing here. *You* did a good thing."

Yes, they had. It felt like a good thing, so why then did he feel so... sad?

"C'mon." Grinning, Severn opened the habitat door, strode in, and flicked on a lamp. "No cameras this time. Just a bed, a roof, and me."

The soft interior full of quilts and cushions looked... exquisite. But the space was so small. His wings almost touched the domed ceiling.

Severn strode to a cabinet and found a bottle of wine and two glasses. "To celebrate." He glanced over his shoulder and his smile ticked. "What's wrong?"

"Nothing." Mikhail forced his feet forward. He rolled his shoulders and let his wings sag. It wasn't so bad. "Where did you find the wine?"

"The local shop outside Haven. Hid the wings and horns, obviously. Well, actually, Solo's tokens bought it. I owe him... a lot." Severn slumped onto the end of the bed, letting his wings drape over the quilt behind him, and smiled sheepishly. His gaze lingered as Mikhail made a slow circle of the habitat. "You're not okay."

"I just..." Mikhail eyed the bed. "I don't know. I feel..."

"Confused? Scared? A little lost? Overwhelmed?"

All of that. He nodded.

"You're not the only one." Severn patted the bed beside him. "Taking Haven was right but also terrifying, because now it's not just you and me, it's Solo too, and the angel with the bent wing. What's his name...? Torand. He cried when Solo told him it was okay to grieve the death of his friend. And the pair who are clearly in love and have only now been told it's real, not some forced mystical bond shit. And the couple with two fledglings. Next week they were due to hand them over for *further training*. *That* conditioning shit's not happening. Ever. Again. They were terrified, and now, they get to keep their squalling balls of feathers, and they don't know what to do with that. We took Haven. We interrupted the cycle. And suddenly everything is a whole lot bigger."

Mikhail sat beside him and accepted the empty glass. Severn popped the cork with his teeth and poured the bubbly wine. He tasted his and hissed. "Holy shit, that's cheap and nasty." Studying the bottle, he asked, "How many bottles do you think it'll take to get you drunk?" He looked up, and the warmth in his gaze suggested he genuinely wanted an answer.

"I don't get intoxicated."

His eyes were even more beautiful golden than they ever had been when angel-blue. They were dazzling with intelligence and charm and the sly kind of mischief Mikhail had fallen in love with long ago. All of it had carried over into his demon form. If anything, he was Severn still, but *more*. Like Mikhail had only ever seen him as a sketch before, but now he was solid and real.

"Challenge accepted." Severn clinked his glass with Mikhail's. Their gazes met, and he paused. "You're better than Seraphim ever was. You're putting it right."

"*We* are putting it right."

"Yes." His teeth flashed. "We are."

The wine wasn't particularly pleasant, which Severn apologized for, blaming his lack of tokens. Mikhail drank a glass, then another, while Severn chatted about the angels he'd met.

Mikhail lay back and listened to his smooth, dulcet tones. Severn's speech pattern was the same, just deeper. And he was right. Whatever happened next, they had done a good thing. It wouldn't ever make up for Mikhail's own mistakes. He didn't expect forgiveness, but as Severn's rumbling voice lulled him to sleep, he did hope for change.

CHAPTER 25

 evern

MIKHAIL LIGHTLY SNORED on the bed, pillowed on his wings, finally relaxed. The serenity on his face was all Severn needed to see. Yes, they were in the middle of a crisis, but Mikhail had been through enough to break most people. He needed some peace. Severn plucked the empty glass from his loose fingers, set it aside with his, and folded the covers over Mikhail.

"Now ain't that adorable, Jasper."

"Caw!"

The voice pivoted him. The old crone sat in the chair by the *closed* window, their rayvern on their knee, its beady black eyes judging Severn.

He had the sudden urge to wrap his hands around their throat and throttle the answers out of them. He rammed his hands into his pockets instead. "You just gonna show up now, huh?"

"Shh, demon!" they tutted. "Can't you see your angel is resting?"

"How did you get in here?" He lunged halfway across the room toward them only to be met with Jasper's spread wings and the rayvern's loud *caw*!

Amii waved a hand but grinned and smacked their thick lips together. "Walked right in, didn't I. Might 'ave been wearin' angel at the time, eh?" They shifted in the chair. "Don't like it much. All them feathers tickle."

"Not in Haven... in *here*?" he hissed. He'd locked the door, hadn't he?

"Pfft, the how don't matter. I'm here, ain't I? Fix me some of that cheap plonk you bought to get 'im sloshed."

He glanced at Mikhail, still asleep, and glowered at Amii. "Get your own wine."

A deep frown dug into Amii's wrinkled face. Why they preferred to wear the crone's illusion when they both knew they were anything but a crone, or human, or female, was beyond him. Amii was a riddle. They showed up whenever they felt like it, clearly knowing a lot more than they let on, and vanished again just as cryptically, usually before some battle or when something horrible was about to happen.

Was that why they were here now? Like a bad omen.

He still glared at them but poured a fresh glass of wine and handed it over. "How come you show up after we've already done the hard work?" he asked, keeping his voice low. Resting a hip against the cabinet beside them, he studied the demon. The layers of shawls and tattered gowns were an act. Everything he knew about them was a carefully crafted façade. They even smelled old, like dried parchment and something spicy, that reminded him of winter nights in front of a fire.

They raised the glass, upended it, and drank the whole thing in one go.

"We could have used you earlier," Severn said. They had a lot more power available than they let on. That's what the spiciness was. Concubi power. Enough to have dissuaded a few angels from attacking Mikhail. "We could use you in what's to come."

They licked their lips and watched Jasper hop from their knee to the windowsill. The bird peered outside, watching for threats. "Believe me, young one. If I could 'elp, I would." They looked up. A touch of crazy glinted in their old eyes. "Got yer skin back, I see. Weren't so hard now, was it?"

"We have different ideas of *not hard*. Mikhail..." He stopped and lowered his voice again. "Even as demon, I couldn't save him from Luxen."

"Jasper don' like him," Amii grumbled. "Lost his way, that one."

"Caw!"

"And the emotional fallout of not knowing if he was still going to love me *as demon*. Then yeah, it's all been real fuckin' easy, Amii."

Their thick wet lips stretched into a wide, unassuming smile, and they slid their gaze toward the sleeping angel. "Worth it though, eh?"

Severn followed their gaze over the spread of black feathers, to where Mikhail's chest gently rose and fell. "Yeah."

"He's special, that one. A bit wobbly to begin with, but

he's comin' good. Seraphim was the same. Massive ego. Absolute fuckin' asshole, he was. The moods! Could flip like a summer's storm. They don' like being alone, angels. Give 'em a bit of lovin', though, and they melt like butter." They lifted their gaze to Severn, rheumy eyes hiding depths that went beyond their illusion.

What if Mikhail was right and Amii was Aerius?

Was Severn talking to a god among demons?

He wanted to ask if Seraphim really died protecting them, if Mikhail was somehow channeling some part of Seraphim, and why, if they were Aerius, they weren't fucking leading the demons in the war against angels. But if he asked any of that, Amii wouldn't answer.

"Funny how you lectured me on wearing lies when you're just as bad," Severn said, angling for a reaction. "The crone, the dead nephilim, even Konstantin. You're everyone else but never yourself."

They snorted. "Think you've figured me out, 'ave yah?"

"Not me." He nodded toward Mikhail. "Mikhail saw it first."

Amii harrumphed. "Never could resist 'em. All them feathers wrapping stupidly fragile souls. Fluffy on the outside, glass in the middle. But there ain't nothin' more formidable than an angel with a cause. Problems come when that cause gets twisted at the root."

Holy shit, he *was* talking with Aerius. The *actual* Aerius. The First Demon Lord. Rayvern King. The one who fell in love with Seraphim.

Jasper, the cryptic clues, the salve turning Mikhail's wings black, the ether overload. All of it.

Severn swallowed his thumping heart, willing his thoughts to slow. Half of him wanted to throw the demon god against the wall, while the other half wanted to kneel. Now was not the time to lose his shit. "Yeah, well, we're working on it."

"Work faster."

Severn bit back the urge to tell Amii/Aerius to go fuck themselves. "Maybe instead of fucking off when shit gets real, you could, yah know, *help*."

"You don' want my help." They rose from the chair, not bothering with the groaning old bones act, and offered their arm to Jasper. The bird obediently hopped on and preened when Aerius stroked its head.

"Demons need *you*," Aerius said. "Not me."

But the return of Aerius could change *everything* among demons. The morale boost alone would be like adding a thousand demons to their ranks. Luxen could fuck off, and with a true leader behind them, Remiel would have to think twice before attacking.

Severn straightened. "Never thought I'd call Aerius a coward."

Aerius glowered side-on. Their lips thinned, pressed together. "You wanna square up to me, youngin?" The chuckle that rumbled out of them came from the untapped depths of whatever Aerius's true form was. "Thinks he can take me, Jasper, he does." The laughter turned to a growl that made the air tremble and had Severn's wings wanting to fling open in defense. "Quit yer bitchin'," Aerius grumbled, "get some rest, and be ready for what's comin', because it ain't getting any easier from here on out." They opened the door and hobbled outside. Severn started after them, but there was no sign of Aerius on the path. He didn't bother looking in the sky. The demon had a knack for vanishing.

Shutting the door, he settled in the chair Aerius had vacated and watched Mikhail sleep. Aerius clearly had their reasons for staying out of things, or maybe his and Mikhail's lives weren't the only ones they interfered with. Aerius wore the humble crone act for a reason, likely so they were overlooked, assumed to be a nobody. And given the threat of that growl, Aerius was not someone to fuck around with.

He could only trust they knew what they were doing.

HE WOKE to the sounds of the shower running. Mikhail emerged moments later, a small pink towel wrapped around his waist and his damp hair plastered down his back. His wings were hidden, but he still looked like sin walking. Powerful thighs, broad chest—for an angel. Droplets of water shimmered on the fine hairs on his skin. Severn had the sudden urge to lick every drop clear.

He shoved from the chair before his cock got too uncomfortable and headed for the shower. Of course, the hot, wet air smelled of sunshine and Mikhail. He chuckled and turned the shower to *cold*.

By the time he was cleaned up and towel-dried, Mikhail was already wrapped up in his rough demon leathers, his hair messily braided. Impossibly *more* of a mouthwatering sight than before.

Severn tucked a towel around his waist, leaned a hip against the wall, and sucked on his teeth, eyeing Mikhail like he was breakfast, lunch, and dinner. Demons didn't waste time with seduction. If they want it, they make it clear. But angels had their allyanse and their excuses and a lifetime of avoiding intimacy. Which was probably why Mikhail didn't even notice Severn's attempts to appear seductive. He was too busy fiddling with his coat buckles, his mind clearly far away, until he must have finally felt the weight of Severn's gaze. He looked up and surrendered a tiny smile. He tilted his head, drifting his own salacious gaze down Severn's naked chest, and now he was in the game.

Severn had absolutely let the towel slip down his hips.

Mikhail broke from his stance, crossed the room with a few long strides, and smothered Severn's mouth with his in a rush of heat and need and a sudden thrust of ether that had Severn's knees buckling. *Yes*, this was what he needed. Mikhail's desire. Even though he shouldn't fear losing it, he did, and probably would for a while, because their love, this thing they had, it was still new and fragile and blinding. Severn feared he'd fumble it, break it, lose it somehow. Mikhail's hands scorched his waist, skimmed his hips, and his hot mouth sucked at Severn's neck, then trailed lower, over his right pec. Mikhail's wet tongue flicked a nipple, and gods, Severn was glad for the wall holding him up.

They should probably discuss the meeting with Aerius and everything that needed to be done to stop Remiel. There really wasn't time for—

Mikhail's blunt little teeth nipped at the rise of Severn's hip. The towel slipped free, pooling at his feet, revealing an interested cock eager for Mikhail's attention. Angel fingers encircled his straining shaft. A curse fell from Severn's lips. Mikhail dropped to his knees and—*holy shit*—his tight, wet mouth sucked Severn in deep. His tongue pressed hard against the underside of Severn's cock, igniting a fire low in Severn's spine, sparks of pleasure needling his nerves.

Severn dropped his head back, eyes rolling. Mikhail licked and sucked and teased. He hadn't planned on this. Some fooling around maybe, he'd get Mikhail off because he loved nothing more, but this... This was divine.

Mikhail shifted, rising off his knees. The absence of his warm mouth sprinkled shivers through Severn. His cock jumped, suddenly cold and more needy than ever. Mikhail pressed in, all over, his smaller body pinning Severn to the wall. "Hm," his angel purred. "I like the way you taste. I want to swallow you down."

Oh fuck, Mikhail getting talkative? Even Severn had limits, and he wasn't sure he could handle hearing filthy words from such perfect lips. He'd lost his ability to speak somewhere in that idea and wasn't sure how to reply, other than nodding and making some kind of strangled moan.

Mikhail chuckled again and lowered himself down Severn's naked body, dragging his hands down Severn's chest as his mouth teased a wet path southward, unraveling Severn's thoughts with every lick.

Wet lips sealed over his cock again. Lips so smooth but deliciously tight.

He thrust his fingers into Mikhail's hair, further mussing his thick braid, and fought to control the urge to pump down Mikhail's throat. Freely given ether tingled Severn's skin, making his concubi heart simmer and consume.

"*Fuck.*"

Mikhail slipped his tongue free, looped its muscular tip around the crown of Severn's cock, and suddenly swallowed him *deep*. The combination of strength and tightness, warmth and slickness, had Severn's hips tilting, seeking *more* of everything Mikhail gave. Then Mikhail pulled back again, swept his tongue over Severn's weeping slit, and swallowed deep. His rhythm was a cruel delight, his tongue a fucking instrument of erotic torture. He pulled free, on his knees, and said, "Come, demon. I want to see your face the moment you lose your seed." Mikhail's fist replaced his mouth, encircling Severn's pounding erection, pumping faster, blurring the strokes into one rolling wave of endless rising pleasure. Severn almost wept, so willingly lost to Mikhail. On the cusp of coming, body flushed hot and his heart pounding, he dropped his gaze and saw Mikhail peering up. His eyes were alight with passion. His fucking little curl of a naughty smile had Severn tipping toward the edge. There was no holding on.

"Come, Severn."

Blinding ecstasy shot threw him, his seed spurted, he bucked erratically and cried Mikhail's name, and then Mikhail was a whirlwind of hot lips and thrusting tongue, mangling a kiss. Severn grabbed him by the back of the head, matching his ferocity, devouring everything Mikhail gave, and giving it right back.

CHAPTER 26

ikhail

"ANGELS WON'T FOLLOW me in battle," Severn was saying as they walked across the sunlit lawns.

Angels bustled to and fro, some chatting excitedly nearby, others taking to the sky to express themselves. Mikhail's heart soared to see them beginning their journey. But as Aerius had told Severn while Mikhail had slept, this was just the beginning, and there was much to be done.

Severn's revelation regarding Amii being Aerius had come while he'd dressed an hour ago, right after Mikhail had vigorously and thoroughly used his tongue to explore Severn's substantial member. Tasting his spicy seed and watching Severn lose his mind with his cock firmly between Mikhail's lips had been more the revelation than Amii's reveal. He could still taste Severn now, and if he let his thoughts linger too long on their fevered kiss, his own body rapidly responded.

"Solo will be their general," Mikhail said, forcing thoughts of tasting Severn's cock aside for later. He could do little about Aerius too. The demon would do as they pleased, despite Severn's insistence they act.

Solo walked alongside them. His tightening brow revealed his concern at his new orders. "I've never commanded so many in battle."

"You have their trust and are more than capable," Mikhail said. "Divide the angels into the flights as Severn suggested, depending on their skills. Once we know our strengths, we can better determine the next move against Remiel."

Solo rapidly recovered his composure. "Yes, Your Grace. On the other matters," he added, "there has been no sign of Vearn, and reports are coming in from the cambion and nephilim that no new flights have been seen entering Aerie. It seems Remiel has enough angels. His attack is likely imminent."

"All right, get the measure of our flights, Solo," Mikhail said. "We do not have long." Solo thumped his chest, but before taking to the air, he lingered, half smiling at Mikhail. "Was there something else?" Mikhail asked.

"I hope you don't mind my saying, but you look different this morning, Your Grace. In a good way."

Mikhail stopped on the path. He was well-rested and had woken feeling more capable than ever, but he hadn't been aware his feelings were so readily on display. "You can see that on my face?"

"Yes," Solo said. "I've never seen you happy before. It

softens your..."—Solo waved in his general direction—"... well, softens you."

He ruffled his wings. "It could also be the post-coitus glow. I've heard from the mated angels that such a thing is real. And as I sexually engaged with Severn this morning—"

"Okay," Severn spluttered, appearing at Solo's side. "I'm sure Solo doesn't want to know about our sex life right now."

A grin brightened Solo's face. "Actually, I'd like to know about the sex—"

"Maybe later." Severn wrapped an arm around Solo's shoulders and steered him away. "Go be a general—"

"Is happiness directly related to the sex?" Solo asked Severn. "I'd like to explore this further—"

"I'm sure you would." Severn chuckled. "And once we've dealt with Remiel, I'll take you to the madam for a thorough exploration of the sex."

"You will?" The red-haired angel beamed. "Your word?"

"On my wings, as a demon of Red Manor."

Satisfied with Severn's word, Solo spread his wings and quickly disappeared over Haven's gardens.

Severn softly laughed and returned to Mikhail's side. "There's a time and a place to tell Solo about you sucking me off, but that time is not when we're facing an imminent battle. We need him focused, not horny for cock."

"Perhaps now is exactly the time, to avoid being distracted by such thoughts." Mikhail caught Severn's hand and pulled him close. "I find your cock entirely distracting." Severn's laugh, with him pressed so close, rumbled through Mikhail, making his wings shiver open.

"Gods, say cock some more, it's wonderful." Severn

snorted, nudging Mikhail's nose with his, teasing the prospect of a kiss. "We're commanding a flight of angry, horny angels. I don't know if they'll fuck Remiel or kill him."

Mention of Remiel soured Mikhail's lust. Reluctantly, he eased his grip on Severn. "About that meeting... I suggest we parley with him as soon as possible."

"You want to chat with Remiel? He's not going to be reasonable, Mikhail. He already knows the truth. He's fully aware of all the lies we're trying to reveal. *He told me.* He'd made it very clear what he thinks of us both. A meeting is suicide."

"Not if we're careful. We must try, or angels and demons will die."

Severn sighed. "He's not Tien or Vearn. He's old, perhaps even one of the original guardians."

"Yes, I am aware of what Remiel is." He still dreamed of Remiel's hard steel thrust through his chest and the icy way it had stolen his breath.

Severn's face clouded, like thunder spoiling a summer's day. "Guardians killed Seraphim. He'll try and kill you."

"I don't intend to let him."

Severn flung his arms around Mikhail's waist, sealed his fingers against Mikhail's lower back, and locked them together, thighs against thighs. Severn was taller now, making Mikhail look up into his golden eyes. "I'm not losing you again, Mikhail."

The temptation of his kissable lips was almost too much to resist. "You won't. You have my word, Severn." Mikhail shifted his hips, pushing closer, and Severn grunted a moan. Their cheeks brushed. Severn's teeth nipped at Mikhail's ear.

"Do you think the angels would mind if I sucked you off right here on this lovely lawn, Your Grace?" he whispered. "A demonstration of what their cocks are really for?"

Mikhail laughed and shivered off the rising lust before he succumbed to Severn's idea. "Now who is distracted, hm?"

MIKHAIL SPENT the next few hours selecting six of the most visually impressive angels from their new Haven flight. Once happy with his choice, he summoned Severn and Solo to Haven's gate. Regrettably, there had been no privacy, and no time to find Severn again and indulge in the caress of his demon or quench his rising desires. There was still so much of Severn's real skin he hadn't tasted and wanted to. Like his wings... They were sensitive. Mikhail knew that much, but would Severn moan when he kissed them? That reward would have to wait.

By the time they'd all gathered, the midday sun was as its zenith.

"Your Grace." Solo dipped his chin. "Have you selected the angels least likely to lose their shit when met with Remiel?"

Solo's choice of phrase had Mikhail arching an eyebrow. Severn smirked to his right, clearly the source of Solo's new phrase.

Each of the angels Mikhail had picked were no strangers to battle and were warriors he personally had sent to Haven years ago. They had the look of strength. He hoped to make up for his mistake in ordering them here, although Solo assured him no angel blamed Mikhail —if anything, they idolized him. A fact that made his wings itch.

Six warriors would have to be enough, any more and Remiel might consider the flight a show of force. He'd barely blink at six. "We have word from the nephilim," Solo confirmed. "Remiel has agreed to meet us on neutral ground at Stonehenge, as was our suggestion."

Stonehenge, an ancient human memorial, was easily located from the air. Exposed on Salisbury plains, the land offered sight lines for many miles. Its neutral status meant it was unclaimed by demon or angel.

"At any sign of aggression, we leave," Mikhail said. "We must not engage Remiel."

"Forgive me, sire, but..." One of the females in the flight moved forward, glancing at her fellow flight members. They nodded her on.

"Yes?"

"Could you not appear to him as the six-winged... god?" She clearly struggled to use Seraphim's name. "Surely that will be enough to convince him our path is righteous."

If he faced Remiel not fully in control of all his *gifts*, the result would be disastrous. He didn't trust himself not to kill every soul there. "We should attempt diplomacy first. My... ability is somewhat difficult to control."

She nodded and stepped back. Nobody here truly believed Remiel would change his ways, but if they tried aggression first, angels would die, and there had already been centuries of unnecessary deaths.

"Truth is our blade, justice our shield," Mikhail said. "We do not need force."

"All right, form up," Solo commanded.

Severn drew alongside him as they walked through Haven's vast, glass, security double doors. Having him close and having them *see* him close meant more than Mikhail could convey in words. Every step they took together was a sign of things to come.

Severn noticed his gaze. His mouth ticked. "You've got this."

Spreading his wings, Mikhail took to the air with Severn beside him. Symbols of hope and change, symbols of the truth. Remiel couldn't fail to witness how change was coming. But more importantly, neither could Remiel's angels.

CHAPTER 27

WITH THE SKY CLEAR, the circular monument of
Neolithic stones at Stonehenge soon became visible in the
distance. The air was warm, the wind gentle, full of
summer's promise. Despite knowing the meeting with
Remiel was unlikely to go well, Severn found himself carefully hopeful. Everything they had achieved was already far
beyond anything he could have dreamed. And if they could
free the Haven angels, have them fly alongside them, then
surely there was cause to hope they might succeed in
more?

There was more chance of Remiel sheering off his own
wings in protest than him listening to Mikhail, but this
wasn't trying to reach Remiel. He'd bring angels, and they'd
see what Mikhail had achieved. Hopefully, seeing Mikhail's
accomplishments, they'd question their own place in the

world and begin to realize the feelings they'd quashed out of shame were actually something to celebrate.

Gods, they were making history right here, right now.

Black dots speckled the blue sky to the east—Remiel's inbound forces. A lot of them. Severn exchanged a knowing glance with Mikhail. He tipped his wings and spiraled downward over Stonehenge's distinctive stones.

The sun had baked the short grass golden. It crunched under Severn's boots as he landed. His wings stirred up pollen and dust.

Humans—who often came to admire the ancient rocks —gawked at Severn, or more likely Mikhail landing beside him, and the other angels behind them. Humans saw demons all the time. But angels were out of reach, unobtainable in Aerie, and bathed in sunlight, they shimmered like mythical creatures.

"Best get out of here," Severn said, shooing them off. "Shit's about to get real."

They drifted away but loitered near the access road a few hundred meters back. Most lifted their phones, taking pictures of a rare sighting of a demon standing peacefully among angels.

"Their presence may work to our advantage," Mikhail muttered.

Shadows sailed over them from above—Remiel and his flight spiraled downward.

He landed roughly a hundred meters away, his battle angels landing wordlessly behind him. And the bastard looked every damn inch a guardian, from his shining armor to his wing tips dipped in gold. The summer breeze teased through his long blond hair.

The humans oohed, earning Severn's glare. The prettier the angel, the higher up the asshole scale they were. Mikhail had been right up there, but he was Severn's asshole, so he didn't count.

Remiel had brought a flight of thirty. A show of force compared to Mikhail's seven. Or so he probably thought. Mostly, it just made him look like an insecure dick.

Remiel started forward—alone.

Mikhail glanced back at Solo, nodded his readiness, and then walked across the grass. Severn matched his stride. No damn way was he facing Remiel alone after the last time. Severn didn't trust the guardian as far as he could throw him.

Mikhail, in his demon armor, with wings and hair as black as night, could have been Remiel's dark twin. Just a shame the pretty golden boy was the evil one.

Humans cooed like a flock of pigeons. They'd begun to creep forward in an effort to get a better look. Their presence was a distraction and might be worse than that. The chance of this meeting ending peacefully was slim.

The soft breeze hissed through the grass and ruffled Mikhail's feathers. Severn lifted his own wings, fractionally opening them, just enough to fill the space around him and brush close to Mikhail.

Remiel halted and lifted his chiseled jaw. "You both return like stains on a clean sheet."

An array of smart-ass, filthy retorts tried to burst from Severn's lips. He pinched his lips together.

"Thank you for agreeing to meet," Mikhail said.

Remiel dipped his chin respectfully. So far, he'd successfully ignored Severn, which couldn't have been easy, seeing as a mass of huge demon was difficult to miss in a wide-open field.

"Surrender Haven," Remiel said, "and you will be forgiven, Mikhail."

Still no acknowledgment of Severn. Not even a glance. He wouldn't be able to ignore a punch to the face. Severn pulled his fingers into fists. Typical angel. Didn't want to see the truth standing right in front of him.

Mikhail's delicate smile somehow managed to appear both polite and predatory. "Haven isn't owned. It's free. The angels you see behind me have chosen to follow Severn and I—"

Remiel's scoff cut Mikhail off. "Nonsense. You exhibited god-like powers so they fell in line. They follow you out of fear, not loyalty."

"I understand why you would assume that, given your well-documented methods of brutal punishment—"

"My methods are the angel way," Remiel's words snipped. "I am a guardian, a true and destined leader of our people. A people you abandoned, Mikhail."

"I am saving our people," Mikhail countered. "Your actions and the battle to come will condemn them to death."

Remiel's right eyebrow ticked. "We fight for what is right, there can be no greater cause."

"You fight for lies."

Okay, Severn could see where this was rapidly headed and it had nothing to do with diplomacy and everything to do with two of the most badass angels getting into it. "Remiel." Severn said his name like a hard yank on a dog's leash, and finally, the angel fucking looked at him, albeit with hatred in his eyes.

"The very fact you stand beside Mikhail is an insult to the millions who have died—"

"Stop!" Severn snapped. "For fuck's sake, we get you love the sound of your own voice, but fucking stop and *look*." His command sailed far, carried on the wind to Remiel's angels, watching on.

A muscle twitched in Remiel's cheek. His hand hovered dangerously close to the angelblade at his hip. "What I see is repulsive."

Severn let a smirk play on his lips. "What you see is the truth *you* told me. *Love*, you said, *was too dangerous a thing. Love kills*, you said. *Therefore we*—the guardians—*kill love. We are not the first demon and angel to fall in love*, you said. Love stands before you now, in the form of eight angels and one demon. We are here for love, not in spite of it. We are here to free all the angels trapped in your lies and the lies of the guardians who killed Seraphim that day. Love *is* dangerous, Remiel, because it will not be silenced. Love is true, and the truth will always prevail."

Remiel lunged, grabbed Severn's jacket, and hauled him off his feet. Severn had forgotten how damn fast he was. But he hadn't gone for his blade, and that was the only reason Severn didn't right hook the prick into the ground and probably the only reason Mikhail hadn't gone full god-mode. A quick glance to the side revealed the humans still holding up their phones, rapidly taking pictures, *filming*.

"The truth is what I say it is," Remiel hissed in Severn's face. "This ridiculous display is over." He spared Severn a knowing smile and threw him back.

Severn spread his wings, catching himself in the air, and dropped to a crouch in time to see Mikhail's wings twitch wider.

Remiel freed his blade. *"Attack!"* His angels exploded into the air. Remiel lunged for Mikhail.

Mikhail skipped back, using the downward draft of his wings to avoid Remiel's slashing blade. "Retreat!" Mikhail yelled.

As much as Severn salivated at the idea of plowing into Remiel and driving him into the dirt, his force was far larger. Severn might get a few punches in, but then Remiel's angels would be on them.

"Retreat!" he echoed, falling back.

Remiel's flight hovered over them, creating a rippling ceiling of feathers and armor. There was space enough to scatter to the four corners of the plains and regroup. Mikhail had made it clear they were *not* to engage.

But Remiel was still charging forward. His blade struck Mikhail's with a loud *clang*, and with Mikhail already unbalanced, the blow further unsteadied him. Mikhail parried blow after blow, backstepping, blocking, never attacking. He could have disengaged. Why draw this out?

"Solo, go," Severn urged. The other angels had scattered, but Solo hesitated, staring at the unfolding battle like he might be about to do something stupid. "Mikhail will be fine. Go."

His green eyes flicked to Severn, then widened in alarm. "Oh no." He bolted forward, on foot, around Severn.

Severn whirled. The flank of humans was impossibly spilling forward as one heaving group. What in the…? Severn made a grab for Solo's wings to try and stop him from falling into the chaos, but his fingers sailed through Solo's feathers. Solo was dashing for the point *between* the humans and Mikhail's battle with Remiel. He meant to stop the people getting too close. And he wasn't going to make it.

The herd of humans, either in stupidity or some oddly placed bravery, raced forward, arms waving, like they'd all collectively lost their minds. This fight had nothing to do with them. They were unarmed, wore no armor, and were putting themselves in danger for no reason Severn could fathom.

But no human was ever to be harmed in battle: Seraphim's Law. That's why Solo ran at them, his red wings waving a warning.

"Mikhail!"

Mikhail's head whipped around. He saw the crowd, saw Solo running.

Remiel's blade came down with the full force of his guardian strength. Mikhail twitched. Severn's heart choked him. Mikhail stumbled to a knee. He hadn't been hit... had he?

"Remiel, *humans!*" Mikhail snarled. "Stop!"

Angels protected humans. It was written into their creation. Remiel would stop, he had to. But Remiel clutched his angelblade with both hands and raised it above his head, the point angled toward Mikhail's chest.

Oh, hell no.

Severn thrust his wings down, vaulting into the air, intending to come down hard on Remiel.

But the humans yelled, spilled around Mikhail, and flung themselves at Remiel. Three tackled the guardian clean off his feet, and for a moment it seemed as though they might actually succeed in pummeling the bastard into the dirt. Then Remiel exploded from underneath them, roaring his fury and spinning his angelblade. He slashed blindly, sweeping the shining sword in a great arc, slicing through human flesh and bone, severing human lives in a blind rage.

Gods, Severn had been caught in the throes of battle and never seen a massacre like it.

He dropped to his feet beside Mikhail, grabbed his arm, and heaved him into the air. Any second now, he'd get it into his head to help the people, and Remiel would kill him. Mikhail found the wind beneath his wings and gained height, rising fast beside Severn. Remiel's flight watched the horror below unfold and let them through like they didn't exist.

"Solo." Mikhail anchored in the air and turned, but Remiel's flight—finally drawn into the fight—descended on Stonehenge. Their numbers were too great.

"Hopefully he got out." Severn hovered, scanning the horizon, but there was no sight of red wings. "Regroup at Haven."

Mikhail met Severn's gaze. "Remiel killed humans."

Remiel's forbidden crime had splashed across Mikhail's pale face, each scarlet drop of blood evidence of Remiel's madness.

"He won't stop there." If Remiel believed himself above Seraphim's Law, there was nothing stopping him killing anyone who stood in his way, including humans. He wasn't just looking to win the war, he wanted London.

They needed a new plan. A bigger force. One to rival Remiel's thousands of angels, one that could stand against him in the inevitable battle to come. Severn knew what they needed, but he had no idea how to see it done.

"We need demons."

CHAPTER 28

*S*olo

THE BLINDFOLD WAS UNNECESSARY. So was the strip of linen shoved in his mouth and tied off at the back of his head and the strap binding his wings together. But none of the angels had seemed particularly interested in listening to his pleas after Remiel had ordered they descend on him.

The air was thin but warm. The sweeping sounds of feathered wings and rattle of armor had always been comforting. Now, a sense of dread settled in his belly. Even blind, he knew this was Aerie. He was home. But on his knees, hands and wings bound, blinded and gagged—it didn't feel like home anymore.

A few jerks at the back of his head and the blindfold vanished. He blinked into dazzling light. Blurred figures sharpened into angels—a lot of them. Catching sight of a

257

few familiar faces, he tried to smile, but the gag inhibited it, and they looked away anyway.

Whoever had whipped off the blindfold undid the gag from behind him and tore that away too. Solo licked his dried lips and coughed the dust from his throat.

Remiel circled around and stopped in front of him. Blood splatters stained his armor. Speckles of blood dirtied his pristine white fathers. The sight of it turned Solo's stomach.

"What do you have to say for yourself?" Remiel asked.

Was this a trick question? There was only one sinful angel here, and Solo was looking at him. Could the others not see the blood? Did they not witness the unspeakable horror at Stonehenge? The angels surrounding him looked on, their faces blank, cold—just like Solo's must have been for so long. How is it they had their eyes wide-open but they were still blind?

Solo cleared his throat. "I am not the guilty party here."

Remiel's backhand whipped across his face. He didn't see the floor rush up but felt it strike his face and shoulder. He blinked his vision clear and found himself on his side. Fiery pain in his jaw and head throbbed. The angels hadn't moved. They had to know this was wrong. They had to *feel* it, like they must have felt their lives had been missing everything that made it worth living.

Remiel jerked Solo back to his knees and stepped away. "Confess your collusion with the traitor Mikhail."

He realized then, with a sinking sense of acceptance, that nothing he said would stop Remiel from killing him. This was a display, a lie, to paint Mikhail as the enemy and to further Remiel's narrative as the guardian of the truth.

He truly believed he was in the right, that his cause was just. Or he was mad.

Solo lifted his chin, and ignoring Remiel's glare, he addressed the angels, his brothers and sisters. "Mikhail fights for truth."

Remiel's fingers snagged Solo's chin, forcing him to look at him and not the others. "You admit it?"

The guardian's eyes were ice-cold, void of compassion. He was a hollow thing. Solo would have him pitied if he hadn't committed the ultimate sin. "You killed those people. You are no angel, and those surrounding you know it. Your time is almost over. It will be Mikhail who finishes you—"

Remiel's next blow knocked Solo into darkness.

CHAPTER 29

$\mathcal{M}$ikhail

SOLO HAD NOT RETURNED, and the flights they'd sent to scour Stonehenge for any sign of him had returned unsuccessful. Though, while there, they had helped the humans collect their dead. They had the evidence of Remiel's crime on their electronic devices, and the shocking footage had begun to spread like wildfire among the people.

Remiel's actions were unforgivable. He would face judgment of angelkind. But flying to Aerie and demanding his surrender and return of Solo would end in failure. Remiel's forces were too vast.

They needed demons.

As Mikhail flew wing-to-wing with Severn toward the north London demon boroughs, the need to help the people, to help Solo, chased the sense of duty around his head. He couldn't do anything to remedy the past, but he could strive for a better future. Solomon would not be forgotten, but first, Severn needed to recruit the demons, and he could not do that alone.

Since his suggestion to ally with his kin, Severn had been subdued, perhaps even fearful. In the years he'd known him, Mikhail had watched for a trio of fine lines on Severn's forehead that would indicate his concern, and now, as a formidable demon, those lines were back, like cracks in his armor.

Severn began a downward spiral through the clouds. Mikhail glanced behind him. A vast line of shimmering angels stretched far. Every Haven angel who knew and understood what had to be done flew in formation. Each of them free to choose this fight. His heart swelled with pride to see so many, but a stutter of fear soon chased that pride away.

Once they dropped below the clouds, demons would see them. Only Severn could convince his kind that a vast angel-flight hadn't come to attack. The entire fate of the two races, and perhaps even human civilization, rested on Severn.

Tipping his wings, Mikhail spiraled through the clouds after Severn's jagged demon outline. Behind, the angels did the same. The air grew heavier and darker as the sunlight that had warmed Mikhail's dark wings vanished, choked off by heavy clouds.

Gradually, the snaking River Thames emerged, winding its way through a gray and battered London. They were north of the river's iconic path, firmly in demon territory but close enough to the river boundary that demons might assume the angels were across the water. Severn had already sent a message ahead for his sister to meet, but what she wasn't aware of was the arrival of almost two thousand angels behind her brother.

Mikhail had felt Djall's wrath. She was not likely to react well to such a sizable force.

Empty, half-collapsed warehouses and old office blocks lined the Thames's muddy waters. Ancient cranes arched over the waterside. Up ahead, a vast rectangular building stood out from the other. An intact glass pyramid made up once entrance, and a stylized sign, EXCEL LONDON, adorned the edge of its enormous, white, flat roof. A roof so large it could easily accommodate their angels.

Mikhail landed beside Severn, near the center of the roof. The flight of angels soared in behind, the combined rustle of feathers like a sudden flood of water.

Severn's frown was not a comforting one, and Mikhail immediately wished he could do more here for him.

"Djall's not here." Severn scanned the skies. "Dammit."

She didn't appear to be here, but demons were notorious for springing surprises. Many buildings loomed around the roof they all waited on, but they were higher, making better perches. Demons could be in any one of those buildings—perhaps all of them.

"I don't like it," Severn grumbled. "We're sitting ducks."

There was nothing likable about any of this. "In your sister's position and had I received word of an approaching flight, I'd gauge your force before revealing my own."

"Is that supposed to be reassuring?" Severn managed a small smile before turning his attention toward the rows of silent buildings and their dark windows. They were the only logical place to hide a sizable force—if Djall had brought her ranks as Severn had assumed she would. "Screw this," he muttered. He started walking forward and threw out his arms. "*Djall?! Come out here!* We're not going to attack. We're here to talk."

The thick silence swallowed his voice.

Mikhail monitored the surrounding buildings, searching for any signs of movement. The stillness of the air had his skin prickling. Old buildings such as these usually housed birds, at the least, but any wildlife had been displaced. The silence lay heavy with unseen threat. Every second they waited on the roof increased the risk of being spotted by Luxen's forces, or even angels from the other side of the river. They were, indeed, sitting ducks.

Mikhail sensed gazes on him. But from where, he couldn't be sure. Djall's forces had the higher ground. They knew the territory. And it hadn't been long ago that Mikhail had led a flight of angels, just like this one, to slay the demons in their homes. An alliance would take a great deal more than words.

He faced their angels. "Lay down your weapons."

Metal scraped and rang and shimmered in the gray light, and the angels laid their blades at their feet. Mikhail took his own from his back. He lifted the blade high, so any observer could clearly see him lay it on the roof.

"A pretty sentiment, angel," Djall's voice bounced around the empty buildings. The hollow spaces played with the sound, making it impossible to trace. "But until you cut off your extra pairs of wings, you're the most dangerous thing on that roof."

Mikhail raised his empty hands and pulled his wings in. "Our intentions here are good. Remiel has an insurmountable force neither you nor I can defeat alone. The time has come to ally."

"The enemy of my enemy is my friend?" She emerged on the rooftop of the nearest building, whip in hand. Mikhail's wing ticked at the memory of that whip finding its bite. Light shimmered along her elegant horns. Her heels clicked her approach. She rested a boot on the small, raised wall at the edge of the roof and braced her arm on her knee. "So many angels. What a lovely sight." Sarcasm dripped from her voice.

"Djall," Severn warned. "Hear me out."

"And my brother, the Angelfucker. I heard you out. And here you are, with hundreds of angels behind you. What am I supposed to think of that? You fucking them all, Konstantin?"

"Sisters," Severn muttered. He offered Mikhail a sorry look and started forward, opening his wings.

Djall suddenly leaped off her roof, glided over the gap between the buildings, and elegantly landed with a few backward flaps in front of Severn. "Hm..." She strode by Severn, ignoring him, and came to a halt in front of Mikhail. "Don't get any ideas, guardian. One word from me and your measly little flock of feathered freaks will die in pools of pretty blood before they've had a chance to look up."

He arched an eyebrow and scanned the empty buildings behind her once more. "You have demons in the buildings?"

"Enough to finish you off." Her gaze stroked over him from head to toe, sunset yellow eyes acutely reading him. "That's Luxen's armor. You choose to wear it after he tried to fuck you?"

Mikhail swallowed. His heart thumped faster. He was not immune to fear, and the experience at Luxen's hands had left him fearing a lack of control. As a concubi, she'd probably already sensed his thoughts before he knew them. "It seemed appropriate."

Poking her tongue into her cheek, she tilted her head and turned her attention toward the gathered angels. "So, what is this? You had a falling out with the prick Remiel and want revenge, so figured you could recruit my sap of a brother to your cause?"

"*Djall*," Severn snapped. "Can you for one second drop the sassy shit. This is about more than us. You know Remiel's forces are too great. When that fight happens, he'll kill us all."

She glared in a way that said she'd heard a lot of words from Severn and none of them pleased her. "What happens when these angels decide they don't want our help? They'll drive their shiny blades through our backs, that's what."

"Betrayal is not our way," Mikhail said.

"Isn't that *exactly* what Remiel did to you, *Mikhail?* Don't try and pull that honorable shit with me, angel. I have more honor in one fucking horn than you have in all your feathered flock."

"Djall—" Severn stepped forward.

"No!" Her face twisted in disgust. "That angel killed all of Red Manor. He butchered all concubi, hung our wings on his fucking wall." She spat at Mikhail's feet. Her eyes flashed. "How dare you come to me asking for help. I should kill you where you stand. The fact Konstantin stands beside you is the only reason you're still breathing."

She turned and marched toward the edge of the roof.

Severn caught her arm, whipping her around. "Djall, wait. Remiel—"

She shook him off. "No, Stantin. You ask too much."

They were losing her. And if they didn't have Djall, they had no chance of allying with demons. The coming battle would be a massacre.

There had to be a way to make this right, to make her see he had changed, *they* all had changed. Angels were not her enemy. Not anymore.

Severn's face was stricken as he looked back at Mikhail's. He knew their survival hinged on this moment.

Mikhail spread his wings and knelt on one knee, letting his wings fall around him, as low as possible. Head bowed, he said loudly, for everyone to hear, "Konstantin, Lord of Red Manor, claimed me under Red Manor. I vow to protect Red Manor and all its kin until I meet my end. I have wronged you in the most terrible and unforgivable of ways." He hesitated, if only because the next words might be his undoing. "I cannot make right the sins of my past, but I can offer you a sacrifice." He closed his eyes and said, "Take my wings."

"What?" Severn spluttered. "No."

Mikhail kept his head bowed. His heart drummed. It was only right. He'd launched a crusade against demons. He'd hunted the concubi almost to extinction, and he'd brutally taken their wings, exactly as Djall had said. There was no redemption for that. He had nothing else to offer, only his wings.

"Djall, no. He doesn't know what he's saying. Stop—"

"Get out of my way, brother." The click of her heels drew closer.

Djall's demon purr rumbled. Her polished leather

boots came into view. She crouched, placed a dagger beneath Mikhail's chin, and tipped his head up. Yellow eyes scrutinized his.

"Mikhail, no..." Severn pleaded from behind his sister. Mikhail couldn't see him, which was probably a good thing. He saw only Djall's smiling face.

"You don't have to do this," Severn said. "We'll leave— find another way."

"You would surrender your pretty wings to me?" Djall licked her lips and ran her tongue suggestively over her sharp teeth.

"Mikhail, don't. Djall, you fucking touch him, I'll—

"Take them," Mikhail said, "and ally with us to end this war."

"Your wings for an alliance," she mused. "Hm... clever angel."

"This is ridiculous," Severn hissed. "We need *him*. You said it yourself, he's the most powerful weapon we have—"

"Severn," Mikhail said firmly. "This is my choice."

"Don't..." he began, then stopped. "Don't do this out of guilt, Mikhail. The past is done."

Djall straightened suddenly. "Hush, brother dear. Your angel has spoken. He gives himself to Red Manor. It would be wrong to deny his request."

"I swear to Aerius, Djall," Severn snarled, using the full threat in his demon voice. "If you touch his wings, I'll kill you."

Mikhail lifted his head but stayed kneeling. "You will not harm her."

"Mikhail, damn you!" Severn bared his teeth to them both. "I can't... I won't be a part of this."

Mikhail closed his eyes. Severn would see why this had

to be done, eventually. Djall's warm hand stroked along the feathered rise of his right wing. Shivers spilled through him. He braced for the agony to come. It would be worth it. He believed it. His sacrifice would save many lives.

"Fuck. No," Severn moaned.

Justice.

His wings for peace.

Yes.

This was right.

A sting pricked his wing. He glanced right to find Djall had plucked a single leading feather from the tip. One of the primary feathers, larger than all the rest. She held up the glossy feather, showed it to Severn, and then raised it to all the angels. "A promise!" she declared, presenting the feather to the empty buildings.

Still on his knee, Mikhail spotted movement inside the windows, and slowly, one by one, demons emerged from the shadows, filling every window and rooftop. So many... and more kept coming. Easily matching their number of angels. She'd been right. She could have slaughtered them all.

Grinning, Djall crushed and presented the feather to Mikhail again. "You have your alliance, guardian, and the protection of Red Manor, but if any one of your angels so much as touches my demons, I will slice the rest of your wings from your back without a care." She chuckled, flicked a finger along his jawline, and rose.

The feather went into her jacket, close against her chest.

Mikhail rose on unsteady legs.

Severn kept his head bowed, eyes downcast. Djall thwacked him on the back and sauntered toward the edge of the roof. "Don't look so worried, Stantin. All you have to do now is convince Luxen to surrender his rule." She took to the air and beat her wings to gain height. "Have your forces follow mine." Her demons joined her, filling the air with their number and the thunderous flap of wings.

"Severn—"

"Later." He was airborne in a blast of wings. Mikhail sighed out the last of his tremors and gestured for the angels to follow. Weapons retrieved, the angels climbed into the air, cautiously avoiding the demons.

Mikhail could only hope they'd done the right thing.

CHAPTER 30

 olo

Solo whispered a prayer to Seraphim, asking for guidance, for a sign, for anything in what would surely be his final hours. He knelt in the same cell Severn had once been locked in. Nobody came with sandwiches, probably because there was nobody left in Aerie who cared.

His wings were still tied, hands still bound at his back. He knew what was coming. But Solo didn't have a Severn to save him from the edge. Or anyone. Just some cats he'd adopted, who by now had probably left looking for someone else to feed them. He'd miss them. Who would miss him when he was gone?

Mikhail had asked if emotions were a curse, and they felt like torture now. But he would not give them up, not even fear. He'd felt more alive in these past few weeks than his entire life. At least he had been free to experience life as it should be experienced, even if for a short while.

The main door lock clunked, and Remiel entered. He unlocked Solo's cell door and swung it open. "Follow me."

Solo shifted onto his feet and ducked out the cell, lowering his wings to fit through. Remiel walked ahead, his white feathers clean now. Solo studied their overlapped pattern. Remiel was the pinnacle of a guardian. He was everything angels aspired to be. Solo had admired him, maybe... desired him. But it was all a terrible mistake.

Spiral stairs took them higher. Solo counted each step. He'd never again see the sunrise above the clouds. He'd never again feel the wind under his wings. He'd fall from the edge, and fall and fall, and then there would be nothing. He'd once considered seeking death but now fiercely clung to life. There was a cruel irony in that.

"I pity you," he said.

They walked through the grand atrium now, Aerie's vast glass ceilings arched so high above them that they blended into the blue skies. There were no angels here. Remiel had them all gathered outside for the imminent battle. A battle to end all battles.

The guardian hadn't replied. He just stared ahead. His mission his only concern.

"To never know love," Solo said. "I'm not saying I know it—but I've seen it. Severn and Mikhail are in love. I see it every time they look at each other. I can feel it in them too."

"Love is cruel," Remiel said.

A strange thing to say for an angel who could not feel. Unless Remiel *did* feel. Solo recalled that horrible moment at Stonehenge. He'd tried to save the people from Remiel, gotten many away, but he'd seen Remiel's face as he'd cut them down. Hate was too soft a word. Remiel despised them. No conditioned angel would do such a thing. No unfeeling guardian would murder with such glee. But Remiel had.

"Who hurt you?" Solo asked.

Remiel glanced over. "What?"

"You clearly feel very passionately about eradicating all evidence that love between demons and angels exists. You've hidden the truth for a long time, like we all have, but what you did at Stonehenge—besides being heinous— was an act of emotion. The murder of so many helpless people had no practical reason. You couldn't kill Mikhail, so you killed the people in your way instead, and it made you *feel*."

"You've had an epiphany so you believe you understand?" Remiel's cold voice matched his cold eyes. "You cannot comprehend what it is to have loved and have that love cast aside for another."

Remiel had loved?

Sunlight shimmered through the great glass doors that would lead them out onto the balcony and to the hundreds of waiting angels.

Solo slowed his pace. If he was to die, then he would die knowing the reason.

Remiel turned. "Do not test me, Solomon."

"Who did you love?"

Remiel sucked in a breath. His wings rose a little but sagged as he sighed. He glanced at the closed door. "He was a wonder, brighter than the sun, and when he graced us with his presence—his touch, his words. He was our whole world. Just to be near him was to adore him. We loved him so thoroughly and so wholeheartedly that it became a madness. You are lucky. You do not yet know love, and that is a blessing."

He spoke of Seraphim. Like all guardians loved their creator. So much so, they'd tried to keep him for themselves *and failed*.

"After all this time," Remiel said, "you would think love would lessen its grip, but love is a curse that lasts forever."

Solo studied the guardian, and perhaps in all of this, there was a part of Solo that understood why Remiel was like he was. Hundreds of years of guilt, of desperately trying to hide the truth, and of trying to *cure* angels of the agony he endured every day. Yes, Solo understood why the older guardians persisted in their lies. But they were wrong.

"Seraphim would not wish for you to suffer as you do."

"What do you know of Seraphim? You're young, barely a few decades under your wings. We protected you. Haven protected you. I protected you. Mikhail seeks to undo centuries of protection. He must not succeed. All of angelkind must be protected from the truth."

"Or they could be free to make their own choice?"

Remiel's dry laugh dismissed him. "And choose to love demons? Come now, it is time to meet your end. I will tell you this, Solomon. You needn't concern yourself with the coming battle. No angels will fall. Your kin will survive. Vearn will end the battle before it's even begun."

"Vearn?" His heart leaped. Vearn had vanished from Haven. They'd seen no sign of her since. "Where is she?"

"Speak a word of this conversation to anyone and your dignity will be taken from you in your final moments. Do you understand? I can make the edge far more painful for you."

Solo's wings trembled. "But Vearn... what does she have planned? Tell me that, at least."

"There's no use in your knowing. It would only further torture you."

They'd missed something. Vearn had an advantage somewhere, somehow. She'd try and hurt Severn and Mikhail. "But—"

The glass doors heaved open and cold air rushed in, ruffling Solo's bound wings and cooling his face. He relished in its touch and the smell of sunshine it brought with it. Angels hovered in the skies or stood back and watched.

He could not fight this, could not stop it.

Aerie's shimmering edge approached. The swathe of blue sky stretched on forever. He'd never find its end, but that was all right. He'd seen enough. He'd seen the truth.

"Solomon, Angel of Aerie. You are hereby found guilty of conspiring against angelkind," Remiel said. "Speak your final words."

The toes of his boots touched the edge. The clouds below looked soft, like they might catch him, but he knew that to be an illusion. Turning his back on the edge, he looked at the faces of the angels who didn't yet know their true selves. Mikhail would succeed. He'd save them all. Solo had faith.

He closed his eyes. In this, his final moments, he'd choose his own fate.

He stepped back.

The wind caught him. Gravity grabbed and pulled, yanking him down so fast that the wind roared in his ears.

Or perhaps that was his heart. Aerie's shining disks faded against the blue and then vanished as the clouds swallowed him.

It would be all right.

He had faith.

He'd die, but the truth was already free and finding its way to winning.

Severn and Mikhail would make it so. He was only sorry he wouldn't be there to see it.

Thank you, Seraphim, he prayed. *For allowing me to see.* The wind tore his tears away. Perhaps the god was listening and would hear him and know all his angels weren't lost. That they could still be saved.

The clouds vanished, shrinking away.

A jagged shadow emerged from the blanket of white with wings so broad they might surely consume the sun. Angular wings. *Demon* wings.

The shadow tucked its wings in and plunged.

His heart pounded, and the wind still roared. He did not want to die.

Demon hands caught his.

Demon wings flared.

And the moment before the terrible force of gravity pulled his conscious away, he knew he was saved.

CHAPTER 31

evern

LUXEN HAD GATHERED the demons together in their dilapidated meeting hall. With no room left inside, demons lined the streets too. Maybe all of them in London. There should have been more, but the war had taken too many, too soon.

Mikhail stood to Severn's right—a pillar of angelness that had the crowd understandably restless. Djall stood at his left, chin up, eyes front. On Luxen.

High Lord Luxen stood on the raised stage area in front of them, wings only half spread, as though this were all a formality. Keeping them closed must have been an effort for him, given the threat he faced. He'd had no choice but to hear Severn speak. And Severn had said everything he'd needed to, about Remiel, about Haven, about Mikhail and Djall, about Luxen's failed attempt to weaponize Mikhail, and his failure to meaningfully prepare for Remiel's imminent attack, painting a damning picture of High Lord Luxen's incompetence. He'd never been a warrior. And now Severn stood in front of him, their differences were stark.

Luxen had listened without saying a word, his face impassive, emotions expertly packed away. He could be furious or resigned, there was no way of knowing. His strengths were in subterfuge. Mikhail would call it lies.

Though, Mikhail was doing a damn good job of appearing impassive too.

"Red Manor has the means and the numbers to adequately defend our land and our people," Severn said, closing his argument. "The time has come to step down, Luxen."

Luxen scanned the quiet crowd. He'd lured them all into loving him, but there was only so much a concubi could do, and no allure would be enough to counter Severn's points.

"It is time for Konstantin to lead," Djall said, adding her voice, and with it, the voices of the demons who followed her. Severn might even have felt something for his sister in that moment. It had been a long time since they'd seen eye-to-eye.

"You surprise me, Djall." Luxen laughed his slippery laugh. "It wasn't long ago you were advocating for your brother's death."

"True, but my personal feelings won't mean shit when we're all dead in the mud. You have no force to fight the coming battle. You threw your lot in with trying to tame Mikhail, clearly failing. Step aside."

Luxen's great angular wings ticked in irritation. He

regarded each of them coolly, then Severn smiled, just enough. They both knew he'd won. Luxen had slithered his way to the top without a true challenger. The other demon lords, now long gone, had fallen in line because it was easy. All of that had changed. "Traditionally, I should challenge you to a dual," Severn said softly, addressing only Luxen. "But we both know who'd win." No longer angel, Severn was larger than Luxen in body and strength. His wings flexed open a little. His were fucking larger than Luxen's—not that they were comparing, but if they did, Severn would win that fight too. They both knew that if it came down to a brawl, Severn would pummel Luxen into the floor. "Do the clever thing and step down."

Luxen's fine jaw ticked. "Very well." He stepped back, his wings lowering, but his gaze slid to Mikhail.

Mikhail stiffened, and Severn fought the urge to fucking rip Luxen's heart out of his chest with his bare hands. The High Lord smiled some secret bullshit smile, hinting at whatever he'd fucking done to Mikhail. Then he knelt. "I abdicate and surrender my title to Konstantin of Red Manor."

An unexpected cheer went up. Severn had been so consumed with getting Djall to stand beside him, and then Mikhail's fucking pledge to give up his wings had so thoroughly unbalanced him, that he'd come here almost numb to the impossible task. He'd expected to have to fight Luxen, probably kill him. He hadn't expected the High Lord to back off, and now he had and the cheers rose up, he blinked awake. As though this was someone else's dream and he'd been its spectator.

"Kon-stan-tin. Kon-stan-tin. KON-STAN-TIN." They chanted so loud that the roof and walls trembled.

Holy shit. That was his name. His real name, and he was really here, with Mikhail and Djall beside him. How the fuck had that happened?

Luxen rose, and without so much as a glance back, he carved through the crowd and left, taking his cloying concubi allure with him.

"That won't be the last we hear of him," Djall warned, but she did so around a grin. "They're cheering your name, brother. As it should be." She turned on her heel and knelt. "For Red Manor."

Then Mikhail knelt, and the demon cheer became a deafening roar. What did they see? A demon who had risen from the dead, allied demons with a flight of angels, and somehow tamed the infamous guardian Mikhail?

Maybe he really did deserve this?

But all those achievements had another side to them. They couldn't see the hurt and sacrifices that had brought him here, to this very stop. He'd lost his wings, almost lost his love, and lost demons he cared for. Ernas among them.

"For our fallen kin, for truth, we will win this war!"

The cheering became euphoric. Wings flapped, demons cheered and roared, and maybe, just maybe they could unite in these final hours. If they didn't, death with gold-tipped wings would surely come for them all.

ANGELS AND DEMONS mingled in the tower that had once been Luxen's and now belonged to Severn. The High Lord had surrendered that too, and as Red Manor's previous digs had been the corner of an empty warehouse with a rusted oil drum for a fireplace, Luxen's luxury pad was a welcome upgrade.

Djall had drawn up a list of rules and stuck the notices to every available surface, reminding demons and angels why they'd suddenly been shoved together in a high-rise building and to make an effort to play nice. It would never last, not least because the Haven angels were all emotional wrecks and the demons all highly suspicious of the angels they suddenly had to bunk with. But they only needed a few days of peace, a week at most. Both nephilim and cambion were posted around London, watching for Remiel's flights. They'd surely attack at any moment.

More good news arrived in the form of humans spreading their photographs and videos of what they'd named the *Stonehenge Massacre*. Their news channels were rife of an internal angel-split, of some angels fighting *alongside* demons, of an angel and demon *affair*. The humans' foolish love of all things *angel* had been rocked now one of those angels had human blood on his hands.

Change was happening with every passing minute, and much of it made Severn giddy whenever he stopped to think on it all.

The stars were out by the time he dragged his weary ass to the suite he'd claimed for himself and Mikhail—one of the larger, top-floor apartments in Luxen's building— *Severn's* building now.

High Lord Konstantin.

It had a decent ring to it.

He chuckled and opened the suite's sliding glass doors wide, revealing London's panorama. Windows this high weren't supposed to open, but someone had retrofitted the doors to allow easy access on the wing. Leaning against the aluminum frame, he breathed in London's distinctive night air, tasting a mix of wet concrete and estuary. It might not have been the most pleasant of smells, but it was home. London below was dark. On clear nights like this, demons knew to stay inside.

The suite's door opened, and Mikhail strode in. His wings were hidden, but his hair had a wild, fresh-from-flight look, making him look haggard and rough, and had Severn's thoughts veering back to how he'd had his hands in all that hair and fucked Mikhail's mouth just yesterday. Then he recalled Mikhail on his knees in front of Djall and how her blade had glinted.

He was still pissed at this feathered asshole for being so blindingly stupid.

"We're the humans' new favorite fascination." Mikhail tossed a newspaper on the coffee table. A large black-and-white picture of them standing side by side before all the shit went down at Stonehenge covered half the front page. Severn drifted over and picked up the paper. Mikhail was in the foreground, his wings half spread behind him. Severn stood in the background. They both looked proud and honorable, like they belonged side by side. That picture had probably done more for demon and angel relations than anything else they'd achieved so far. It was just a damn shame it had come at such a high cost.

Looking up from the newspaper, he watched Mikhail a few strides away, his quick fingers flicking open the buckles of his jacket. The damn proud, stubborn, self-sacrificing fool.

"No mention of Solomon," Mikhail added, pulling open the jacket and running his hand through his hair, gathering the long locks over one shoulder.

Solo's capture and the humans killed at Stonehenge had not been part of their plan. Solo was a fighter, but Remiel was a guardian. If Remiel wanted Solo dead, Solo wouldn't be able to stop him.

When Mikhail looked up, his face had paled. "It doesn't seem right that he should fall."

Solo wasn't dead. Severn refused to believe anything else. "I've had the madam ask the nephilim to watch the skies for him. Hopefully we'll get word soon."

Mikhail nodded, but the worried pinch of his brow stayed. "You're very quiet."

"I'm still pissed at you." He threw the newspaper onto the coffee table.

"Yes, I gathered by the lack of eye contact since your... promotion?"

"Don't change the subject, angel."

Mikhail's mouth did a little half tick as he tried to suppress a smile. Gods, he was so fucking adorable when he tried and failed to hide his feelings. But Severn wasn't falling for that smile. He could keep his hands off him until he'd said what needed to be said. "We're supposed to be a team. An example to all the demons and angels currently throwing shade at one another in all the rooms below us. Proof this can work."

Mikhail's cheek ticked. He'd never taken criticism well. "How are we not those things?"

"At ExCeL, you ignored my protests—"

"I heard every one."

"But you didn't *listen*."

"No, you were being... emotional."

"Yes, I was fucking emotional. She was going to cut your wings off. You might not care, but I fucking do. You shouldn't have done it. Djall could have hurt you. Regardless of what I feel for you—which is a whole fucking lot, by the way—we need you for the battle."

"I understand your sister more than you realize," he said calmly. "We are both warriors. She could not accept anything less than my absolute subjugation for the sake of the demons who follow her and for the pride of Red Manor."

How was he right and wrong at the same time? Also, when exactly had he become such an expert on demons? "You didn't know she would take a feather. She *could* have taken your wings."

"Yes, and it would have been worth it. You are High Lord Konstantin. You command a force of demons and angels and have a chance to stand against Remiel." Mikhail moved closer and grabbed Severn's hand. "You command demons and angels *together*." Severn's hand was so much larger than his. His nails sharp, while Mikhail's were blunt. "As we are together," Mikhail said.

Oh gods, this was an attack on his heart and soul, and Severn was already beaten. As Mikhail lifted his face, there was nothing Severn could do but kiss his amazing angel who would have so foolishly surrendered his wings to his enemy.

His mouth was soft but quickly became demanding, his restrained passion fast unraveling. Severn couldn't kiss him enough. He wanted to kiss him until Mikhail gasped and moaned. Instead, he broke from the kiss and rested his forehead against Mikhail's, careful to keep his horns high, and looked into angel eyes. Eyes full of feeling. "I can't stay mad at you." Mikhail's fucking smile pierced Severn's demon heart. "I don't understand how you came to be here, with me. I don't know how to say the things you deserve."

Light fingers danced up Severn's cheek, then wrapped around a horn and pulled. "Then show me."

The sudden demand sent a dart of lust straight to Severn's balls. "Show you?" His grin twitched. He bowed his head, breathing in at the curve of Mikhail's neck. *His* angel. The warmth and familiarity had Severn's own wings unfurling behind him, his mind too distracted to keep them hidden. "Careful what you ask for, you might not be able to handle what I give."

Mikhail's hand slipped between them and startled Severn by grasping his semi-erect and eager cock through his trousers. Mikhail had him by the horn and by the cock, and fuck was there anything hotter? Severn exhaled hard.

"I can *handle* anything you care to give."

Oh gods. Did that mean what he thought it meant? Mikhail had always had a preference for submission, a desire Severn fucking loved, but things were different now. It was one thing to bend for another angel, another to do the same for a larger demon.

He licked his lips, afraid his voice might quiver. "Mikhail..." Yeah, there was the tremor. "Do you want me? Like that?"

Mikhail freed his horn but only to grab Severn's chin. His guardian eyes burned with lust. "I need this, with you. Control me, like before. I want this. I want you, in all ways."

Pure lust ran tingles down his spine, collecting in his cock, hardening him. He somehow blocked a groan behind his teeth, but with Mikhail's warm hand on his cock, there was no hiding the very visceral response to his words.

Mikhail wanted the real him. All of him. To hear him say the words, to see the raw need in Mikhail's eyes, Severn felt as though he were falling. Gods, his angel was everything.

"I'm sorry..." Severn whispered. He flicked his eyes up. "That you had to face Luxen earlier, after what he did."

Mikhail gave a small shake of the head and spread his hand across Severn's cheek, urging Severn to lean into him. "I had my demon beside me."

"Did you..." He had no right to ask, but he had to know. The not knowing was eating him up inside. "Did you and him—"

"No. He dared not, or could not." Mikhail nudged his mouth, seeking Severn's kiss. "Your touch is my only desire. The feel of your lips on mine fills my dreams now."

Severn teased his lips over Mikhail's. Their breaths mingled. Hunger and passion sizzled between them. "You truly desire me... as demon?"

Mikhail's beautiful eyes lifted. His dark lashes fluttered, their strokes so soft, like his feathers. "Demon or angel, I desire *you*."

He hadn't understood how much he'd needed to hear the words, and to believe them. And believe them he did. "I love you so much, Mikhail. When you offered your wings to Djall, it almost destroyed me *again*. I forgave you long ago, it's time you forgave yourself."

Mikhail tried to turn his face away, and that too made Severn's heart ache. He thought he didn't deserve forgiveness. Severn could only try and show him how wrong he was. He captured him with a kiss, swallowed his sigh, and wrapped an arm around his back. With a gasp, Mikhail tilted his head back, exposing his throat to Severn's bite.

By Aerius, he was weak for his angel, would do anything for him, protect him, love him, save him from himself.

He grabbed Mikhail by the hips and turned him to face away, ducking beneath his sweeping wing. Locking an arm around Mikhail's chest and the other around his waist, Severn hauled every inch of Mikhail back, plastering his body against Mikhail's back and ass, Severn's thigh crowding Mikhail's, holding him in. Black wings framed them, glossy feathers shining.

Severn nipped the base of Mikhail's neck. Mikhail gasped and shuddered, his body reflexively arching, surrendering to Severn's hold. Severn drove his needy cock against Mikhail's lower back, needing to *feel*. Mikhail's hand came around and grabbed Severn's hip, locking him there. Mikhail's intention was clear. He wanted *more*.

"Undress, Your Grace," Severn whispered into his hair, stealing a moment to breathe his scent in deep and capture it inside, holding it close to his heart. "I'll be right back." He may have said it with too much of a growl, but Mikhail's over-the-shoulder, knowing look did cruel things to Severn's body, set him ablaze.

Mikhail sashayed toward the bed, wings leisurely spread, swaying a little in time with his hips and ass.

Tease.

Leaving Mikhail was the last thing he wanted, but they were going to need some help for what came next. Lux's penthouse was next to theirs and still trashed. Severn rummaged through the drawers, soon finding the toys. Maybe another time Severn would be a bit more thoughtful of his selection from Lux's bewildering array of dildos, butt plugs, and straps, but right now, he just needed the lube.

He returned to find Mikhail sprawled naked on the bed, on his side like a sculptor's Adonis. His wings painted the bed black. His naked body demanded to be licked and nipped—teased between Severn's fingers. His cock hadn't lost any interest during Severn's absence either. The long, veined shaft lay erect against his natural V, pointed toward his hip.

Severn's mouth watered to take that piece of angel meat in deep and make Mikhail grunt like the animal they both knew him to be.

Mikhail's gaze dropped to the small bottle in Severn's hand. He raised a questioning eyebrow.

"For this, we'll just need a little help."

Tossing the bottle onto the bed, he strode across the room, quickly unbuttoning his trousers. The *angel delight* spread out like an all-you-can-eat buffet of sin had half Severn's mind lost in the play of muscle while the rest of his thoughts had funneled into his cock and were now lost there.

He stumbled the last step, kicked the tangled trousers away, then growled as one trouser leg caught on his foot. Fucking Haven, he'd set the damn things on fire if they didn't let go.

Mikhail's luscious chuckle was the final straw. Severn forgot the trousers, crossed to the bed, and prowled up Mikhail's strong, warm legs, stroking over his calves and skimming his knees. Mikhail's legs fell open, shamelessly inviting him higher. Severn licked up Mikhail's inner thigh, swirling his tongue, and gently held him down by his knee. Mikhail gave a strained groan, and in reply, Severn nipped with sharp teeth. Mikhail hissed. His cock twitched against his lower belly. The sight of it had Severn's wings shuddering.

He probed his tongue higher, flicked the tip over Mikhail's balls, and grinned as Mikhail's hands suddenly wrapped around Severn's horns, locking Severn firmly in place with his face buried between Mikhail's legs.

Sucking the soft flesh between his lips, Severn brought a hand under him and stroked a finger behind Mikhail's balls, hinting at where his fingers would explore next. Mikhail squirmed, but his grip stayed firm on Severn's horns.

Had Seraphim grabbed Aerius by the horns when his demon was giving him head? Severn chuckled at his own thoughts and slid his tongue higher, up the veined base of Mikhail's cock, and hummed low in his throat, sending the small vibrations through his tongue.

Mikhail panted, like he'd been flying hard. Or fighting. He was only now beginning to realize there were other passions in life. Severn would make it his mission to explore every one with him, find Mikhail's likes and dislikes, what drove him wild and what made him lose his mind.

Flattening his tongue, he swept up Mikhail's cock and slipped his wet lips over the angel's swollen, sensitive crown. Mikhail bucked, driving his cock deep over Severn's tongue while yanking Severn's horns down. The dual attack slid Mikhail's cock over the roof of Severn's mouth and down the back of his throat.

Severn spluttered from surprise.

Mikhail's hands vanished from Severn's horns. His body suddenly turned to stone.

Shit. Severn lifted his head, sliding his mouth off

Mikhail's cock, and knew the expression he'd find on Mikhail's face. Sure enough, his eyes had blown wide, his mouth open.

"You didn't hurt me." Reaching up, Severn wrapped his fingers around Mikhail's cock and stroked his fear away. "Just surprised me. I can take a whole lotta cock, especially yours, Your Grace."

He still looked concerned, and that would not do. Bracing his free hand beside Mikhail, Severn shifted himself higher, forcing Mikhail's knees farther apart to accommodate Severn's hips. Mikhail dropped his head back, pillowed on all his dark hair and feathers. His lashes fluttered. The dark pupils in his blue eyes were full and deep.

With their gazes locked, Severn brushed his thumb over the wetness leaking from Mikhail's cock, brought his hand up, and licked the angel's saltiness from his thumb. The concern on Mikhail's face vanished, replaced by the raw look of a male who now only had one thing on his mind. One need.

Mikhail's arm looped around Severn's neck and yanked. His tongue thrust between Severn's lips in a sudden, savage intrusion, his passion a force neither of them could control. He tore free, gasping, and his angel eyes weren't so soft now. "Fill me."

Severn's rattling heart might explode if he kept up those demands. "Hm..." he purred. "In good time, Your Grace."

"Now."

This Mikhail was the cruel one, the Mikhail who commanded flights and waged wars. And Severn was gonna fuck him so damn hard he'd be feeling demon cock for weeks.

"Are you sure?" Severn rumbled. He wrapped his fingers around Mikhail's cock again, sweeping up its eager wetness, using it to make his grip glide. That part of Mikhail was *very* sure.

"Ask me again"—Mikhail's hips jerked—"and you'll no longer find me submissive."

Severn ducked his head and smiled against one of Mikhail's pert nipples. He still marveled at the fact he'd been admiring these little nipples for years—every damn time Mikhail sauntered half naked about Aerie—and now, he got to suck them. Mikhail's hand grabbed a horn again, urging him *down*. His hungry angel had waited long enough. Severn grabbed the bottle of lube and rose onto his knees to admire the spread of hot, writhing angel beneath him.

A flush had worked its way up Mikhail's chest. Precum dribbled from his cock and glistened in the dip of his hip. Severn had never seen anything or anyone more fuckable. Lubing his fingers, he warmed them, grabbed Mikhail's leg to hold him still, and teased his wet fingers around the puckered edge of Mikhail's hole. Mikhail's mouth fell open in a silent plea while his glare burned for more.

So fucking accepting. Severn slowly inched his fingers in. Mikhail's lashes fluttered. His back arched some, driving himself down over Severn's fingers, instinctively seeking that part inside that would make his cock tingle.

Severn's fingertips found the risen nub and stroked it. The effect on Mikhail was instant. His hands scrunched the bedsheets in his fists, he locked his jaw, and his flushed cock jumped. Severn stroked that pleasure point more, and Mikhail squirmed, melting in Severn's hands. He could make him come like this and was briefly caught between doing exactly that or fucking him blind.

"*Severn.*" Mikahil's eyes snapped open, and the heat in his stare burned through Severn. "*Now.*"

Dilemma solved for him, Severn grunted—words didn't cut it now—pulled his fingers free, slicked his own aching cock, grabbed Mikhail hips, and yanked him down the bed, lifting his ass, slightly bending him, *opening* him. Mikhail's legs rested over Severn's shoulders. Fuck, the sight of his glistening hole shredded the last pieces of Severn's control.

Grasping his cock, he pressed the slick head against Mikhail's warm softness, shifted his hips some, and eased its thick width into Mikhail's sweet, clutching tightness. All reason and thought vanished. Nothing existed outside of the tight sensation of Mikhail's ass swallowing Severn's cock.

Mikhail had hold of the sheets again. He bit his lip with tiny white teeth, his gaze on Severn's face, his expression locked in raw, desperate need. It took every pound of Severn's heart to make himself ease in every excruciatingly wonderful inch at a time—until he was seated deep, balls to buttocks. And fuck, he braced against Mikhail's thigh briefly, panting, shuddering, resisting the need to just fuck his hole like a starved incubi pup.

Mikhail's fingers dug into Severn's arm in a silent plea. "*Move!*" he grunted, not so silent now. Angel-ether saturated the room, unseen by Mikhail, but gods, Severn was fucking losing his mind to it.

Easing out was a new kind of torture. Then back in. Sensation pooled into one maddening stream of ecstasy.

Mikhail took it all. Mikhail's cock lay so fucking hard against his belly that Severn needed it in his hand. He took that cock and pumped it as his own slammed deep to the sounds of skin slapping skin. A tightening spiral warned Severn he was close to coming. The last thing he wanted was to stop, but by some miracle, he stopped thrusting and stilled, allowing the tingling pressure to dissipate. It wouldn't take much more than a twitch from Mikhail for him to come, and he didn't want this to end.

He'd fucked Mikhail's ass before, but not in his true skin, not like this. This was something else. Something that transcended angel and demon. A joining between two beings destined to be together. He'd never felt so fucking free.

A knot tried to choke him, emotions rising.

"You stopped?" Mikhail enquired in a small voice that had no right coming from him.

Severn laughed softly. "I just need a second."

"Do you want to stop? I thought—I'm sorry—"

"Fuck. No." He laughed, looking up at Mikhail. Gods, he looked thoroughly fucked, flushed and sweating, hair tangled. Severn stroked Mikhail's cock some more, preferring to focus on him so he didn't spill his load too soon.

Mikhail groaned and dropped his head back. His throat undulated, and his cock wept pearly precum. Severn salivated to take him between his lips again, but to do that, he'd have to unseat himself, and if he moved an inch, he was just as likely to tip himself over the edge.

Mikhail's panting quickened. He lifted his head and stared daggers at Severn, daring him to finish him. What was Severn to do but obey? Severn gladly pumped him, relentlessly gliding his hand back and forth. Mikhail's stare faltered, his breathing stuttered. His small gasping groan turned deep and gravelly, then his hips jerked, his passage flexed around Severn's dick still seated balls-deep in his ass, and his cock spurted, dashing cum across his glistening chest.

Severn had a weakness, and it was watching Mikhail come while buried inside him. He grabbed Mikhail's thighs, yanked him hard, and fucked him like a maddened beast. Mikhail watched him with sexed-up eyes, dashes of cum all over his chest, and *fuuuuck*... Severn came so hard his wings beat as his cock unloaded pulse after pulse. His own cry echoed in his ears. And he fucking flew somewhere far away, to a place full of stars.

He came back to himself, looking down at the thoroughly smug-looking angel. And just to torture him some more, Mikhail ran his fingers through his spilled seed and brought those fingers to his lips. He licked them clean, his eyes on Severn.

"Oh, my dear... you're really not innocent, are you?" Severn ran his hands up the insides of Mikhail's thighs, reveling in Mikhail's absolute surrender. He really could get used to this. He could especially get used to seeing his dark demon cock buried deep in Mikhail's lily-white ass.

"Come here," Mikhail growled out, his command rumbling.

Reluctantly withdrawing, he danced his fingers over Mikhail's dribbling hole as a parting gift, making him shudder, and then climbed over Mikhail's bent leg and lay alongside him, atop his soft wing, pinning Mikhail down. They should get cleaned up, but he didn't feel much like moving.

Mikhail's fingers stroked absently over his horn, so he

tucked his head in closer and listened to Mikhail's thumping heart.

"An angel and a demon fell in love..." Severn mumbled, his thoughts fucked and dreamy. But now he'd spoken, he wasn't sure how that sentence ended. How could it end? He didn't want to think on it, fearing the ending was not the one they wanted.

But he needn't have feared because Mikhail finished it for him, "And they changed the world forever."

THE BUILDING WAS quiet beneath them. Either their flights of angels and demons had killed one another, or there was peace between them, for a night, anyway. A breeze rippled the drapes over the open door, blurring the dark London outside. Severn had Mikhail tucked close, facing him, and absently skimmed his fingers up over his hip. Mikhail's eyes were heavy-lidded, his lips soft and slightly swollen. He had the smug, satisfied look of someone thoroughly fucked, and Severn's demon heart swelled to see him so content.

This was them now. Two leaders. Together. He supposed he had Seraphim and Aerius to thank. Had they not fallen in love, perhaps none of this would have happened.

"Their love was true," Mikhail said softly, clearly thinking along the same lines. Mikhail's fingers trailed over Severn's right pec, teasing around a nipple. "I feel it. Seraphim's rage is monumental, but so was his love. The guardians feared his wrath." His voice rumbled in the dark and quiet, slow and smooth, like honey.

Severn propped his head on a hand. Mikhail's wings lay over his side of the bed. A sheet lay over his legs, but the rest of him was naked and gleaming in soft moonlight.

The next few days were going to be tough. The battle would be bloody. Angels and demons would die. Quiet moments like these would have to see them through. It wasn't just Mikhail's body he admired. His mind too was a marvel. Mikhail had been manipulated since his birth by the very people who should have protected him. He'd seen his errors, knew he'd fucked up, and he was trying to fix it. But as strong as he was, Mikhail was also vulnerable.

Luxen had seen that.

The High Lord had rolled over too easily. There were many demons who despised Mikhail. Demons who might take the coming battle as an opportunity to stab him between his wings. Djall had feared angels betraying her, but Severn feared demons doing the same to Mikhail. And if Severn should fall in battle, he'd have nobody to protect him. "If something happens to me—"

Mikhail's hand captured Severn's and raised it to his lips. He looked up, meeting Severn's gaze. "There has never been a more capable High Lord, except perhaps Aerius himself. I have faith you will not fail."

Maybe. He pulled Mikhail close, breathed him in and reveled in angel. Had Aerius held Seraphim and told him how they would both survive the battle to come, told him of the dreams he had of their long life together? But those dreams had not come true. Love may be immortal, but angels and demons still died.

Severn hooked a leg around Mikhail's, trapping him close, and hugged him to his chest. Mikhail's soft laughs gently shook them both. "You know I am not some fragile angel needing protection?"

"Hm," Severn mused. *Fluffy on the outside, glass in the middle.* Aerius had lost his angel. Severn would not lose his.

"To ease your mind, will you indulge me in something?"

The tentative way he asked had Severn arching a brow. "I'm intrigued."

"Your wings... may I kiss them?"

Seraphim, help him. He swallowed hard, lifted his shoulder, and arched his right wing over, slowly lowering its leathery peak to within Mikhail's reach. Mikhail studied the wing a while, his gaze almost as tangible as his touch. Then he lifted a hand, hesitated long enough for Severn's heart to pound, and settled his fingers on the leading edge. Sensitive was one word. Dazzling was another. Severn let his eyes close. Mikhail's gentle strokes were almost painfully soft. The bed rocked, and then warm, soft lips brushed lightly. It hurt—in the best way. He tucked his chin into his chest, squeezing his eyes closed, so Mikhail didn't see how his tears leaked through.

Mikhail's fingers glanced down Severn's cheek to his lips. "They're wonderful, as are you."

olo

"THIS IS COZY. Did you build it yourself? I like the rug. Very... rustic." Solo was sitting against a corrugated tin wall, his bound wings pinned behind him. The little tin hut was barely big enough for his feathered arches and certainly wasn't big enough for him and the enormous demon bumbling about the tiny space, shoving logs into a tiny stove and grumbling to their rayvern companion.

Solo wasn't sure who he feared most, the demon who had plucked him out of the sky, or the rayvern who eyed Solo like it had taken a shine to his green eyes and wanted to keep one.

He'd been quite happy to accept the demon's help, preventing his body from shattering all over London. But now he was trapped, the situation was less amusing. He also wasn't entirely sure *why* the demon had caught him.

Maybe the rayvern wasn't the only feathered pet the demon liked.

"Your rayvern is—"

"Caw!"

"I was just—"

"Caw!"

"Going to say—"

"Caw!"

"I have cats, and I really need to get back to them." Maybe the demon would understand that and let him go? "Pets can be very demanding, as I'm sure... you... know..." The big demon slowly turned and eyed him hard.

They really were *big*. Thighs the width of Solo's waist, shoulders like boulders. Glossy skin, though. He knew that from the demon's gentle hold.

"An angel with cats?" the demon grumbled.

Gods, they had a voice like thunder. It was a wonder the resonance didn't collapse the hut around them.

"Er... yes. It's a new experience. I'm not entirely sure how it happened. I think perhaps they adopted me."

The big demon chuckled.

"Caw!" the rayvern said.

"He's very talkative, your bird."

"Hush. Both of you," the demon groused, turning back to the countertop. Their huge body prevented Solo from seeing what they were busy preparing. "I'm tryin' tah think 'ere."

So, if the demon had caught him and brought him to their... den? Was that what they called their homes? Then surely they didn't want to kill, Solo. Not all demons were bad. Severn was evidence of that. Severn was reasonable.

Maybe this one was too? "It's just... the ropes are chaffing. Could you untie me, please?"

"You're more polite than the other one." The demon turned again and thumped over, trying not to knock over all the bowls and pans and strange pots of grasses and things, then leaned over Solo's head and reached behind him. The demon's chest was suddenly all Solo could see. Abs like iron bars. Nipples like—

Solo squeezed his eyes close.

The ties at his wrists fell away, and after a snip, his wings sprang free—the left shot toward the ceiling and arched over their heads—a red canopy. The right punched out, knocking a tin door over. "Sorry."

The demon tutted. "Illusion them away, angel." They inched their bulk back in front of the stove.

The wings vanished with a thought. He'd have done it sooner, but banishing them when they were tied took greater concentration, and he was having a hard time focusing on anything other than surviving. "You should maybe build a bigger hut?"

"Well, I ain't normally this size, am I. Needed wings, didn't I. To catch falling angels." They waved a thick finger at him.

"I certainly appreciate your help, so thank you... for, er... saving my life. But I... I really need to get going." Remiel had made it clear Vearn was planning something. He had to find Severn and Mikhail and warn them.

The demon eyed him like they might cut him up and use his remains as kibble for the bird. Yellow eyes peered into Solo's soul.

"Have an important meeting, do you?" the demon asked.

"We've got movement." A smaller, cloaked figure appeared in the hut's doorway. "Oh, hey. You have an angel."

"Hello." Solo waved.

"Hi." The figure came forward and extended his hand in greeting, like humans did.

Solo gave it a welcome shake. The figure dropped his hood. Stumps of what would one day be large horns marked him as demon. That and his inky blue skin. This one was much less threatening. "Nice tah meet yah. I'm Ernas, and I guess you already met—"

"Shh," the big demon grunted. "Your prattling is distractin'."

"Caw!"

The hut was getting very crowded.

"Remiel's angels are on the move," Ernas said. "He's heading for the killing fields. He means to battle in the open because angels are stupid—oh, sorry, mate, didn't mean you."

Solo shrugged. He knew some pretty stupid angels. "It's valid."

The big demon rattled off a string of words that sounded like curses to Solo, but they were so deep and spoken in one long breath they were hard to make out. He eyed the open doorway. Maybe he could make a run for it, fly to Haven, find Mikhail, and hope Vearn hadn't gotten to him already.

"Word is, Mikhail was seen with a flight of angels near the docks, but there aren't any reports of attacks, an' there's nothing out that way, so seems kinda weird he'd be there," Ernas continued. He occasionally glanced warily at Solo.

"Mikhail is in London?" Solo asked. Why would he come here if not to attack? For Severn, surely. Oh. To recruit more forces. They'd gone to the demons! Would Mikhail being away from Haven be enough to stop Vearn's plan?

"Ernas, can you take this one back to Mikhail?" the big demon asked of the little one.

"I don't need an escort," Solo said, rising to his feet and brushing dust from his clothes. "I can just see myself out..."

Their collective frowns were not impressed. Even the rayvern looked at him like he was an idiot.

"If you want your wings pulled off, sure, waltz right out the door." Ernas grinned.

That was another good point. He didn't know where Mikhail was, and although Severn had shown him some parts of London where demons and humans mingled, he couldn't just walk through demon territory—or fly through it—and ask after Mikhail or Severn.

"An escort it is," Solo agreed cheerily.

"You comin'?" Ernas asked the big one.

"Can't," they replied gruffly. Their shoulders drooped and they went back to busying themselves with the bowls and herby pastes.

"Why not?" Solo asked. They'd left the hut to catch him, and a big demon like them would be a huge asset in their ranks.

"That's enough of your chitter." They waved him toward the door. "Off you go now. And hurry. They don't have much time."

"Who doesn't?" Solo asked. Ernas hovered an arm at his back, ushering him toward the door. "Why don't they have much time?" he called back. It seemed as though the big demon knew things, important things, and that they might be a lot more important than he'd given them credit for.

Outside the hut, drum fires illuminated halos around a dark street. Ernas flicked his hood up and blended in with the shadows along the tightly packed shanty-style old London street. Similar huts to the one they'd just left lined the street. Demons loitered in their doorways, watching him pass by, their yellow eyes keen and hungry.

Unarmed, and wearing just his Aerie prisoner linens, Solo had rarely felt so exposed.

"Demons ain't so easy to kill when you're on your own, eh?" Ernas smirked.

Solo hurried to keep up with the young demon's loping gait. "We could fly?"

"Not yet. Too close to angel-town." Ernas flung an arm around Solo's shoulders and pulled him into a rough side-hug. "The boss says you gotta get to Mikhail, so I'm gettin' you there. But just so you know, I kinda hate you, and everyone who's watchin' us? They kinda hate you too. It's not personal."

Solo swallowed hard. "Then why are you helping me? And why did the boss save me?"

"Dunno. The boss saved me too." He pulled his arm back, stuck his hands in his pockets, and kicked a can into the gutter. "Scooped me right off the street after I got jumped. I'd have died if not for them. So now I do what they say, and you should too. They don't talk much about themselves, but I listen an' watch. They have a plan, right? Konstantin, us, we're all part of it."

The big demon *was* powerful. "Does the boss have a name?"

His eyes sparkled. "I got some ideas on that, but you'll think I'm nuts."

"I don't know... I've seen some strange things lately. The world is changing around us."

"Nah," Ernas smirked. "It's you who's changin'. Feels good, though, don't it?"

It only really occurred to him then that he'd been pushed off the edge of Aerie, and he'd survived, and now he was here, deep in the heart of demon territory, speaking with a demon, with demons all around. He should have been afraid. Not long ago, he *would* have been afraid. But now he wasn't.

"Yes," he told the pup. "Change feels good."

evern

"—Grab his wings."

A jolt to his back sent his thoughts reeling. He stared at the floor, between his hands, wondering how he'd gotten there from the bed. Muddled from sleep, his thoughts took too long to align.

Hot, heavy hands pulled again at his wings.

Others were here. He heard their breathing. Heard the sweep of demon wings and the lighter, softer gasp of angel feathers. He smelled *angel*. And not his angel.

Intruders.

His growl came unbidden. Severn twisted, swinging his arm out, intending to rake his nails through whoever had pulled on his fucking wings, but something else swung in. He didn't feel the blow so much as blink awake from it, his cheek against the floor and ears ringing. Two figures stood between him and the sliding door, backlit by the moon, like enormous gargoyles.

Sickening heat throbbed down the side of his face and neck. Instincts had him reaching for his face, but the effort cost him, and his hand flopped back down. Blood on his fingertips. Blood on the floor. He could taste it now too. His gut heaved. Shit, shit, shit... the head wound was bad.

The smaller demon of the two came forward. His boots clunked on the floor. Leather creaked as he crouched. "For what it's worth, I'm sorry it had to come to this."

"Samiel?" How was he here? Flown in through the window... And the other slim figure was Luxen—holding back because he damn well knew Severn would rip him apart. Samiel and Luxen *together*.

Mikhail?!

The room twirled, the floor tipped. Severn grabbed the edge of the bed. Bloody handprints stained the sheets. His skin tingled, half his body numb and his head a ragged mess of throbbing pain and broken thoughts. He had to get to Mikhail. Screw Samiel... he had to know Mikhail was all right. Lifting his head above the edge of the bed, he saw Mikhail's face. He slept, he was safe. But a shadow lay over him. A shadow made by an angel. She stepped into the throw of moonlight. Vearn?

A needle glinted in her hand.

What was this? Gods damn them! *"What... have you done!"* Severn grabbed for Mikhail's arm, desperate to pull him free. His fingers brushed his skin, smearing blood. *Cold. Why was Mikhail cold?*

"Mikhail?" No... No, this couldn't be... He reached for his upturned wrist, his pulse.

Hands gripped Severn's wings and yanked him off the bed, dumping his ass on the floor. Oh, they were going to fucking regret this. Severn snapped out his wings, throwing the grip off. He lunged toward the bed, for Vearn.

White-hot agony cracked through his wings and down his spine. He jolted to a stop and dropped. His knees cracked against the floor. His wings... He pulled. Fire tore through his shoulders, tearing a cry from his lips. *No... his wings!* He swung his head around, searching for Samiel, and saw instead how a pair of angelblades pierced both wings, pinning him to the floor like a butterfly pinned to a board.

Shock drove a ragged sob up his throat. His heart thumped too hard, too loud, filling his head with its roar, and his breaths hissed through gritted teeth.

The pair of demons stood back, still bathed in moonlight. They'd pay for this, they'd all pay. But he had to get to Mikhail.

"It is done," Vearn said.

He didn't want to know, didn't want to hear her next words, didn't want to *see*. Mikhail still breathed, didn't he? His chest still rose and fell. But shock had his body trembling, and he couldn't tell, he couldn't be sure. *"What. Have. You. Done-to-him!?"*

"Euthanasia is a more peaceful death than that of Our Grace Seraphim's death," Vearn said. "Be grateful for that."

Euthanasia? What? She looked peaceful, as though her work was over. No... no-no-no. He couldn't think it, couldn't draw the line. Seraphim had been killed... His gaze fell to Mikhail... not moving, not breathing.

The roar that surged through him came from the very depths of his concubi soul. It might have shaken the world. Strength poured through his limbs and pulled his wings against the edges of the stuck blades. Steel sliced through flesh. Didn't matter. Pain was a distant inferno. None of it mattered. He had to get to Mikhail. Sleeping Mikhail. *Not dead.* He refused to believe it, or think it.

"And on the eve of the Battle of a Thousand Stars, the great god Seraphim was killed for the protection of angelkind forevermore." She fucking said it like a prayer, like some divine messenger, and smiled her sweet smile over Mikhail's motionless body.

Vearn knew the past.

She'd always known the truth.

He slipped on spilled blood and shuddered to a knee. The wet metallic smell filled the air. Its wetness streamed from his wings. He didn't care. He didn't need wings. He'd cut them to shreds to have Mikhail back, but damn them —they wouldn't let him go.

"Samiel?" He wasn't even sure why he'd said his name, perhaps out of some foolish hope that somewhere inside that lying shell he maybe cared. That Samiel wasn't a stranger after all and might still be his friend. The Samiel he'd known hadn't been this cruel. The Samiel he'd played with in London's streets and later loved. He would not do this, not even out of jealousy.

"Please." Severn sobbed, breaking, coming apart.

No, Mikhail... Not his Mikhail... Not like this.

"I can't do this," Samiel muttered.

"You must," came Luxen's reply. "Traitors must be punished. This is how it ends."

"He's dead. This is cruel. Let Stantin go to him."

Mikhail's face, so pale, so peaceful. He couldn't be gone. He was too bright a star to die like this, to fade away as though his life meant nothing. No, it wasn't right. Severn refused to hear it. Wings twitching, bleeding, Severn staggered to his feet and heaved against the blades holding him down. He heaved until every damn muscle screamed and his blood ran in rivers. The pain came, not from the steel blades, but from inside—from his heart, where a terrible, hollow, hungry agony threatened to spill over.

His right wing sprang free. He staggered, twisted, almost fell, and then the left jolted free. He fell onto the bed and froze on his knees, afraid to reach for Mikhail, afraid to *know*. Because he already knew.

Like Seraphim... angels always died for their demons.

His mouth twisted and trembled, his heart burning up and crumbling to ash.

Not his Mikhail. Long ago, the angels had taken Seraphim from Aerius, but they would *never* take Mikhail.

He leaned in, folded his wrecked wings around them, and brushed bloody knuckles against Mikhail's cool face. "Mikhail?" he whispered. "Please... I can't do this without you." Mikhail would wake if he could. He'd tear their enemies apart if he could. But he didn't move. Severn bumped his forehead against Mikhail's. Mikhail's eyes were closed. But he lived. Severn knew it. Mikhail just... needed help. "Seraphim," Severn whispered. "Help us." If any of this had meant anything, if any part of this was more than just an angel and a demon in love, if the god was here in some form, either for vengeance or truth, then now was the time to make his presence known. Now was the time to make right the terrible past. *"Make it right, Seraphim. Save him. For love."*

CHAPTER 34

*M*ikhail

MIKHAIL BEAT HIS WINGS, *but with every stroke, they weighed him down. His heart pounded, his chest ablaze. He couldn't stop, couldn't rest. If he fell here, there was nothing below to catch him. He had to reach Severn. Severn was his sanctuary. His savior. His everything.*

Light flooded all around, burning through Mikhail's eyes. He stalled in the air, hastily adjusting his flight to keep himself aloft. The world was a blur, the light too blinding. Which way was the right way? Tiredness tugged on him, trying to pull him down and down and down. He could not fall, to fall was to surrender.

A dark, throbbing heart at the center of the light grew bigger. And as it grew, it formed the shape of an angel. An angel framed by six dark wings, each feather as black as night. The angel's shining armor was not designed to be seen, and neither was his face —hidden now by a gleaming helmet. He knew this angel. He was fierce and terrifying, a force who could end worlds, but he was not perfect. He made mistakes, he laughed as easily as he raged. But he was loved. And that love had made him better, made him see his faults, and made him want to change the world for good.

Was this light a mirror, or was this shining figure truly a god?

Power jolted through Mikhail, lancing up his spine. He bucked, opened his mouth to scream... And fell.

∾

THE BLURRY SIGHT of Severn's stricken face filled Mikhail's vision. Tears shone like diamonds on his dark skin. His amber eyes widened, though the pain in those eyes only seemed to intensify. Severn flung an arm around Mikhail, looping it behind his back, and hauled him close. *Blood.* The air was saturated with the smell of it.

Severn whispered three words into his ear. "Vearn. Samiel. Lux."

Three names. Enemies, all.

Three people who had dared hurt *his* demon.

The sluggishness cleared, leaving his thoughts as sharp as glass.

"That's enough!" Vearn's cry rose. "Kill Konstantin and let's be done with this."

"Do it yourself, angel," Samiel snarled.

"Cowards. Both of you."

Luxen's resonating growl followed. "The deal was to bring you Mikhail. You said nothing about killing Konstantin. I do not surrender demonkind to angels. It's time you left—"

"Then I'll do it myself!"

Severn was exposed. His back to their blades.

Wounded. Weakened. Nobody would *ever* hurt Severn. Power surged through Mikhail's veins, driving out the chilling effects of whatever substance Vearn had pricked into his arm.

With strength not entirely his own, he shoved Severn aside and reared up on his knees, six wings blasting open.

Vearn's trajectory had her rushing forward, the angel-blade thrust out, destined to sink into Severn's back. But Severn was no longer where he'd been. Mikhail had taken his place. A memory flashed—not his own—of an angel protecting his demon. As was right. That guardian's blade had shattered a god's heart.

Not this time.

Mikhail twisted away, thrust his forearm up, and as Vearn toppled forward, Mikhail landed an open-palmed strike into her middle. She flew back, struck the wall, dropped, and sprang forward again, screaming with the full force of a guardian's misplaced righteousness.

She hadn't seen Severn retrieve the second blade from the floor. And she didn't see him now, that blade raised above his right shoulder. Her unwillingness to see anything but the path they'd all been forced to follow left her blind.

Severn brought the blade down with lethal accuracy, sliding its great weight into and through her neck. Her eyes flew open. She grasped for Mikhail, and even in those final seconds, the devout belief on her face didn't falter. Then the blade tore free of her flesh. Her body fell, her head beside it.

Severn stood gasping, the bloody blade limp in his right hand. His torn wings streamed blood behind him. And behind them stood two demons.

"Konstantin..." Samiel began. He almost sounded sorry.

Severn whirled, roared, and lifted the sword.

A blur of something solid and demon-shaped plunged through the window, shattering glass. Wings flew open, and the demon plowed into Samiel's back, slamming him to the floor. The figure pressed a boot to Samiel's back and retracted his wings. He flung back his hood and snarled, "Didn't see that comin', did yah, *bitch*."

The pup Ernas.

Luxen spread his wings, about to leap free of the building.

He had to be stopped.

"Luxen, you motherfucking bastard!" Severn started forward too.

Outside the window, a wall of red feathers blasted open, blocking Luxen's only exit. Solo arched a russet eyebrow. "Going somewhere, demon?" His red hair stuck out at odd angles, and his feathers appeared ruffled.

Solo was alive. Ernas was alive. And they were both here.

Severn dropped his blade and staggered, about to fall. Mikhail threw his arms around him, crushed his bigger body close, and felt his silent sob. He breathed him in. His sanctuary. His life. "You're safe. We're safe. I have you."

The sob into his neck had Mikhail squeezing his eyes closed. He hugged his demon tighter. So tight, the lines between them blurred.

"I thought you were gone," Severn mumbled. His big hand stroked down Mikhail's hair. "I thought... like before. Aerius lost... and I couldn't, Mikhail. I couldn't lose you."

"Not us," he said with force. "Never us." Severn went

to his knees. Mikhail crumpled with him, his vast wings reflexively curling in, the feathers like bars keeping the world at bay.

Severn's sobs slowly leveled, leaving him breathless. His wings still wept blood. Mikhail brushed tears from his face, and Severn brushed his cheek against Mikhail's palm. He grumbled a moan of protest. His thick fingers curled around Mikhail's arm, holding tight. "We aren't alone, are we..."

"No."

"Ernas?" Severn lifted his head, and Mikhail lowered his wing.

The pup beamed. "Back from the dead, bitches. Yah missed me, right?"

"I'm gonna need a minute." Severn slumped into Mikhail, but he smiled, and that smile was Mikhail's world. They were both naked, bloody, and bruised. The air smelled of blood and death. Of demon and angel. But Mikhail didn't want to move. Not yet. Not when Severn was so obviously hurting.

"You need medical attention," he whispered.

"Stantin... I'm sorry," Samiel's muffled voice piped up.

Ernas stamped on Samiel's back. "Shut it, numbnuts. Ain't nobody wanna hear shit from you right now. One more word and I let Konstantin kick your ass, and you'd better know he'll kick it halfway across London."

"Solo?" Severn shifted, easing from Mikhail's arms. "Shit... Solo? You're safe?"

Still hovering outside, his attention on keeping a quiet Luxen contained, Solo thumped a fist against his heart. "You won't believe it. But a demon saved my life."

Severn huffed a half laugh, not quite managing a full one. "I believe it."

~

THE NEXT FEW hours were a blur. Ernas found Djall and, together with Solo, dealt with Vearn's body and escorted Luxen and Samiel to a nearby building for secure holding until their judgment could be determined. Djall had delivered the dire news of Remiel's forces gathered on the edge of the killing fields. Demons attended Severn, carefully wrapping his wings, while Mikhail dressed and kept a watchful eye on their work, never moving more than a few strides away. Severn eventually grew tired of the fuss and dismissed them.

After gingerly dressing, Severn muttered, "Let's get out of here."

They found a smaller apartment a level down, and as dawn's red light flooded through London's quiet streets outside the window, Mikhail sat with Severn on the edge of the bed.

Severn stared at the window. He couldn't fly. That put them at a distinct disadvantage. Their forces were a fraction of Remiel's. And the power Mikhail had summoned last night had been different, controlled and precise. In clearing his veins, he feared it had also burned out. He wouldn't be seeing Seraphim again.

"Can we just..." Severn began, then with a sweep of his arm, he gathered Mikhail to his side. His trembling was back, and as Severn slumped against him, Mikhail guided him down to lay his head in Mikhail's lap. He stroked

Severn's dark hair, tucking it behind his horn, until his tremors subsided.

The attack had shaken him, perhaps more than anything else in all the time Mikhail had known him. In the years past, they'd returned bloody and exhausted from battle, but Severn had always kept his head high. Mikhail didn't need to smell emotion to know he was scared.

"I'm going to find Aerius," he said, breaking the comforting silence.

Severn turned his head and blinked. "Don't. They won't help."

"The demon who saved Solo—"

"Was Aerius? Yeah, figured as much," Severn agreed. "But they won't be pulled any deeper into this. I tried."

Mikhail laid his hand on Severn's chest, over the *thud-thud* of his heart. "They're afraid to."

"Afraid," Severn huffed. "Aerius doesn't fear."

"I would not be so sure."

Severn turned his face toward the window, and Mikhail stroked down his horn again and skimmed his fingers along the fine line of his cheekbone to his neck in a gentle caress. "You told me they said we did not want their help, remember? And it struck me as a strange wording. Had I died last night, you would have blamed yourself."

Severn's brow pinched.

"Aerius blames themself for Seraphim's death, even after all this time. They're afraid if they interfere, the same thing will happen again. Love makes us stronger but also gives us fear."

"Mikhail..." When Severn looked up now, his face betrayed the very fear he'd spoken of. "Don't go. Stay with me. Remiel can go fuck himself, the demons and angels can fight their own war. I don't care anymore."

"You don't mean that."

He pushed up suddenly and braced an arm against the bed, peering into Mikhail's eyes. "I preferred it when you were clueless about emotions and I could talk you around any argument."

He remembered those days well. Severn trying to explain both sides to Mikhail, Severn trying to lessen the risk of casualties, always trying to mediate. He was brilliant, but not even Severn could stop Remiel. "We need Aerius."

Severn rubbed at his face. "I'll come with you."

"No, stay. Rest." Mikhail rose from the bed.

"I don't..." Big demon eyes pleaded.

"There is no time. I must go now."

Severn pressed his lips together. "Now? Fine. So I'll just rally the angels and demons and somehow get them all armed and to the killing fields without you? Is that what you're telling me here? Because, I gotta say, I don't think angels much like me, and now my wings are fucked, I'm basically useless—"

Mikhail swooped in and cupped his face, cutting off his rant. "The last thing I want is to leave you." He bowed his head and pressed a small kiss to his forehead, between the horns. "You have Solomon."

"Yeah, but he ain't you, Mikhail." Severn's sudden grin was all the warning he got. Suddenly, Severn's arms looped around him and yanked him down, his back on the bed, with Severn poised over him.

Mikhail laughed.

"Nobody is you." Severn nuzzled his neck, sucked a

pinch of skin between his teeth, and nipped. "Tell me we can fuck right now and forget everything else."

Mikhail let his eyes fall closed and imagined exactly that—Severn's warm hands riding over his skin, his wet mouth in soft, vulnerable places. "Hm..." he groaned. "I want to." But Severn was also recovering from terrible wounds and hurting, inside and out.

Severn chuckled and splayed his hand over Mikhail's hardening cock. "I know. Gods, you're practically glowing with ether." Severn's mouth hovered over Mikhail's. "Let me drink every drop," he said, enunciating every word. "Won't you satisfy your wounded demon?"

There were those big, sorry demon eyes again, reaching into Mikhail's newly excavated feelings and squeezing them.

He chuckled. "You are terrible."

"Hm, yes, exactly the way you like me."

Gently, Mikhail levered him off and managed to squirm free of his grip. Severn flopped back onto the bed. He'd regained some color, and a smile. He made no attempt to hide the obvious rod trapped inside his trousers. "Such a tease, Your Grace."

"Later. A promise."

All the precarious joy snuffed out of Severn's eyes as his thoughts returned to the battle to come. "Then I guess I'll see you on the killing fields, Mikhail."

"I'll be there." He left the apartment, and his demon, behind.

evern

As Djall talked numbers and weapons and locations and tactics, and demons marched toward the killing fields, Severn's heart thumped so hard it had to be trying to break through his ribs and make a run for it. He'd never been fucking scared to fight. He'd feared battle, but that wasn't the same as this gut-liquefying terror. And he'd always overcome it. This was different. Sharper... real, less easily shoved aside. He didn't want to be here, standing at the front of a few thousand demons and angels, about to march most of them to their deaths. Including his own.

And he definitely didn't want to be here without Mikhail.

The bloodred of dawn had given way to a crisp early summer's morning. The soft sweep of angel wings accompanied the heavier sounds of demons on the ground, armor and weapons clanging. The air smelled of river, just a note away from blood.

Remiel's forces shimmered far across the churned-up killing fields, so far away that they almost disappeared in the morning light. Tufts of grass and stubborn weeds had sprung up between the two fronts. London was trying to heal the land.

Gods, he was going to throw up.

Vearn's attack had fucked with his head.

He wanted to find Mikhail, curl them both into a ball, and hide. But Mikhail had to be Mikhail and go off on some righteous quest to find a demon god, leaving Severn very much alone.

"Hey, you all right?" Djall grabbed his shoulder hard enough to startle him out of his thoughts.

"Yeah, fine."

"Shake off last night's shit, okay?" Her glare hardened, like she could sense weakness. "We need Konstantin. We need our High Lord. You said you could do this, so fucking do it."

He brushed her hand off. "I said I've got this."

She grunted and marched back down the line of demons. Severn rubbed his hands on his leather armor, drying them. If he fumbled his sword today, he'd die. If he couldn't clear his head, he'd die. When had the threat of dying become so fucking terrifying?

He paced over the cracked ground, spotted a mound of rubble, and climbed up to get a better view of their forces. A front of demons speckled with angels spread before him. Maybe five thousand strong. That alone was a fucking miracle.

The background grumbling and murmurs began to

fade, probably because their High Lord had found some higher ground, making him visible. His bandaged wings twitched. Shit, he was going to have to say something rallying when all he really wanted to do was call the whole pointless thing off.

Where the fuck was Mikhail?

"Angels and demons, together." Raising his voice, the thousands hushed until just the wind could be heard, rifling through feathers and over demon wings.

He was committed now. Best think of something inspirational, these could be his last damn words. Dammit. His wounded wings throbbed. He placed a boot on a concrete block and pointed across the fields toward the sunlit force of angels.

"There's a guardian angel over there who knows the truth. Remiel wants us dead. He knows his past is a lie, he knows this war is a lie, but he'd rather see angels and demons die than admit he—and all the guardians—are wrong. He appears strong, but he's weak. He appears to be righteous. He is wrong. The angels who stand with us now, know my words to be true. Prisoners in their own lives, they are now free to fight. And they join us today—not to fight Remiel, and not to fight their kin—but to fight for truth."

His heart thumped, pumping burning blood through his veins, filling that ancient concubi desire to lead. *"We've been fed their lies long enough."* A small cheer bubbled through the crowd. *"No more demons will die for lies!"* The resounding cheer grew louder, building on itself, turning to a roar, and Severn's heart soared. *"Today, we end it. Today, we win, and no demon or angel will die for lies again!"* The roar sailed on and on, across the field, filling the air, the streets behind their ranks, and thundering the ground.

Severn bared his teeth, if only to hide the quiver in his lips, and wished Mikhail would hurry the fuck up and get Aerius here, and maybe, just fucking maybe, they'd have a chance.

CHAPTER 36

 ikhail

ERNAS LANDED in a run in the midst of a shantytown full of strings of lights, tin roofs, drum fires, and cambion demons. Mikhail landed behind the pup and folded his wings in, keeping them from filling the narrow street. Yellow demon eyes regarded him coolly from their makeshift homes.

Ernas whistled between his teeth. "C'mon, angel. They're right up here." He skipped over some rubble to a rusted shack, larger than the rest, with a slight slant to it, like the structure might collapse at any second. "Angel inbound!" Ernas announced, then rapped his knuckles on the tin wall.

The demon that ducked their head out of the doorway had to be eight feet tall, not including the two great curved horns adding at least another three feet. Huge shoulders held up a body that wouldn't fit through human doorways. Their skin shimmered a glossy, silken brown. Mikhail was not small by angel standards, but this demon was like none he'd ever seen, making him feel vulnerable. His wings fought to flare wide as a threat. But he held them tucked close.

The demon took one look at Mikhail and said in a voice like thunder, "Bollocks, it's you." Ducking their head, they vanished back inside the shack.

Ernas shrugged. "They get like that."

"Oh, I know. We've met." He hadn't been armed with all the facts when he'd met Aerius, but he was now. "Give me a minute, Ernas."

Ernas narrowed his eyes, assessing him. "Only because my man Konstantin trusts you an' all."

Mikhail dipped his chin. "Thank you."

The shack was almost identical to the one Amii —*Aerius*—had kept him in before. Slightly larger but the same stove, the same rickety old table, and same sweet-smelling herbs. However, this demon definitely was not an old crone.

"Stopped hiding your true form, have you?" Mikhail asked.

"Don' you get all high an' mighty with me, angel."

Mikhail leaned against the doorframe. It creaked, threatening to collapse. He quickly straightened again, crossed his arms, and studied Aerius while they were faced away. The muscle and build screamed concubi—the *first* concubi. Seraphim's creation. Their wings would be enormous and stunning. "Why do you hide who and what you are?" He knew the answer—at least, he thought he did— but wanted to hear it from Aerius.

They busied themself at the table, grabbed a pinch of herbs from one plant, then another, and tossed them in a small bowl to grind up, all while deliberately facing away. "Didn't work out so well last time, did it."

"You're a hypocrite. You set Severn and I on the path of truth because you're afraid of it." They didn't reply, so he continued. "You talk of love, about demons and angels, and you make us live out your fantasy because you're too afraid to face how yours ended."

Their shoulders locked in a hard line. If they were angry, good. They should be.

"There is a battle about to rage, a battle for what's right. You're the first demon, the Rayvern Lord, and you're hiding in a rusted hut."

"Angel," Aerius grumbled. "You don' know the first thin' about me. Go do your fightin', my being there won't make no damn difference anyway."

Jasper decided to make an appearance by swooping in through the grubby, cracked window and landing on a stand made from some sort of metal bar sticking out the wall. *"Caw!"* he accused Mikhail.

Mikhail swallowed bitter frustration. "Why won't it make a difference?"

"Because..." They turned. "Wars ain't won by fighting. Blood spills blood. Always been that way. Your battle will fail."

"Not if you help us."

"And what can I do? Kill more angels?" They crossed the shack in one stride and rapped their knuckles on Mikhail's forehead. "Use that pretty head a' yours."

More shocked than anything else, Mikhail blinked and

329

slowly unfolded his arms. "I don't understand what Seraphim saw in you."

Aerius blinked and grinned. Thin lips peeled back over sharp teeth. "He couldn't get enough demon ass. You have that in common!" They grabbed his shoulder, leaning in too close. "And the wings, I s'pose."

He shook them off. "We have more in common than that."

"Caw!"

Jasper sounded sympathetic for once. "Your bird agrees," Mikhail added.

Aerius threw their hands up and backed off. "Ganging up on me, eh. Pah!"

"A guardian attacked Severn and I last night, as we lay together. She tried to kill me. I saw... I think I saw Seraphim. I can't explain it, but he was there. He's been with us all this time, yet you stand back?"

"What happened to the guardian?" Aerius asked carefully.

"Severn decapitated her."

They pursed their lips and nodded. "A happy ending for you. Enjoy it while it lasts."

"Today we face Remiel—"

"Remiel?" they grunted, and all the softness in the demon turned to stone.

Mikhail expected them to say something, anything, but Aerius just sniffed. "And tens of thousands of angels who don't understand the truth," Mikhail added. "Severn is wounded, and whatever you did to my wings, is gone. Burned out."

"Pfft, I just healed your wings. The rest is in yer fluffy head."

"Now who's lying?"

Dark eyes flashed a cold warning and the temperature in the tiny hut plummeted. "What do you want from me, angel? I'm busy."

"Busy hiding, busy pretending you're someone you're not, busy watching others try to right *your* wrongs?"

"Ain't that what I just said. Now go. Shoo with yah." Aerius waved him back.

Fine. He was done here but for one last thing. "You believe you failed Seraphim. Perhaps you did. Perhaps he died because the demon he loved did nothing. And perhaps thousands of angels and demons will die today, because you did nothing. You're so worried about history repeating itself, but the most you can bring yourself to do is push and pull Severn and me. It's not enough, Aerius. Angels and demons need you. Seraphim doesn't blame you, so stop blaming yourself and help us." He recalled Severn's words then, so bright and sharp. "It's time you forgave yourself."

He left the hut, nodded at Ernas, and quickly took to the skies. The battle awaited, and so did Severn. Before the day ended, the fate of the world would be decided. He could only hope he'd done enough.

Demons and angels stood in a long line at the northern fringes of the barren killing fields. Mikhail swooped in low over their heads and spotted Severn's large, distinctive figure at the front next to Djall's angular outline. He beat his wings to a landing beside the pair.

The relief on Severn's face tugged at Mikhail's heart, but his relief soon fell away.

"They're not coming, are they?" Severn asked.

"No."

"Didn't think they would." He swallowed hard and clenched his jaw, casting his gaze across the scarred landscape toward the shining line of angels—so thin and bright they looked like the edge of a blade. Remiel's numbers were vast. Easily three times their own. They couldn't win this.

He regretted all the years he'd spent turning these fields red with spilled blood. Blood spills blood. If only there was another way to end this.

Solomon's wings flicked up dust as he settled beside Mikhail. "Your Grace."

"Solomon," Mikhail acknowledged, relieved to have the warrior back on their side. He wore demon armor, like Mikhail's. And it suited him. Several blades glittered at his hips and ankles.

"Fuck me, Solo." Severn grinned. "You look good enough to eat."

Solo cleared his throat. "It's very comfortable and doesn't weigh one down in flight. I'm uncertain why angels prefer heavy metal armor that inhibits our ability to move."

Severn snorted and spun his blade in his hand. "With angels, it's all about the shiny."

"Metal armor is very affective at deflecting demon axe-blades," Mikhail defended, although not entirely sure why when he too wore similar demon armor and agreed with Solomon's assessment.

"It's also easily grabbed and makes you easy to yank out

of the air. I told you this years ago. You flicked your hair, looked down your nose, and said angels had always worn polished steel and would *continue to do so*."

He did recall a conversation along those lines. "I should listen to you more often."

"Fucking Haven, we really are about to die if you're suddenly humbled."

Djall chose that moment to remark on the tightness of the armor's fit around Solomon's rear, which flustered Solomon enough to have him blushing the color of his wings.

"Sister, admire all the angel asses you want later," Severn advised. "Red Manor has a war to end." Severn lifted his blade in signal and started the slow walk forward. "Move up!"

Half their forces lifted off the ground in a blast of wings, angels and demons flying side by side.

Djall flanked Severn's left, Mikhail strode at Severn's right, and Solomon paced at Mikhail's side. Two demons, two angels. Whatever the outcome, they'd already made history.

A huge flock of rayverns startled from their hidden roosts among the grass and flew into the air, cawing chaotically, the flap of their black wings suddenly loud.

Remiel's shimmering line slowly grew as his angels took to the skies, their front line expanding. Thousands and thousands of angels who each believed they fought for what was right, and would die for it. Another avoidable tragedy about to unfold.

Solomon's expression was grim, his face pale. He'd be thinking of all those they'd lost in battles like this one, and how each death had chipped away at the lies surrounding him. Solomon was a brave soul. Every angel was, in their own way. And behind them, the demons marched, facing certain death. Each and every one strong, fierce, amazing. *Inspiring*. It was wrong that their lives should end now, when they should be beginning.

He couldn't allow this.

Their steps cracked the old, hard mud. Bones of the dead lay beneath their feet. And if Mikhail did nothing, more would join them.

No, this could not happen. Not like this.

There *was* a way to end it.

A shadow fell over the killing fields. Mikhail lifted his gaze, fearing another flank of angels, but the source was clearly demon in shape, the wingspan mythical in size. The spooked rayverns suddenly flocked together, chittering and cawing. They spiraled higher, encircling the demon in the sky, while darkening the killing fields below.

"Aerius," Severn whispered, then grinned at Mikhail. "You did it."

Whispers passed through their ranks. *"Aerius."* The whispers resonated, growing louder. *"Aerius... Rayvern Lord. He's here..."*

But Aerius wasn't descending. They hovered high above, looming, waiting, their rayverns circling. Battles didn't win wars, Aerius had said.

Mikhail knew how this ended. He fell into a loping run, fanned his wings, and caught the air, quickly lifting him off the ground.

"Mikhail, *don't*!" Severn's cry chased him.

Severn would hate him for this, but that was how it had begun between them, so it seemed only fitting that perhaps it should end that way. He couldn't look back. If he looked back, he'd falter and fall.

Faster. His wings carried him low over the undulating ground. So many years spent cruelly slaughtering his enemies right here. Cutting them down as though their lives meant nothing. He'd been so wrong. He could not bring them all back, like he had Severn. But he could end it. Or try to.

Remiel's expanse of white wings caught the morning sunlight and lit him up like a star as he flew in fast, mirroring Mikhail's approach.

A glance back revealed enough ground lay between him and his demons to buy him some time. Mikhail landed, kept his hands off his blade, and watched Remiel soar in, the tips of his wings flashing golden.

The guardian gracefully landed. His armor shone as clean and smooth as his face. But his lips hinted at a cruel smile. "Surrender now, and perhaps I'll spare your flock, Mikhail."

Remiel's forces were fast approaching—angels Mikhail had commended in the past. Angels blinkered to the world. Angels just like Solomon, who may not know their lives were missing heart and feeling, but were honorable and admirable nonetheless. He believed in them. That hadn't changed. He loved them, even. They should hear the truth.

Remiel's hard face tightened into a frown. "Well? What is your reply? Surrender and spare us the bloodshed."

Remiel would kill the demons. There was no deal to be made with him.

Closer, Remiel's angels came. Some now close enough

to hear his words. The wind would carry his voice to the rest.

"No." Mikhail met Remiel's blue-eyed glare. So cold. If the angel had a soul, it had long ago been lost to ice. "We will not surrender."

The guardian's laugh was smooth and sweet, like poison. "You think that demon in the sky makes a difference? My numbers are thrice yours. You will fall beneath my blades, and your bodies will rot in the sun, carrion for those rayverns."

Reaching over his shoulder, Mikhail grasped his angel-blade, slowly pulled it free, and lifted it vertically, high in front of him. Sunlight shivered on the shining steel.

This was the only way.

Now was the time to end it. *Now or never.*

Blood spills blood.

Reversing his grip on the blade, Mikhail plunged the angelblade into the ground. Remiel stepped back, reflexively grabbing his own blade, but when he saw Mikhail's thrust into the earth, he snarled and spat a cruel laugh. "What is this? You surrender then?"

"No, I do not surrender." Spreading his arms and wings wide, Mikhail stepped back. *"There is no war. There never was."* The wind carried his voice to Remiel's angels. *"Open your eyes and choose your fates."*

Feathers ruffled. Blades shone. Angels looked on, proud and resplendent. Each one a beacon that had lost its way.

Remiel's laugh sailed through the quiet. "You're insane. Driven that way by the allyanse gone awry. You destroyed Haven, and now you seek to destroy Aerie. I'm impressed you managed to gather yourself a following, but that's all it is. If you do not pick up that blade and fight, I will simply take your head."

Rage made Remiel's words brittle, as though he might break at any moment. He'd killed humans. He'd stabbed Mikhail through the back. Behind the dazzling picture he made lay an ancient desperation.

The swirling wind brought with it the sound of Severn's ranks gaining ground. Once the two fronts met, only the blade in the ground would keep them apart.

"Angels," Mikhail said. Their collective gazes land on him. *"You each served under me. I believed we were right. But we were weapons of a war we had no choice in. A war born of wrongness."*

Remiel's glare flicked behind Mikhail, reading the approaching line of demons. His snarl twitched. "This has gone on long enough." Lifting his blade, he started forward. "Pick up your blade or die in the mud."

The sound of a sword punching into the ground rose from behind Remiel. Just one blade. The guardian turned.

There, in the ground, an angel had driven his blade. Mikhail couldn't see his face behind his helmet. He couldn't be sure if he knew him. But it didn't matter. He'd listened and heard, and he'd driven his weapon into the dirt.

"Traitor!" Remiel yelled. He sprang off his back foot, lunging toward the angel who had staked his choice, his rage all-consuming. He would kill that brave soul—an angel of his own flight. An angel who did not deserve to die for having a heart to feel.

Mikhail grabbed Remiel's wing and jerked him back. The guardian's blade sang, sweeping at Mikhail lightning fast. He ducked, more out of reflex than thought, and twisted away. Unarmed, he had nothing to parry with and no means of defense.

"Die, scourge!" Remiel thrust his sword at Mikhail again, and again Mikhail danced away.

A blade chimed as it struck the earth—another driven home by one of Remiel's flight. And another. Sunlight made the surrendered blades shine. And more... the sigh of blades leaving their sheaths and then the dramatic thrust as their points drove into the dirt peppered the air. More and more followed.

Remiel stumbled, recoiling from Mikhail. He saw each blade and winced as each one was thrust home, as though those blades struck him, not the ground.

Rows of blades shimmered, like silver tombstones marking the countless dead who lay buried and forgotten.

Remiel hunched over, his wings rose, guarding against his pain. "No... no... you fools!"

Severn raised his blade and plunged it into the ground. *"This battle was over long ago,"* he hollered, drawing Remiel's horror-filled gaze toward him. "Guardians lost."

Demons drove their edged weapons into the killing fields. The Haven angels landed and did the same. The ground trembled under the thrust of thousands of blades, London shivering for the thousands of souls laid to rest.

Djall stared at her whip's coiled length before lifting her gaze and scanning the jagged rows of inverted angel-blades. She wasn't the only one just now understanding the future that had begun to unfold around them. She tossed the whip to the ground, then spat at Remiel's feet.

"No," Remiel muttered. "No... don't you see? I tried to protect you! If you cannot love, then you cannot hurt!" He spun on the spot, stumbling around, perhaps hoping to see just one angel still standing in defense of his lies, but none did. "This is a mistake! Seraphim deserved to die! His love of a demon destroyed him before we did! I was there! I saw it! He'd come to despise his angels, and we just wanted his love... just his love..."

Remiel's angels murmured among themselves. They'd seen their guardian attempt to murder Mikhail for reasons that now began to unravel. They'd seen Remiel murder innocent humans, and now, in his desperation, he revealed secrets none of them had known. He finally revealed the truth.

His flight shifted, becoming restless, and a current of tension simmered in the air around them. Remiel's unbalanced floundering suddenly steadied. He tightened his grip on his blade and faced his angels. "You are all wrong. *All of you!* The guardians kill demons and control you to protect you!"

A few of the leading angels from the front of the flight stepped around their inverted blades and started forward. Remiel backed up, stumbling over his heels, into the waiting throng of demons. Demons shoved Remiel forward, bouncing him back to face his fate. More angels started forward. He looked up—toward his only escape— but Aerius was still above, and the keen-eyed flock of rayverns cawed their warning.

"You can't do this. Guardians are sacred! *We correct and control you!*"

An angel grabbed Remiel's arm. He yanked free, twisted on his heel, and bolted for Mikhail.

Mikhail hesitated. Remiel dropped his heavy blade and slipped a dagger free. Hatred contorted his face.

"No!" Severn yelled.

A wave of black swooped over Remiel. Caws and screeches and the crack of rayvern wings buried the guardian's screams. White wings flapped, oddly out of sync, and then vanished under the heaving mass of pecking beaks and black talons.

Severn suddenly shoved at Mikhail, rocking him back, planting himself between the rayverns and Mikhail.

The screams eventually died. The rayverns squabbled and chittered, fighting over feathers and strings of wet flesh and blood.

Mikhail looked up, saw Aerius's great wings blot out the sun, and watched them soar away, leaving only their rayverns behind.

Angels stood still. Waiting.

Demons watched on. Waiting.

Only the sounds of the birds feasting disturbed the quiet of the killing fields.

The blades stayed thrust in the dirt. And one by one, Aerie's angels took to the air, until the sky was full of sunlight and angel wings.

Mikhail slipped his hand into Severn's. "I think it's over."

Severn swung him a glare. "You and I are going to discuss what you did back there."

"Are you angry?"

"I'm thinking up multiple ways to make you pay."

The suggestive threat had Mikhail's heart quickening for very different reasons than violence. "I look forward to it."

"Your Grace." Solomon cleared his throat. "What do we do with... them?"

The demons and Haven angels scanned the skies, waiting for Aerie's angels to turn around and attack.

Djall glanced over. She plucked Mikhail's black feather free from inside her jacket and handed it out. It was scrunched some, but intact. Mikhail lifted his gaze to Djall's face. "A promise kept," she said.

"Keep it, please."

Her lips thinned as she pressed them together, and then in a sudden blast of wings, she shot into the air and hovered a few meters above. "Demons—and angels—go home. We're done here. We're safe. Red Manor watches over you."

There were no cheers, no raucous, angels and demons, quietly stunned, just left, one by one, making their way home. Solomon left to check on Samiel and Luxen. Mikhail stayed, watching the flights and ranks peter off, until the sun had begun its descent toward the horizon. As twilight set in, only a few stragglers remained. But the thousands of blades still shone in the dirt.

Severn had stayed and found a mound of rubble to crouch on and stare out over the empty fields.

What was left of Remiel's body lay glistening and raw. Bits oozed from inside his tarnished armor. Aerius had finally gotten his revenge.

Mikhail approached Severn but stayed at the foot of the mound of rubble, looking up. He had not expected to end the day alive. Everything they'd been through, every battle they'd fought, every death, every attack, every nightmare. Had it truly ended?

The angels in Aerie and those across the seas would need help to adjust. The demons would be confused too.

They'd spent their whole lives defending against brutal angels, and now they were expected to be neighbors?

"I have no idea how to make this work," Mikhail admitted. *Make us work.* Mikhail should go to Aerie. Severn would need to return to his people. They would all need guidance.

Severn climbed off the rubble, tucked his thumb into his hip pocket and regarded Mikhail with a raised eyebrow. "Nobody knows how this works. Before we try and figure it out, I need to say some things. Remember I said you don't listen, and you accused me of being emotional? You remember that conversation?"

"I do." Mikhail pulled his wings in, sensing a few harsh words were about to be aimed his way.

"You left me back there, Mikhail, knowing I couldn't damn well come after you. Those were the longest few hundred meters of my fucking life, and then you throw your blade away? Why didn't you just offer Remiel your wings too, huh?"

He seemed as though he genuinely wanted to answer. "Blood spills blood. It had to end."

"Yes," Severn snapped, "but if you keep looking for death, it's gonna fucking find you."

Severn cared. He cared so much that Mikhail's action had hurt him, again. He'd known his actions would cost a heavy price—the risk of losing Severn. "I have to go to Aerie."

The city sparkled over London, swept by thin clouds. Tiny flecks of white dusted the skies around the glass disks —angels.

"You gonna go alone?" Severn asked. The question sounded like a simple one but was far from it.

"No," he said firmly. He didn't want to go alone. He never had, but he'd understand if Severn chose not to be with him. "I'd like us to go. Together."

"Fuck, Mikhail. You know I'll go anywhere for you." Severn was in front of him suddenly, so close he couldn't think around him and didn't want to. Demon heat enveloped Mikhail, chasing off the chill. "I don't do well with being left out of that head of yours." His hand grabbed Mikhail and crushed him to his broad chest. "I've almost lost you twice in a day. I may look like a hard-ass who chews up angels for lunch, but that's just the demon in me. In here"—he squeezed Mikhail's hand over his heart—"I'm all glass. Please, don't break me."

His warm lips skimmed Mikhail's forehead in a chaste kiss, and the second Mikhail banished his wings, Severn's arms folded around all of him, crushing him close.

Mikhail tucked his head beneath Severn's chin, melting against him. "Forgive me."

"You know you don't need to ask."

Oh, but he did. Severn's embrace eased, and Mikhail slowly separated, immediately missing his warmth. He cast his gaze to Aerie, his angels calling him home.

Severn's fingers still held Mikhail's and tightened. "Are your angels gonna descend on us like they almost did Remiel?"

"I hope not."

Severn snorted and reeled Mikhail against his side. "Will you save me, Your Grace," he asked, "if they do?" Severn's golden eyes glistened in the fading light, full of warmth and softness.

"I will always catch you, Severn, should you fall."

Severn's face lit up. "For a heartless guardian, you turned out to be quite the romantic."

"I'm learning..." He chuckled.

As Severn's gaze found its way back to Aerie, he sighed. "Does it ever scare you," he whispered, "the times we tried to kill each other? What if we'd succeeded?"

So fragile, this demon. So full of feeling and love and understanding. "If we can find love," Mikhail said, "anyone can."

CHAPTER 37

evern

SEVERN ARRIVING in Aerie had caused a stir among the angels. They had observed him like a strange exotic animal, fascinated by having a demon among them without the urge to stab it.

Once angels figured out demons weren't meant to be killed, a whole new world of possibilities would open up to them. But it would take some time. Time Mikhail had bought them.

Mikhail answered their queries with patience and honesty, while Severn hung back, quietly watching Mikhail glow among his kind. Gods, if Severn were any more in love with him, he'd burst.

Days went by with only a few reports of scuffles among the demons and Haven's angels. Mikhail had ordered Haven's gates permanently opened to any angel who wanted to take some time to relearn what it meant to be an angel at their own pace.

The rayvern, Jasper, appeared on a late summer's evening a week after the battle. The huge bird cawed at him from a streetlight as Severn wandered the demon streets, making himself accessible as their High Lord. Keeping himself grounded—though his sore wings helped that too.

"You." Severn glowered at the big rayvern. "Where's Aerius, huh?"

"Caw!" Jasper cocked his head, then hopped and flapped to the next streetlight. He looked back, cawed, and hopped again.

"All right, fine, bird."

Severn followed the caws through the streets, down back alleys and across a strip of old railway tracks, before finding a row of abandoned terraced houses. An ominous place, but Jasper cawed from the rooftop somewhere, urging him on.

"Dammit, bird." He pulled off the bandages keeping his wings clamped and flexed them wide. They weren't fully healed, but they'd get him on the roof.

After a few painful flaps, he landed to find Aerius crouched on a flat section of rooftop, staring toward the west, where the sun was fast setting behind jagged rooftops and chimney pots. The setting sun lit him up like a mythical creature, pooling in his wings.

"You did what I failed to do," Aerius's voice rumbled. They glanced back and offered Severn the softest smile he'd ever seen from them. "You saved your angel."

Severn approached but left them enough room to stretch his wings. "I'm pretty sure Mikhail saved himself."

Aerius tutted. "I ain't talkin' about the end. I'm talkin' about the beginnin'..." They looked over. "Do yah really think he coulda done any of it without you? You being there, by his side for years—when he needed you. Angels and demons, they need one another. They go together like... like jam in a Jammie Dodger." Shrew eyes narrowed. "The cream in a Custard Cream? A biscuit... the cream in the middle, biscuit on the outside—Oh, forget it. We need 'em, and they need us. It's all, it's enough, and it's everything."

Severn did know, but he'd grown fond of Aerius's wily ways. And they were right. Angels did need demons. And demons, he suspected, were better off with angels too. He certainly was. Mikhail gave him a purpose that had nothing to do with picking up a blade and everything to do with hot, late nights tangled in his limbs and wrapped in feathers. "I'm sorry you couldn't save yours. Your angel, I mean."

Aerius sniffed and looked toward the setting sun. "Magnificent, he was. Just like yours. Just as stupid, mind. None of 'em are too bright. Heads full of fluff."

"You miss him?"

"Every damn day. He was beautiful, an' terrible, and I'd give my wings to 'ave 'im back." They sighed at the last rays of the sun as it dipped behind the roofs. Stars had already begun to speckle the blue-black sky high above.

"I know the feeling." Severn's wings still ached at the memory of the blades pinning him down, but he wouldn't hesitate to go through it again to save Mikhail. "You came through for us, Aerius, in the end."

"Nah... I jus' wanted to kill that mouthy blond twat Remiel. Been tryin' to smoke 'im out 'is nest for years. An' when it looked like you were gonna get to 'im first, well... I said to Jasper, I said, *we can't 'ave that, can we*. Remiel was there, mind... when it happened, all them years ago. *When the guardians took my angel*." Their voice gave a dangerous growl, and the big demon flicked his wings. "Remiel was the last."

Jasper cawed from a nearby chimney pot and ruffled his feathers.

Aerius shrugged a beefy shoulder, and the dying light cascaded down their wings. "Was never about me though. Or Seraphim. Or even revenge, like you learned." Their gaze found Severn again and landed hard, like a hand holding him down, making sure he listened. "It had to be you. You had to prove to 'em that love is worth fighting for, and sometimes, worth dying for. Or they'd never see it. Stupid angels."

Severn shoved his hands into his pockets and lowered his wings. Aerius was saying more than they ever had before. This felt a whole lot like it might be goodbye.

"Whatcha gonna do with the young one who betrayed you?"

So they knew about Samiel. He deliberately hadn't thought about Samiel still in the cell, awaiting the judgment of the lords—which was, he supposed, his job now as High Lord. "I don't know..." Half of him wanted revenge, the bitter half.

"You gonna forgive 'im?"

"One day. Maybe." He didn't feel much like forgiving him. "Ernas reckons we should put one of the humans' ankle tags on him and give him a chance at redemption."

"Samiel beat the pulp outtah that pup. Almost killed 'im. So if he can forgive, maybe so can you, eh?"

Severn was too close to this one to make the call. Djall would be better placed to decide his fate.

"Listen to the pup," Aerius said. "He's a good pup, that one. You look after him, right? He prattled on about *Lord Konstantin* like you were the best thing since sliced bread. Clearly, he ain't seen you passed out on ether."

Gods, that memory was enough to make Severn cringe.

"And Luxen... eh?" Aerius asked.

"Can fuck all the way off."

Aerius's heavy laugh rumbled through the roof. "He was tryin' to do right with the tools he had. Tryin' to protect his kin."

Severn definitely wasn't going near Luxen. He didn't trust himself not to punch the bastard through a wall and have him accidentally fall on a blade. "Like I said, he can fuck all the way off."

"Or maybe... he's just desperate for angel cock, eh?"

"If he goes near Mikhail again, I'll cut his cock off."

Aerius's laugh deepened. "You gonna do good, Konstantin."

"It's Severn now."

"Yeah, it is." Aerius lifted their head and squinted at the stars. "See that star there? The brightest one. Brighter than all the rest?"

He saw a whole lot of stars, but there was one to the north that shone steady and true. "I see it."

"Seraphim told me if yah fly hard enough an' high enough, you can reach that twinkly spec."

Severn was fairly certain that was impossible. A few miles up and the air became too thin to breathe. But who was he to argue with Seraphim? "Yeah?" He side-eyed Aerius.

The Rayvern King smirked, and there was a whole lot of feeling in that one smile. "You got this, Severn, High Lord of Red Manor. No longer lost."

An unexpected lump of emotion lodged in his throat. He tried to swallow it, but the damn thing didn't budge.

"You ain't gonna need me again." Aerius stepped from the edge of the building. Their enormous wings opened like the sails of a ship and quickly took them skyward— toward that star. The smaller black-winged rayvern sailed alongside them, cawing over London.

Severn watched them climb higher and higher until they vanished in the darkness between the stars. "Go find your angel."

CHAPTER 38

M ikhail

THE WARM BREEZE rifled through his feathers and kissed his cheeks as he looked from the Aerie balcony upon a vast blue sky. Voices echoed through Aerie's high spaces. Some of them demon. Mikhail turned to admire the demons wandering Aerie's glass halls, guided by curious angels. The demons' hard, dramatic lines and iridescent wings stood out in remarkable contrast against Aerie's glass backdrop.

Severn was approaching, with Djall alongside him, both deep in conversation. Murmured voices filled the quiet. An occasional bark of laughter echoed through the halls.

This was how Seraphim imagined his world would be. Angels and demons working together to protect their human charges.

A dancing couple drew Mikhail's eye back outside—

dark wings against light feathers. A demon and angel pair. He watched them swoop and dive, heard them laugh. The demon caught his angel, and together they spiraled, disappearing into the clouds. His heart swelled, emotion rising. He knew not to stifle such feelings. They were a part of who he was now—the new Mikhail. Someone he was still discovering. With Severn's help.

While he'd watched the pair, Severn's presence settled beside him, so comforting, like his wings had wrapped him close. Severn's gaze found his, and the weight of all they'd achieved spoke in his demon eyes. He'd aged in a way that didn't touch his skin. There were no more lines than there had been years ago, when they'd fought, but the weight of the past made his expression shimmer with knowledge and understanding. "Djall has taken herself off to check the perimeter. So she said. But I figure she has her eye on one of the Haven angels who did his best to fluff his feathers every time she looked his way."

Mikhail raised a brow.

"He'll be fine…. I'll go check she hasn't killed him and stuffed his body in a closet later."

"Yes, I think that would be wise."

"She also gave me this." Severn produced the black feather from inside his coat. "Said it didn't feel right her keeping it when she had your word." He could barely contain his grin.

Mikhail gave his wings a little contented twitch. Being accepted by Djall was an important step. Severn had a lot to do with that. He smoothed the way with demons, while Mikhail calmed the angels. Together, they really were making a difference. He took the feather and examined it, then flicked it into the air. It twirled, the wind caught it, and then it was gone. Like Mikhail's six wings. Now just a pair, or so Saphia confirmed with her routine examinations. But still black. He preferred them that way.

Mikhail closed his eyes and breathed in the sweet air and the spicy scent of demon. "Hm..." His hand found Severn's without looking. "How are *your* wings?" Opening his eyes, he saw Severn give his wings an experimental stretch—the left, then the right. Golden sunlight stroked over their midnight expanse. Tiny shimmering embers fizzled. Mikhail's breath hitched.

"They're good."

Severn's grin turned sly, probably because that very morning Mikhail had thoroughly lavished attention on those wings with his tongue, chasing those sizzling embers while learning all the ways in which he could make Severn gasp.

"Wanna try them out?" Without waiting for an answer, Severn stepped off the edge of Aerie and yanked Mikhail with him. The wind rushed. The sense of freedom and peace washed over him, clearing his mind of everything but wonder that he could fall and fly with no fear.

Severn's wings bloomed, curling around them. Mikhail unfurled his, mirroring Severn's, and together they spiraled, swooped, and climbed to the beat of two hearts, two lives, entwined together. Forever. Where they belonged.

EPILOGUE

 olo

"ANGEL, you cut the crusts off these sandwiches. I'm not a pup to be mothered." Luxen shoved the plate of cucumber-tuna sandwiches back under the Perspex door, sat down on the bench, leaned against the wall, and folded his arms across his naked chest, and there he smirked, like he'd won a battle Solo hadn't known they were fighting.

"Then stop complaining like one." Solo shoved the plate back again and straightened. "I have six friends who will happily eat all the tuna out of that sandwich. Don't try me, demon, or you don't eat at all."

Luxen snorted derisively. "I don't believe you."

"Mikhail gave me the authority to withhold food as punishment—"

"No, the friend part. Angels don't have friends." He leaned forward and rubbed his hands together. There wasn't much light in the cells, and what light they did have was refracted through all the transparent plastic walls. So when it reached Luxen's golden skin, it had softened some and tended to pool around the defined bicep muscles and stroke down the ripple of exposed abdominals. He'd taken to removing his shirt during the last few days. Maybe it was hot down here? It did feel rather warm. Perhaps Mikhail would be open to the suggestion of making it more comfortable for their two prisoners.

Samiel, the second of Solo's charges, dozed in another cell, stretched out on the floor with his hands folded behind his head. Their crimes were many, and in a few days, their fates would be decided by the new lords of the demon manors. Angels would have bound them both and tipped them over the edge—*before*. These two were lucky things had changed for the better.

"Something on your mind?" Luxen asked, drawing Solo's gaze back to him.

"I was just thinking it's warm."

Mikhail hadn't said anything about not speaking with Luxen, but engaging with either demon seemed risky. He was to monitor them and see that their needs were met.

"Hm..." Luxen got to his feet, ignored the plate of sandwiches, and approached the clear plastic wall. The building the two demons were contained in had long ago been a zoo, and what were now cells had held large, exotic reptiles. It almost seemed fitting. Lux moved like a snake, like something smooth and silky, like Solo supposed apex predators moved. His cats moved like Luxen when they stalked the mice that dared enter their shared house.

Luxen stretched his arms up and spread both hands against the plastic wall. He tilted his hips, putting his weight on one leg. The trousers rode low on those hips. And without a shirt, of course, the rest of him was right there, suddenly in front of Solo. His gaze traveled all the way down the ex-lord's chest, getting hung up where the beginnings of that delectable V dipped below his waist.

He swallowed. Goodness, his throat was dry.

"Those demon leathers look good on you," Luxen remarked with a jerk of his chin. "Turn around for me."

Annoyance ruffled Solo's feathers. "No."

Luxen's smile grew. "Where's the harm? There's Perspex between us." He rapped his knuckles on the plastic wall. "I just want a look at you?"

"You seem to be confused. You're a prisoner. You don't get to make demands."

"It wasn't a demand. I was asking. You seem the sort to enjoy being admired. Was I wrong?"

Solo's heart fluttered, making his breath come a little too fast. His face was warming too. "No. I mean, yes, you were wrong."

Luxen dipped his chin and peered through his dark lashes. His horns were really quite lovely. "And I thought angels didn't lie?" he purred.

Gods, what was he doing? Luxen was a terrible person! He'd tried to manipulate Mikhail. He was a thoroughbred concubi. He could make angels *feel* things. "I know what you're trying to do. It won't work. I'm immune to demons."

"From what I hear, and from my own admittedly limited experience, it seems the opposite is true. Angels have a weak spot for demons, when you aren't trying to kill us. I didn't believe it, but then there was Severn, and well... then Mikhail."

Solo blinked. Mikhail had spent a long time with Luxen. In the same room. Together. Rumors were the lord had tried to seduce him. "Did you and Mikhail..."

"Did we what?" Luxen purred.

Solo couldn't say it. The idea seemed so wrong. But by Haven, after Severn had taken him to the nephilim, he'd imagined such physical meetings. Demons and angels together, like Severn and Mikhail were together. Having the sex.

"Did we fuck?" Luxen whispered, the question barely finding its way beneath the plastic to Solo's ears.

Heat blazed through Solo's face. "Did you?"

Luxen's lips twitched. "No. A kiss, nothing more. Mikhail's seduction was a delicate one and the first I've ever failed in. Perhaps I should have aimed lower, tried to snare one of his angel friends? Like you?"

Folding his arms, Solo lifted his chin, strengthened by the demon's failure to seduce Mikhail. If Mikhail could withstand this fiend's tricks, then so could Solo. "You're not that special to look at." He shrugged.

"No? You wound me, dear Solomon." Dropping his arms, Luxen stepped back from the edge of the cell and breathed in, expanding his marvelous chest. His wings shimmered into sight, unfurling like two great dark canvases of browns and golds. It was all Solo could do not to gasp. Ever since demons and angels had stopped fighting, he'd been desperate to touch their wings. Without feathers, they should be cold, but he'd heard talk they were flushed with blood, hot and *very* sensitive.

Luxen shrugged a shoulder. "For what it's worth, your ether tells me you're desperate to fuck my every hole, and I've already seen your ass, every time you walk away. I'd prefer to sink my teeth into those cheeks than your delicate little sandwiches—"

Solo fled the cells and slammed the door shut behind him, then pressed his back against it. Oh dear. He had to speak to Mikhail. No, not Mikhail, he'd be mortified. Severn. Severn would know how to handle Luxen, and Solo's, er... problem. He looked down his body, at the jutting evidence of how his anatomy liked the sound of Luxen's bite.

He'd only recently realized he was a sexual creature. It was all very confusing, and now... he was apparently attracted to a demon? And a very bad, very powerful demon. He was out of his depth, and his cock was getting *harder*, not softer. He bit his lip to stifle a groan. There were lots of other demons to desire. Severn had even promised him a trip to the madam to explore more of the sex. So why couldn't he stop thinking about *this* one?

"Leave him be, Luxen," the other demon, Samiel, said —his smooth voice sliding under the closed door. "He's clearly confused."

What did that demon care? He was just as mean as the other one. And Solo *wasn't* confused. He was just... thinking things through.

"Fine, angel," Luxen's dulcet voice crooned, slithering beneath the door. "I'll eat your little sandwiches. If you come back in here and talk with us? All nice. Like friends."

He shouldn't go back in there. Luxen was a powerful concubi. This was all an act to get Solo to free him. Yet... he did rather enjoy the way the demon looked at him, undressing him with those sultry eyes. It felt good to be admired. To be *wanted*. It felt right to have his body thrumming this way. And Severn had said these feelings weren't shameful. He *knew* they weren't shameful. And he knew... since the nephilim, he'd wanted to feel them again. *Lust*, Severn had called it. Solo had an uncomfortable amount of it.

"You still there, angel? Or did I frighten you off?" He sounded forlorn. He was down here for most days and nights. It must have been terribly depressing. "Tell me about these friends you claim to have?"

Solo willed his body back under control with thoughts of how the cats would be most unimpressed with all of this. Collected, calm, and with his heart now settled, he vowed not to be manipulated. He would be the one in control. Luxen *wanted him*, and that gave Solo power. By Haven, even that thought was arousing. But he could do this. Angels and demons had not been made to war. They were made to love. Mikhail and Severn had set that truth free.

This was a new world, with new, exciting opportunities. And Solo ached from his heart to his wing tips to experience them all.

He opened the door.

Thank you for reading the Primal Sin trilogy.
If you enjoyed the series, please take a few moments to leave a review.
Every review really does help new fans find great reads.

ALSO BY ARIANA NASH

Please sign up to Ariana's newsletter so you don't miss all the news & get a free short story.

www.ariananashbooks.com

Also by Ariana Nash

Silk & Steel Series

When Eroan, one of the last elf assassins, is captured trying to kill the dragon queen, he knows his death imminent. Until the queen's youngest son, Prince Lysander, inexplicably lets him go.

Eroan expected death, but in the darkest of places, when all hope is lost, love finds him instead.

This epic fantasy adventure topped the Amazon charts for months. Discover the darkly delicious world of Silk & Steel today.

Click here to start the adventure with Silk & Steel, Silk & Steel #1

Prince's Assassin Trilogy
(now complete!)

Soldier, Nikolas Yazdan, survived a brutal eight year war, but can he survive the wicked and cruel Prince Vasili Caville and the lies within the Caville palace?

Read King of the Dark, Prince's Assassin #1, today to find out!

ABOUT THE AUTHOR

Born to wolves, Rainbow Award winner Ariana Nash only ventures from the Cornish moors when the moon is fat and the night alive with myths and legends. She captures those myths in glass jars and returning home, weaves them into stories filled with forbidden desires, fantasy realms, and wicked delights.

Sign up to her newsletter and get a free ebook here: https://www.subscribepage.com/silk-steel